AN UNBELIEVABLE HOOT

JEFFREY KERSHAW

authorHOUSE®

AuthorHouse™ UK
1663 Liberty Drive
Bloomington, IN 47403 USA
www.authorhouse.co.uk
Phone: 0800.197.4150

Published by AuthorHouse 07/12/2017

ISBN: 978-1-5246-8315-3 (sc)
ISBN: 978-1-5246-8314-6 (e)

HENRY REDFIELD - THE CHANGE OF LIFE

There is a point in everyone's life when they may feel a need to square accounts, when reason or conscience may engender a review of irresponsible behaviour or an unconventional life style. For a while out there, it looked as though Henry Redfield was flying on gossamer wings, which would take him off into infinity. His playboy life style would have been the envy of any 'Riley' worth his salt. Sleazy up-market night-clubs, where the drinking and dancing and general revelry continued till dawn; casinos, where the entertainment lasted as long as his credit; beds, in which he never seemed to outstay his welcome.

Henry was just a whisker under six foot tall, with a thick shock of dark brown wavy hair, and eyes which occasionally qualified as blue-green with a hint of tan - depending upon the light. His face which was rather long, clear skinned and intelligent, was, more often than not, divided by a brilliant white streak of a smile. He had once been accused of being handsome by a near-sighted, octogenarian aunt, but even younger lovelies seemed to find him far from disagreeable. He appeared to discover the whereabouts of money, or 'the material girl', whenever the need arose, even if, upon occasion, it was a close run thing.

The real problem was that he had recently become aware of the need arising less and less. Perhaps it was the effect that the champagne, good food and high living were having on his expanding central zone, his rising cholesterol level, and his contracting bank balance. Whatever the cause, it slowly brought him to the realisation that something had to give. Perhaps, he thought, that intangible and incalculable abstraction, 'Change', should give deep thought to putting itself 'in the wind', a place where writers of both fact and fiction have frequently located it.

The idea that manifested itself to his mind, that wet Thursday in March 2008, was that it would be a race to the wire, as to whether that which would finally give - would be his ever tightening trousers, or his solvency. One thing he was sure of was that any giving, would not likely be done by his Bank Manager. Too many cheques written out to casinos, night-clubs and restaurants told their own tale, with no need for illustrations by *Manet*. 'There would be no more *Monet*'!

Henry had made a killing in the 'excessive eighties,' in property dealing mainly, earning into six figures net each year. He had previously developed an expanding lawyer's practice in central London. However, his outside earnings ensured that he was able to retire from that practice (although only the ripe old age of thirty-six at the time) and set up residence in Cyprus, which was the warmest European tax haven. This he did before reaping the aforementioned profits of his labours and shrewd investment. The easy money, and lack of real challenge, had led him to seek fulfilment elsewhere. These opportunities for personal satisfaction arose, more often than not, after the sun had set.

2009 saw the beginning of the decline of both his, and Britain's fortunes. Their descent was achieved hand in hand either into, or by, the "Recession". It was never clear as to whether the Recession was the cause or the effect of one's personal, or one's country's, economic decline. It certainly provided a convenient excuse for politicians, otherwise lost for an explanation, for the general financial malaise.

It certainly is a strange state of affairs. If one says that the recession is the cause of our economic decline, that is like saying that hunger is the reason for starvation; or that our trains on the South Eastern Railways (more properly called *'Ailways'*) do not run on time, because they are usually late. Henry had often thought that if more people used the trains the Railway Companies would have more revenue and could become more efficient. In turn this would relieve traffic on the roads, and cut down on pollution, one of his pet concerns.

Although this rather technical analysis was not occupying the mind of Henry Redfield just now, his particular recession (not his hairline, which was doggedly holding its own) was a matter for growing concern. His pocket felt as though a hole had been slowly and deliberately singed into it. Henry saw a pressing need for a new, positive direction in his life. His old ways were wearing as thin as the fragile toilet paper provided in some of the less salubrious hotels in the Eastern sector of the continent of Europe.

However, that particular Thursday was to augur in a sea change in his life. Through that fine old tutor "Pain and suffering" he was to find that new direction, and the fulfilment, that his spirit was beginning to crave. He was currently on a visit to London, staying in one of the two flats in Regents Park that he had previously purchased for investment. This trip, from his little yellow and white three-bedroom house by the clear blue Mediterranean, in the sunny isle of Cyprus, was related to a possible resale of an industrial investment in the North of England, that he had purchased six months previously at auction. The prospects were not rosy and it certainly appeared that this time, a net loss would be indicated.

The Buttersoft Industrial Estate, Sheffield was, ironically, melting, or so it seemed, into the earth from which it had originally sprung. The more recent buildings comprised small industrial units. These included - a car repair centre - 'Fix me Quick!'; a double glazing manufactory - 'Paines Panes'; Kash and Karry Kitchins. There was also Dakers Diggers, farm and digging equipment hire. All were all independent businesses that now had leases from Henry of the purpose built units, which had been erected upon the site of a old demolished chemical factory.

Unfortunately, fumes had started rising through the earth from some of the chemicals from the old plant, which had not been adequately buried beneath and around the now uncertain foundations. These possibly dangerous compounds had caused an outbreak of, something similar in its symptoms to rabies, in both the local pig, and the farm labourer population. It also appeared to be having a strange effect upon some of Henry's tenants, their customers, and the passing pedestrians.

Complaints had been made by one such passer-by, Doris Freebody, to the local constabulary. Her complaint was about men, working on the building site at the North East tip of the Estate, who slavered and drooled at the mouth whenever platinum blonde Doris passed them, in her micro-skirt and frilly blouse, cut off both at the midriff, and again, narrowly above the nipple. Although young Constable Perkins, the receiver of this information, had played it down initially, showing wisdom beyond his years and station, the swooping, scooping, snoop of the Daily Spread, Norris Parker (Nosey to his friends) had spread-eagled the story across the morning edition.

3

Henry Redfield thought that the paper should be renamed the 'Mourning Edition' having regard to the murderous effect that the article would have upon his tumbling investment. The suggestion in the story ran that the workmen, overcome by the fumes seeping from the soil, were unable to control their feelings of lust and manly desire for the delectable Doris. As a consequence, their saliva stirred by the joint pressure of the chemical gas and the short skirted, appetising, long-legged, young titbit passing by within eyeshot, had initiated a general dripping, or dribbling, from their lower lips.

As Henry was, directly or indirectly, the owner of this drooler's paradise, the balding moustachioed, imitator of the 'Fleet Street Newshound', Parker, sought to interview him. Feeling that this was an exception to the rule about discretion being the better part of valour, HR decided to face the music. They met by arrangement at a famous old Elizabethan public house in Buttersoft, 'The Cheddar Cheese'. Over a pint of milk stout and a ploughman's lunch, Norris fired his questions nasally, being endowed with one of the finest examples of a patrician hooter on this, the Yorkshire, side of the Pennines, one of the peaks of which it was curiously reminiscent.

'Tell me Mr. er. Redwood..." he intoned.

'Redfield, actually' interrupted Henry.

'Er, yes, quite, no relation then eh? Ha! Ha! Mr. Redfood did you seriously not know the history of this site before you purchased it?'

'No. I bought it recently at auction. My solicitor negligently failed to ask if any occupants at the estate had been seen, drooling at the mouth when the local beauty queen paraded past them, wearing little more than a couple of carefully glued-on lace handkerchiefs' Henry responded dryly, with more than a peck of sarcasm.

He continued on a more serious note, 'my lawyer had no information passed to him either by the Vendors solicitors or the Local Authority about the previous use of the site. It is my own opinion, that the building works undertaken by one of the tenants, Dakers Diggers - the equipment hire people with the largest unit - have, unfortunately, opened up this particular 'can of worms'. They were excavating foundations, prior to building themselves a new showroom.'

'Well now, Mr. Redgrass', whined Nosey mainly through his right nostril, his left having been blocked by the 'latest bug that was going round' but which could still offer the odd snort for emphasis or punctuation whenever required. 'Well now, I think I must correct you on a matter of definition, Mr. Redford.'

Henry searched the heavens for assistance but none came, the heavens were obviously busy elsewhere. 'This is not just a 'can of worms' that has been found on your land, but a veritable 'viper's nest' 'and Parker stood up straighter and leaned backwards, like an artist surveying his handiwork with considerable satisfaction. Henry half expected Parker to close one eye and raise his thumb as artists habitually do.

Nosey continued 'do you realise how serious the threat to health is from the poisons that are seeping back to the surface of the ground?'

'If I am honest I must say that I don't, and for that matter, from what I understand, neither do the Government boffins sent in to test the substances, or anyone else who has examined or tested the gasses. Apart from the ectoplasmic effect that the chemicals seem to have on horny humans and herds of hollering honkies, the sight of people dropping like flies with dreaded beriberi, seems conspicuous by its total absence.'

'Too soon to say, too soon to say' Parker honked in apparent sympathy with the future, possibly trottered, victims of some unspecified and unspeakable plague. 'Are you not concerned, Mr. Redstone, with the likely effect that this unfortunate emission, with all the attendant publicity, will have on the value of your land?' 'Bloody right, I'm concerned, and my name is Redfield, Redfield for crying out loud! My investment is taking what you reporters will no doubt refer to tomorrow as a 'Nosedive'. You, in particular, should appreciate how painful that might be!'

Norris Parker found this last allusion to his prized proboscis rather out of taste, but his most prominent feature was not all that he had in common with that magnificent beast, the Rhinoceros, his skin being extremely thick and durable. The pinprick failed to penetrate. Nosey also had made generous allowances for the interviewee's present painful circumstances.

Successfully catching the penultimate train of thought, he continued, nose to the grindstone:

'How much do you expect to lose?'

Henry sighed. 'Too early to say how much, but a goodly sum for sure. I may have a claim against someone for non-disclosure or misrepresentation, and I will be taking advice on that and every other possible score.' 'But you are a lawyer yourself, surely you know where you stand?' pursued the bloodhound, sniffing a fresh scent.

'Haven't you heard the old adage, that a lawyer who represents himself has a fool for a client?' Henry threw the ball squarely back at Nosey.

'No, this is not my area of legal specialisation. Anyway I am semi-retired. I will consult the specialists and consider my position. I have not yet ruled out the possibility of an insurance claim, and it is early days yet.'

'I thank you Mr. Red-field for such an invaluable contribution. I am sure I can speak on behalf of all our readers.' Parker acknowledged that the interview was ended by a slight inclination of his considerable nose, and off he went haring after the public telephone to relay the valuable exchange to his employers on the Daily Spread and anyone else who wanted it.

Henry felt dejected. He knew that any claim he had would take years, and that court action he might pursue was highly unpredictable. He was going to take a pasting on this venture. In the meantime, the likes of Doris and the digging workmen, not to mention Uncle Tom Cobbly and his crowd, might well commence an action against Henry Redfield for damages. 'We live in an unjust world' he thought as he left the olde world pub and wandered along the hot and dusty street, the odd thought of playing with the traffic crossing his mind, only to be instantly and thankfully rejected.

He trudged to Buttersoft railway station and caught the 13.35pm train via Sheffield to London Euston station. In order to lift his sombre mood he treated himself to a late lunch of poached salmon with all the trimmings. To compliment the meal and make inroads into his mood he helped himself to half a bottle of Moet Chandon. 'Now that's better!' he thought and launched into the Telegraph crossword to help pass the time on the train and keep his mind off the Dakers site.

NOSEY PARKER, DORIS, HER LEGS, AND DAI

Norris Parker, having made good his report to his newspaper and also to Reuters, went off, nose to the ground, in search of the delicious Doris. The precipitator of what was becoming known as the 'Slavering Sickness' was to be found in the beauty parlour having a pedicure. Norris entered this perfumed garden sniffing the wonderful scents, which hung heavily upon the air.

'Yes, can I help you?' asked a pretty brunette perched daintily on a stool at the reception desk.

'Er, yes, my name is Norris Parker of the Daily Spread. I am a reporter. I'm looking for Doris Freebody.'

The brunette touched her hair as the thought of instant fame touched her hair. 'Doris is over in Number 1 Beauty Room, having her nails done. My name is Mavis Masterton by the way' and she fluttered her substantial heavily laden eyelids and crossed her somewhat too powerfully built legs. Norris, deftly managing to avoid catching either her fluttering eyes or her simpering thighs, simply nodded and toddled off nose in the air in the direction indicated, and knocked on the door.

'Come in' said an inviting female voice. Norris entered to be met with the picture of a heavily made up manicurist holding Doris's foot, which was raised and rested on a pedestal. They both looked at him.

'Parker of the Press' he said nostrilly.

The girls looked at one another and simultaneously pronounced 'Ooh!'

'I have come to interview Doris on her recent unfortunate experiences near the Buttersoft Industrial Estate leading to her report to the local police. May I sit down please?'

Without waiting for a response he sat, positioning himself strategically opposite the 'afternoon delight' with her left leg raised up and away from her right, so that her dainty toe-nails could be attended to by Clarissa the Carefree, Colourful Clipper. Parker recognised the tell-tale label of M&S peeking out from the right leg of her frilly knickers. Although Doris was uncomfortable about her unladylike position, the thought that she was to be front page news kept sending thrills, almost reaching those frills, as they travelled joyfully down her perfectly formed spinal column.

Nosey looked around anxiously for Dai Evans, his unreliable dark-haired, lean, Welsh photographer, who, if he arrived quickly, could capture the splendour of delectable Doris, legs akimbo, before the Clipper put away her incisors. Luckily for Norris, Dai did arrive a few moments later, with the usual clatter, which announced that his tripod had snagged on some inconveniently protruding hairdresser's rear end, and had fallen noisily to the floor. Without knocking, Dai barged into the manicurist's parlour with all his clutter.

Norris put his index finger to the side of his nose a code indicating to Dai that a perfect pose was available if only he could move along sharpish. The photographer was about six feet tall, slim athletic build, dark brown hair and ice blue eyes. His skin was a shade darker than the average, and he had the benefit of high and pronounced cheekbones. Denim shirt open at the neck revealing the regulation hairy muscular chest, and wrangler jeans completed the picture of a casual handsome fellow who would be very much in place in one of those cigarette adverts that are now, thankfully, banned from public display. Not a bad looker, our Dai, all things considered.

Every inch the professional, with all the inches required, and a few in reserve, Dai, in a single continuous movement, swept up his Nikon and starting snapping like a crocodile on a frosty day. Doris had been chatting cheerfully to Clarissa about the new pair of blood red, skin tight, hot pants she had purchased from 'The Spider's Web', the youthful and sexy boutique in the High Street, when her pretty little ear caught the repeated click of the camera.

'Ooh! You mustn't; not with me legs like that. Stop it!'

In an attempt to belatedly bring her knees together into more ladylike pose she straightened her legs and kicked out. Clarissa, suddenly chaotic, scissors waving wildly, leaned backwards to avoid taking the blow on her fulsome twosome but, temporarily unbalanced, she fell backwards, her own legs coming back up with such surprising force that her unerring right foot found Nosey's groin. Doubling up with the pain of this ferocious, not to mention entirely unwarranted attack, Nosey fell forward and landed heavily on top of Doris, who, opening her mouth to protest vigorously (and actually forming the word "Ooh!" for a third time) found Parker's huge hooter had landed deep inside it.

The weight of the ungainly arranged pair, with the added momentum of Norris' heavy descent, was too much for the lightweight chair on which Doris had been sitting. It swayed nervously back and forth, wobbled, and finally toppled backwards taking both of them with it. The pain and shock of the fall, with Parker landing heavily on top of her, caused Doris's perfectly formed mouth to snap shut with considerable force. Dai, in the eye of the storm, and every inch the professional, seemed entirely unmoved by this unusual turn of events, but snapped up all the photographic gems on display for future reference.

The damage to the Nose of the Daily Spread's finest was considerable. Blood flowed profusely from both faces of the monolith; it had already swollen to twice its normally considerable size. The imprints of Doris's tiny teeth were to be evident for at least four weeks afterwards. Poor Parker was admitted to casualty in the Buttersoft General and consideration was given to a stitch or two and a protective bandage. Thereafter he was kept in for observation. A full x-ray of his distended nasal region was put in hand. He was not in the slightest mollified by the Doctor's observation that a lesser nose would not have survived the terrible assault from Doris's deadly dentures.

Norris was properly incensed when he overhead doctors discussing in the corridor outside his room, where the medics were dryly indicating their preference for more orthodox plastic surgery. They deprecated the rather primitive do-it-yourself version apparently attempted by Norris, without notable success, in the instant case, or, indeed, wherever any adjustment in the nasal region might be required.

Tears streamed unabated down the face of the Daily Spread's "man in Buttersoft", until he perked up, and was consoled by a visit by an anxious Dai. When the photographer had recovered from the sight of Nosey's extraordinary bandage, which was tightly wound round his nose like the covering of a squash racket's handle, he confirmed that a memorable selection of photographs of delectable Doris would be Nosey's for posterity.

9

'Mind you' Dai said 'I don't think any of them is really very suitable for the front page, far too revealing, if you ask me. Here, I had a set developed on the quick like, for you to look at, look you.'

Nosey had a double take at Dai's use of the double "look, and then buried his nose in the sizzling selection of saucy snaps brought by his friend, famous for "flicking the fastest foto-finger in Forest Fawr". Not of course that there were many such fertile fingers in this rather unknown reach of the Welsh hinterland.

Nosey pulled the bandage down slightly so that it did not interfere with his vision, and reviewed the very provocative snaps of Doris, who, in his judgement, would make a super page three girl, or even possibly qualify for the glossy magazines. "With the right management and handling", he envisioned particularly '*the handling*', she would be a tremendous success.

At just that moment the ward doors opened, and in walked the very same Doris with a large bunch of daffodils and a diminutive dress. Her long slim legs were truly superb he thought.

'Up to her armpits, they are' muttered Dai reading Nosey's mind word for word.

Parker, coming back to his senses, hastily stuffed the photographs under the bedclothes.

'How are you Mr. Parker?' Doris enquired? 'May I sit on the end of your bed.' She began to assume a sitting posture her small firm round rump held momentarily, and teasingly, frozen in mid-air awaiting the patient's assent.

'No. Why don't you sit on the next bed opposite me - all the better to see you with' he suggested, once again anxious for the best possible view of her legs.

'Thank you very much for the flowers, it was a sweet thought' Norris beamed at her.

Doris composed herself. 'Listen Mr. Parker, I wanted to speak to you about those photographs. I am worried sick. If me Dad sees me with me legs wide open on the front page he'll take his belt to me and beat me black and blue.'

She shifted uncomfortably under Norris's gaze, which rarely seemed to stray above her waist. Crossing her legs, she again revealed too much leg, and she sought in vain to drag down the hem of her tiny dress from its permanent position just above her thighs.

Well I don't know ...' said Norris with a conspiratorial wink at the photographer who was slipping his Nikon out of its cover once more.

'You see Doris, I have a duty as a reporter to show things which are news and which will increase circulation.' Nosey's own circulation had almost reached fever pitch what with the photographs Dai had brought him, and now, Doris's legs, as it were, in person.

Dai, in the meantime, had dropped to the floor with the flimsy excuse that he was searching for Parker's bedpan, Nosey having begun to demonstrate signs of discomfort in his nether regions. Dai was now flat on his belly under the bed snapping Doris from every conceivable, and even the odd inconceivable, angle again.

'But please, Mr. Parker! Why on earth would anyone want to see my knickers? she expostulated shrilly.

'Why indeed my child? I ask myself the same question' Nosey snorted trying desperately to retain his composure. His eyebrows reached for his hairline as if to emphasise the fact that it was a mystery to him that anybody should want a peek under Doris's minute ensemble. He spoke as clearly as he could enunciate the words with both nostrils now out of action. The letter 'N' seemed to have given hirn particular difficulty.

He continued 'you have a bright future with a body like yours my child, provided you are handled properly. Now I might have a word with my editor about these pictures if you go to the studio with Dai and have some proper photos taken. You know the sort, "Glamour Photographs". We can offer them to Mayfair and Penthouse but definitely no clothes.'

'Oh no! Oh no! Nothing will be left to the imagination!' moaned poor Doris.

'Let's hope not' replied Nosey thoughtlessly. 'Er-er, I mean, of course it will. These days, the top girlie mags take great care to be tasteful'. As if to emphasise his point Nosey licked his lips, and made a weird sucking noise, which instantly brought back to Doris the spectre of Hannibal Lecter's last scene in the "Silence of the Lambs", where he smacks his lips at the thought of having a friend for dinner.

Parker was already busy using a great deal of his own imagination, conjuring up pictures of Doris wearing even less than she was at that particular minute.

'Now' he advised 'you'll need proper management, and *handling*, of course, and I can take care of that. Doris you are going to be a very wealthy girl. Who knows you may even become a top model. Have you any idea how much they can earn?'

Doris's eyes began to open wider and cracks appeared in her resolution, but not, of course, in her smooth clear skin. She wavered at the thought of stunning new clothes; holidays abroad on sun-kissed islands surrounded by muscular brown suitors swooning over her with bars of chocolate covered coconut; cocktails served on chairs placed in the sea; oodles of *fifties* in her handbag; and her photograph on the cover of Vogue.

Adjusting her voice so as to appear only minutely interested, she said hesitantly, 'well ... if you really think I could be a success, then I suppose I might give it a try'.

'Oh goody, goody, goody!' Nosey rubbed his hands with glee. 'Now off you go with Desperate Dai to his studio.'

It must have been his overweening professionalism that prompted him to call after the retreating pair 'and Dai, I say, Dai, the full works OK? I'll need at least a hundred colour shots in different positions to make up a proper collection. Jump to it. And remember, au naturel. Au revoir!'

Dutiful Dai and Desirable Doris drifted docilely downstairs, and Norris was left to play over the possible arrangements of, and with, Doris in his mind's eye, whenever the insufferable pain in his nose wasn't playing havoc with these tortuous mental gymnastics. He riffled and shuffled through the photos that Dai had left him and then picked up the telephone by his bed and dialled.

GOING TO LAW

In the meantime, our redoubtable retired retainer, Redfield, had requested Rossitter of Blake, Nethergood and Rossitter, solicitors of Bedford Row, to fix up a consultation with Godfrey Hammond QC of the Temple, to advise upon the quandary in which he now found himself. Howard Rossitter was the picture of how one expects one's solicitor to look, especially having regard to the inexplicably enormous amounts of hard-earned, tax paid, cash that one is obliged to pay him. Standing six feet two in his stockinged feet, which, of course, he was not on this occasion, much preferring his Church's brogues, he wore that die-hard uniform of the City Lawyer, a navy chalk-stripe suit.

Being of the old school, Howard still wore a stiff collar. 'Can't break the habit old boy' he confided to a chum he bumped into in the Strand. 'Forced as a youngster to wrestle with a stiff one at Eton, now I can't work up any interest in a floppy one. Here you have a feel.' The chum opened his eyes wide in surprise and a modicum of terror at this off-the-cuff admission, and the intimate invitation proffered by Rossitter, and belted off down the street. Rossitter watched his retreating form with puzzlement. 'I think old Berryman is definitely losing it' he murmured to himself.

The picture was rounded off by his old school tie.

His hair, which had once been black, had the regulation, perfectly dissected parting that he had acquired during a spell in the Officer's Corps at Sandhurst. It was swept across his forehead with a flourish. His face, reminiscent of a youngish Anthony Eden, usually bore a warm, welcoming smile that told its own tale about the state of his bank account, or his marriage, or both.

Rossitter grasped Henry's hand with a firm, thorough and wholesome grip as though it was already full of fifty-pound notes for onward transmission to Howard's private banking account.

'How are you my boy? Bearing up under it? The strain I mean. Don't you worry; My choice for Queens' counsel, Godfrey is the top man for your type of case. Of course, he doesn't come cheap, (*but then, neither do I! Ha! Ha!*, he thought), but you get what you pay for, as you well know.'

Henry smiled faintly, and his knees began to buckle. He took a deep breath and he murmured 'good to see you Howard. Thanks for responding so quickly in my hour of need.'

They had arranged to meet at Counsel's Chambers. The rooms seemed as though they had been eked out of a period house from a bygone age. Henry had mounted the ancient, rather decrepit wooden staircase to the first floor of No.12 Chancery Chambers, thinking of the thousands of Clients who had climbed these well worn, sagging, steps before him. These visits had taken place over hundreds of years, by poor and wealthy litigants alike, who sought assistance from the learned Counsel within the elderly Tudor white walls with their blackened wooden beams. On occasion, the barrister might himself *beam* at a Client to whom he had painted a black picture, but who must nonetheless pay for the privilege of hearing the bleak forecast from his Counsel's lips.

No sooner had Rossitter greeted Henry, than the Clerk, Thomas, appeared to ask if anybody else was awaited. On receiving a double negative, he offered deferentially 'well then, very good. Mr. Hammond is ready for you now gentlemen. Will you both take tea, or do you prefer coffee?'

Tea was unanimously carried, and brought in by Delia the pretty brunette typist of whom Thomas at once confided in a whisper to Henry "she has more legs than sense." Henry appreciated the full aptness of this comment as Delia leant over slightly to pour the milk. He couldn't help musing that if Thomas was wrong in his assessment, that Delia would have to be very bright indeed.

Godfrey Hammond (known in the trade as '*the Ham*', from the manner in which he treated each Court in which he made an appearance. It was as if it were the 'Old Vic' or the Royal Shakespeare Theatre at Stratford upon Avon. Hammond had a regal bearing, and a voice remarkably similar to that of the late Richard Burton. His looks however, owed far more to Charles Laughton than to Mrs. Taylor's late husband. He rose ponderously to greet his newly arrived paying guests.

'How do you do Mr. Redfield?' 'Hello Howard, good to see you again so soon. Please sit yourselves down and be comfortable. Now who is having tea? Oh! And thank you Delia. Ah! Hmmm! I adore chocolate digestive biscuits! She does spoil me you know. Must be paying her too much. Extraordinary legs don't you think. And people complain that you can't get good staff these days. They are not looking in the right places, eh what?'

Henry's eyes immediately sought out the right places as Delia turned to leave the room.

'Excellent choice you made in Delia, Godfrey. Does she often have to work late?' Howard teased.

The Ham's naturally pink complexion darkened slightly and he laughed a trifle nervously. Recovering himself he began to address the issues in the case. His luxurious deep bass tones filled the ancient room with its solid blackened oak beams, and rather cheeky sketches of past High Court Justices of note. Surely Henry was getting good value just having the opportunity to hear that voice which, in itself, must be a real gift from the gods.

'Hmmm. Now from Howard's brief I have a clear picture, Henry. You bought this property at auction. I have reviewed the conditions of sale, and unless we can find additional facts to demonstrate misrepresentation, there is no claim against either the auctioneer, or the Vendor. The Buttersoft Town Council, however, which provided replies to the search and enquiries made by your solicitor, are not in such a happy position.

In his additional enquiries made of the Council before you entered into the contract, your conveyancing Solicitor specifically asked them: -

'Has any previous use of the site or any land done, or will any future proposed development do, anything which might damage or otherwise cause financial or other harm to a proposed purchaser or user of any part of it.'

To this they answered a simple 'No, not to our knowledge'

However they knew about the previous use, and presumably the method of demolition and disposal of the chemicals, having overseen, and possibly licensed, the entire operation. They also had notice of your tenant's proposed digging operations, having granted consents to Dakers Diggers for the works to build their new showroom extension.

Although the position has not yet entirely crystallised, there may be a claim here, and you might even be able to require them to purchase the land from you. About that possibility we shall learn later, if all else fails.

For starters, I suggest that Howard here fires them off a letter, telling them he has taken leading Counsel's advice, setting out your tale of woe, and demanding full recompense or purchase at previously established values. Howard, I will email a suitable form of wording across to you. Now, so far as the delectable Doris Freebody is concerned, and for the sake of completeness, I throw in the workmen's, and any other potential claims against you, I would say this. You were entirely innocent of knowledge surrounding the burial of the chemicals. If they have not escaped from your land onto the property of others, but have only affected people actually working on the land or passing over it you may be able to defend any such claims. Where the fumes escape onto the land of others you may not be so fortunate.

Furthermore, as the symptoms exhibited by the victims appear to be limited to slavering at the mouth whenever Doris or a similarly attractive girl walks by, I cannot at the moment see any real damage for which a claim for damages would lie. I remember forwards from our rugby blues behaving in a similar fashion at the Michaelmas Ball at Oxford without the excuse that they had been subjected to noxious gasses. No proceedings were issued, even though the odd grope was seen to occur in the corners of the dance floor. I seem to recollect a brassiere replacing the Union Jack on the college flagpole. A substantial improvement I thought at the time.'

Henry, who had heard from Nosey Parker about the budding new career of the soon to be ubiquitous, Doris, piped up here.

'Mr. Hammond, or Godfrey, if I may, I have news regarding the pouting, pretty, platinum-plaited passer-by. The bloodhound reporter from the *Daily Spread,* Norris Parker, telephoned from hospital today to give me the latest regarding the delicious Doris. It seems that she will actually *benefit* from this turn of events. He is fairly certain that, on the back of the notoriety she has already achieved, as "the girl who has them drooling instead of drilling with their pneumatics". She may make a breakthrough as a model of sorts.

Miss Freebody is now, through the good offices of Parker himself, likely to be paraded in all her glory across the centrefold of certain of the less acceptable glossies. You may be aware that these are generally available only on the top shelf of your broadminded newsagent's display. These pictures of the desirable delectation may even make page 3, or is it 5, of one of the national newspapers.

I must say that I do not fully understand why she ferociously attacked and bit the reporter's nose, and landed him in hospital. She doesn't look the aggressive type, but they are evidently the best of mates again now, as she is posing for his photographer in the altogether.'

'Well she hardly appears to have suffered directly from the inhalation, or so it seems. Women, thus far, don't appear to be much affected by the gas emission' added Howard. 'Here's the latest edition of the Daily Spread. Doris is on the front page in rather an unusual pose. She appears rather awkwardly balanced on some sort of stool, with one leg raised high in the air. Maybe she was doing aerobic exercises or yoga, at the time. One does have a fine view of her frilly underwear. M&S I would hazard. Hmmm, Parker has outdone himself this time. I agree Henry, the Nationals are sure to want this now.' He held his reading spectacles in his right hand and lifted them back and forth over the photograph to obtain a better magnification.

'What about the pigs?' asked Henry

'Why? Have any complained?' offered Godfrey, failing to suppress a snigger that slowly rumbled and rippled through his body until he burst out laughing.

'Seriously my dear boy, animals do not have legal rights in themselves. There are statutory bodies such as the RSPCA, who can punish by prosecution, wilful harmers of the dumb animal, and of course owners can claim for the value of their loss in proper circumstances.'

The consultation ended on that lighter note and Henry leaped into a cab in Fleet Street, asking, as he bent to enter it for 'Cavendish Court, Wigmore Street please.' He was visiting his accountant to try to estimate the damage in more precise financial terms. The news was grim indeed.

He had finally escaped from his accountants' office and stood in Wigmore Street, wet inside from the whisky that had been proffered, and soaked through from the rain that had reached the street with considerable force, just as he himself did. As is often the case, his umbrella was sitting perfectly furled in his coat-stand in the hall of his residence. To make matters considerably worse, he was minus two thousand pounds in accountancy fees, let alone the likely ten thousand property loss that he might make even if he played his cards right. Then there were the legal costs. If he were sued, even if he won, there would be a substantial bill.

He could fare worse still if he held off from selling immediately. The market was entering free fall. Who knew when values would finally bottom out?

He sought a taxi back to his flat, waving an imaginary umbrella prodigiously, but entirely in vain, and decided to run the three-quarters of a mile to Chester Gate. The white stuccoed elegant fascia would surely frown from its clear and clean windows, at the sodden and bedraggled creature that was about to seek ingress into its stately portals.

DIMITRI, JOSEPHINE AND ISABEL

As he ran, his feet and the rain beat an uneven tattoo on the pavement in the outer ring of Regents Park. He was not tempted, as he had been on better days, to wander (now dripping) through the rose gardens, admiring the burgeoning multi-coloured blooms and blossoms of early spring that adorned the flower beds to his left. The air he sucked in voraciously in the Park compared favourably with the mixed and potent gasses in the busy Marylebone Road in Central London. This dual carriageway he had just crossed at considerable risk to life and limb and some actual bodily harm (*a.b.h.* in the criminal fraternity) to eardrum and lung. The carbon dioxide that he exhaled probably contained nine parts of alcohol, derived from the discreet softening of the financial blow delivered by his accountant, Anthony Goldburg, in an impersonal, but highly dangerous, unsealed window envelope with the whisky.

As he arrived, breathing heavily and alcoholically after the painful sprint, he searched for those elusive keys that were the precursor, *the* sine *qua* non, to the hot bath and tea that awaited him within. All around him the street was awash. Steam rose from the drains carrying that unmistakable odour from the nether regions. Damn! Where were those keys? Water, untouched by the stress and panic felt by those unfortunate enough to be caught in its steady flow, trickled lazily down the back of his neck finding new, exciting, untouched territory in the small of his back. Finally, shaking off the extraneous drops like a soggy canine, he undeftly removed the recalcitrant clinking items from the detritus of his left jacket pocket.

Once inside the hall, with its ceilings delicately plastered with the inventiveness of a former generation, he was able to take a seat on the white marble floor and pause for breath, for a puddle to form, and moments later, for thought. What day was it? Thursday the fourth of April! Uncovering his Rolex he registered that it was also five in the afternoon. Oh yes, he remembered 'the Greek' was due, and from all accounts he was bringing company.

Henry's telephone answering machine was programmed to start speaking his messages as the front door closed behind him. One of these proclaimed in bellowing terms that 'Dimitri' was on his way over. Henry, having finally entered his flat, immediately peeled off his suit and shirt. Discarding these carelessly on the hall floor he fell into the bathroom. The welcome shower jets pulsed down, like a blizzard of hot hailstones, onto his eager scalp in never ending torrents, providing a hot contrast to the cold shower he had just stepped out of. As he dried his body, noticing the unwanted, one might say superfluous, inches around his middle section, the doorknocker pounded like a brass cannon. This was Dimitri for sure, why in heaven's name was he actually early for once in his life?

Grabbing the bottle green track suit he had long eschewed, preferring, as he had of late, the dressing gown, hot coffee, and warm, soft croissants and jam to the cold morning jog, he wrenched it on, and ran his hands through his damp, unkempt hair. Barefoot, he sprang open the door like a conjurer, to reveal not Dimitri, but a stunning blonde. Her eyes twinkled merrily at the sight of the stunned playboy lawyer, of whom she had been told so much, in such evident disarray standing on his recently abandoned clothing.

'I am Josephine' she said with a playful, teasing smile. As though that explained everything.

Henry's evident bewildered puzzlement - he still held the door just ajar thus barring her entrance, whilst staring at her all the while with his mouth at half-mast. She was tempted to burst into uncontrolled laughter. It was barely stifled. To assist his speedy return from Catatonia she explained:

'I am French, and Dimitri, who is not French but Greek, he is parking the car. He has the problem to find the parking place. Why is that so difficult on an 'orrible day like this one? I cannot understand why you English want to drive to the Park in the raining. What do you do there, just sit in the car and watch the trees?'

Henry resisted the impulse to venture a guess at what one might do in the car in the park on such a day, but his arched eyebrow and half-smile (his lips had found each other once more) betrayed his answering thought.

'On fait l 'amour??? Lovemaking in the rain! I don't believe it! You can't be serious!' Josephine interpreted merrily.

Henry, without confirming or denying her assumption, and having recollected himself, drew her into the hall and out of the rain. Her hair, though now rather damp, was still truly astonishing, it seemed to descend from her pretty head forever. He suddenly realised that he had not actually uttered a word and was probably, once again, gaping at her like one of Shakespeare's "cream-faced loons".

Magnanimous as ever, and in accordance with his invariable custom, he forgave himself for staring immediately. She was indeed a truly magnificent specimen of the female race. Her nose, which was unretouched, was small and straight. Her eyes, a surprising chestnut brown, were large and warm, and he selfishly, but not unreasonably, interpreted their gaze as inviting. Her face was a perfect oval with unblemished pale smooth skin, with a hint of having seen the sun somewhere recently. She must have been a little over five feet six inches in her stockinged feet, which had just emerged prettily and glistening rather from elegant brown court shoes. Her sensible, Burberry raincoat slipped from her shoulders to reveal a form, which caused Henry to seek to catch his breath once more. He was so mesmerised he nearly dropped it!

Who was this angel and how had she been catapulted into his home and his life without warning of any kind? Coming out of his reverie he shook himself and asked her at last 'Can I get you some tea? I think I have some digestive biscuits.'

She looked scandalised. 'Tea? *Ma fois* you British! *Non merci*, but if you 'ave some coffee, that would be nice. *Tiens*! No sugar! I have to watch my form you know!'

Henry nodded vigorously, thinking that he would be happy to watch it for her on an indefinite basis. Tearing his gaze most reluctantly from the object of his growing interest, and to ensure that it did not grow any more for the time being, he turned instead into the small crevice off the hall, which passed for a kitchen. His entry was accompanied by some percussive and brassy sounds, very much like saucepan lids, falling from their precarious balance on the sink unit, where they would have been drying for days in company with the rest of Henry's pans and crockery. Some of the latter now had apparently joined company with said lids on the marble floor.

'What part of la belle France do you come from Josephine?' he yelled, ducking his head briefly out from the kitchen.

'Paris. Can't you tell from my accent?' she jested

'Er, of course, of course! I realised that you come from Paris! Paris where else would you be from with an accent like that?' He responded with similar irony. 'What I meant was, what part of Paris? North or South?' said he breathing deeply hoping that his bold and entirely false presumption would not be exploded.

'*Naturellement!* You are 'ercule Poirot, or 'omes Sherlock, the famous detectives, and you cleverly recognised my Paris Accent, 'ow, I do not know. 'owever, you are not sure which Porte or part of Paris I come from. Well, I can tell you that I live in Versailles, or near there. Do you know the Palace at Versailles?' she asked.

'Like the back of my hand' he vaunted as he sauntered back in. He was entirely unaware of the failing elastic in the trousers of his sagging, jogging suit, laden as he was with dainty Doulton china teacups, and small plates with the bits of mature cheddar, (whose maturity had developed so far, that it would almost certainly qualify for a pension). Alongside, there were also what were apparently, remains of digestive biscuits, perhaps of archaeological interest, that he had dug up from various niches in the crevice. These last, Josephine decided to give a very wide berth indeed.

He found her sitting demurely on the sofa. He could not fail to notice her lightly tanned legs, which were not only crossed but also unquestionably superb, and which were thankfully, but not mercifully, for the most part anyway, on public display.

'Do you live actually within the palace?' he asked with mock innocence and a certain assumed hauteur..

'In the palace? No it is not possible. Not any more, the guards, they don't like trespassers or squatters. They force me to leave with the other visitors. Why should I? I told them. After all, the palace, it belongs to the people. I would like to sleep in one of those palatial bedrooms where Napoleon had his Josephine. Bah! Those pigs of security guards. I should start another revolution.'

He laughed at her Gallic improvisation, and prepared to offer her the coffee from the tray he was carrying with his own, best *Earl Grey.* Josephine watched with considerable interest as Henry's jogging pants suddenly accelerated down towards his knees, their mainstay elastic having given up the challenge. Henry blushed as his more personal regions drifted into view, and, having dumped the tray hastily on the resilient marble coffee table sought to recover his dignity with his trousers.

There was another, still louder, report at the front door. Someone was evidently trying to send the brass Lion knocker right through the door. Enter stage left, Dimitri the huge Greek, his silky, shiny, silver, soaking suit sagging sadly, and clinging, but hardly alluringly, to his incredible hulk. In his considerable wake there followed a second girl, also French by her coquettish appearance. The leonine knocker had evidently knocked its last as it reposed sadly in the outsize paw of the Athenian. 'Henry!' he boomed in that rich deep bass of his.

'What's the matter with your trousers?' he bellowed. 'Not been at it with Josephine already have you?' he smiled as he marched into the hall.

'Henry, listen to me. Why don't you buy a house with a godforsaken garage? It is impossible to park here. They will tow my Rolls away! Now would they really tow Rolls Royces away?' Then with due and proper reverence and solemnity at its passing, he handed the remains of the knocker to his bemused host.

'I don't think they'll tow you away Dimi. Not today anyway. The wardens have run and dove for cover and refreshment.'

Looking down at his jog suit he explained 'elastic failure I'm afraid. I accidentally gave Josephine a sneak preview' he giggled. He proffered a large mug of steaming brown toward the huge hand of his friend and client, and placed the deceased and now permanently silenced lion knocker on the hall windowsill.

With no hands to support them, his trousers started a downhill run again. He stuck out his stomach to delay the descent.

Dimitri rejected the proffered beverage. 'No thank you. Give me something stronger. Don't you have any Scotch? How would it be if you pour it into the tea? Then if the police stop me for driving whilst drunk I can blame you for lacing my drink! I am innocent!' he howled, acting out a piece.

Je m'accuse! I accuse! I accuse Henry, the hopeless hack, of hiding hooch in my holy, hot chocolate! Then you will defend me for free, and give evidence admitting that I was a palpably pristine, perfect, pawn in your pustuled, prickly, perfidious possession. I will be set free, and you will be forced to eat bread and water for six years!'

'How does one eat water you Greek imbecile?' retorted the house host, Henry.

Ignoring the response Dimitri turned and indicated his companion. 'By the way, this is lsabel she has travelled tirelessly from Toulouse, just to meet me, fall hopelessly in love, and submit to my terrible embrace!'

lsabel uttered a shriek of absolute denial. 'No way! You are too large in the wrong place! You would kill me by flattening.'

Dimitri bellowed an unhesitating riposte 'flatten you? So what if I do. Don't worry, I loves *Crepes.* You will be "Crepes lsabel" with two large scoops of vanilla ice cream on top please! To represent your hair, we could arrange for oodles of chocolate sauce. Ha! Ha!"

lsabel whose dark, attractive eyes had looked to the heavens for aid and support at this last, inexcusably sexist not to mention gourmandising, vision, was also a French lovely. Her hair was almost as long but coloured an unrelenting black. Her eyes were brown but almost black also, and her figure was slightly fuller than her fair friend's, but there was not an ounce of fat on her, or so it appeared. No doubt careful investigation by one of the experts, in whose hands she was evidently about to place her life, if not her body, would confirm this initial appraisal. She also wore a mischievous and cheeky look, both on her face, and when she turned suddenly, by a flash of firm rounded flesh revealed under her swishing skirt, which was evidently manufactured during a period of severe cotton shortage. All in all, there was something about her which boded (or bodied?) well for someone's future.

The Greek grabbed his friend's arm and yanked him into the hall so they would not be heard, and whispered in a quieter version of his normal gravely tone:

'We are going out tonight, the four of us. You can pay.' Henry's eyes pleaded for mercy. Dimitri continued unabated 'we will have Dover sole and champagne at the 'Elysee' and compete for who can break the most plates.'

Henry's knees started to sag again now accompanied by his trousers as the tiny remnants of his bank balance began to filter away and disappear before his mind's eye.

'Henry! Don't worry you can afford it. By the way, I am after the blonde, so no monkey business! Eh? You don't like Isabel? Eh? She is sexy no, look at those Sheffields eh?'

"Not Sheffields you nincompoop, Bristols!"

However, Henry recognised the power and force of these 'arguments', which had firmly made their impression. However for Henry, Josephine had sparked off something different in his mind. Something truly Napoleonic! Isabel's appeal was a physical sensation not unlike numbness, which probably generated a feverish movement of men's hands in her general direction. But Josephine, Josephine ooh, la, la!

'Now listen, Dimitri, I have had a bad time today, what with my industrial investment leaking a gas which causes men to salivate furiously; an accountant's bill to knock your socks off; and a lawyer's bill yet to come which will dwarf the accountant's charge into insignificance. I just cannot afford another wild spree. However, as regards the choice of target for the evening, you choose.'

Reluctantly, dragging his very mild apprehensions along, he submitted to the Greek's urgings for wild fun that evening, and hoisted his trousers once more. To give Dimitri some credit, he read his friend's mental anguish and understood his predicament.

'Come on Henry! Let's have some fun. What about if I pay?'

'That'll be the day' Henry sighed ruefully.

He remembered the last time Dimitri paid, it was in the South of France, on Henry's birthday nearly a year ago. The starlets were out in force in Cannes and the "Terrible Two" set about them with vigour. Henry remembered the incredible dinners when champagne and the best wines flowed freely. He revisited in his mind the glorious sunsets seen from his room in the Carlton Hotel whilst cradling a scotch on the rocks in his left hand and a French mam'selle in his left. 'Ah yes!' thought Henry in the immortal words of Maurice Chevalier, "I remember them well."

Unabashed and not to be outdone, Dimitri pulled a sodden bundle of fifty pound notes from his back pocket as a clear statement of intent. Then without pause, he visited pocket after pocket withdrawing larger and larger wads.

'There must be thousands there!' groaned Henry wistfully.

'Don't tell me. You have raided some unsuspecting Casino in the dead of night and raped and ravaged its cash balances.'

'Enough! I confess everything' confirmed his Greek hugeness.

'I left them for dead. I played roulette at Maxim's. Number 8 came up four times consecutively. I had two thousand on it by the last spin of the wheel. So don't despair. I am even going to pay that exorbitant bill of legal fees that you sent me last year. How much was it? I think it was five or perhaps, ten grand? Look here's fifteen to cover the interest for late payment.

Oh! And here's another thirty to hold for me, so I don't give it back to them. Now I want you to listen to me carefully Henry!' he bellowed. 'Whatever I may say to you don't give this back to me. Look here's another five for yourself as a fee for resisting my every entreaty when I beg you for it to gamble with. OK?'

'All right, all right!' Henry murmured, thinking. 'But if push comes to shove, by law you can demand it back, and I can't refuse. Suppose I establish a trust for your children by deed, then you won't be able to get at it?'

Dimitri hesitated for a moment, considering whether he really wanted to be parted from such a large sum in this rather rare moment of lucidity. Then, without more, he uttering a Greek imprecation which, fortunately, the girls could neither hear nor understand, and grumbled grudgingly in the affirmative. 'Yes, but do it quickly before I change my mind.'

There it slipped out, didn't it? Dimitri was married unhappily - that is, *his wife was unhappy*. Dimitri was the typical absentee husband and father. His children, despite (or as a result of) paternal absences, were enjoying a good upbringing, attending the best schools, and being showered with the best educational and expensive toys.

In the meantime, the girls had been talking a stream in their native French, interspersed with the odd French giggle. Dimitri re-entered the drawing room and announced,

'You girls take a cab and go home to change. We are all going out for dinner at eight. Put on your sexiest dresses, that is, if you really must dress, it does seem such a waste. Anyway, get ready for the time of your lives. We'll pick you up later. Come on! Run along! *Vite, vite*! We don't want to be kept waiting! *Endaxi*? OK?'

DAI AND DORIS

Up in parochial Buttersoft, the English countryside is suddenly broken by a sprawling hotchpotch of residential streets, a few shopping parades which had changed little since the war, and an area of industrial buildings including the estate owned by the luckless lawyer from London. Here we find that Dai Evans and Doris Freebody had arrived at Dai's ramshackle studio/flat, within a terraced house, on the edge of that industrial area in the fringes of the residential sector. They reached the house in which the studio was situated in similar weather to that being suffered by Henry & Co. in London. Doris had tried manfully to keep the rain off her hair but she was more than a little damp, when the cab dropped them off at the ineptly named *Sunny Rise*, as indicated, on the residential outskirts of town.

Dai, fairly dripping himself, but a gentleman to the last, considerately allowed her first go in the bathroom, even promising her the use of a hairdryer he would borrow from his landlady. She was a Mrs. Soames, a thirty-five year old redhead divorcee, who actually lived on the premises, in the flat on the ground floor of the building. When Mrs. Soames heard that our Dai was entertaining, she insisted on providing a warming cup of tea, offering to bring a tray upstairs. Dai's protestations were to no avail, and he accepted her kindness and returned to his flat clutching the hairdryer.

Doris had decided to remove her dress. It was rather wet and she was to pose without clothes anyway. She stood in front of the large mirror over the navy blue ceramic sink considering her body. It would soon be seen in many households in the land. She gave a little shiver of expectation and excitement. It was really quite thrilling all things considered. Dai knocked on the bathroom door, and told Doris that the dryer awaited her in the bedroom on the right, and that he would wait for her in the large studio down the hall, second on the left.

Doris had many talents, but she had no sense of direction whatsoever. She opened the bathroom door and looked about her. With one hand over each pretty breast, and only a pair of skimpy knickers to cover her virtue, she tripped along the passage seeking the bedroom and the hairdryer. Turning left instead of right and taking the first door, rather than the second (which actually would have led her to the studio), she found to her surprise that she had walked out right out of the flat. As she turned back to re-enter, she discovered that the front door, which was on a spring, had slammed shut. She was on the common staircase wearing nothing but a flimsy pair of panties and her hands.

She was about to bang on the door for Dai to reopen, when Mrs Soames appeared on the staircase with the tea tray. 'My goodness!' she exclaimed 'What on earth is going on? Why are you standing nearly naked in my house? What is Dai up to? I thought he was a good boy!'

Doris was uncertain how to explain her presence. She suddenly decided to opt for the truth. 'We were caught in the rain. My dress was soaked, and I took it off to dry. Now I took the wrong door and have shut myself out. Ooh! I am so embarrassed!' Tears began to form in her magnificent large blue eyes. As they dripped down the perfect cheeks, only pausing momentarily in their matching dimples, the self-righteous landlady began to thaw.

'Oh! You poor thing' said Mrs. Soames caressingly, changing direction like a weather vane in a shifting breeze, now entirely mollified. 'Let's get that Dai to open the door then.' She knocked loudly and shouted 'Dai come and open up! Quickly man!'

Dai was there in an instant and was covered in confusion when he saw Doris in her knickers and hands, in company with his landlady and the tea, all standing prettily on the Axminster carpet.

'Oh my goodness! What has happened?' he asked.

'Your guest was locked out. Now eyes back in sockets, and fetch her a dressing gown. I'll set the tea down in the bedroom and she can warm up. Poor, poor thing' Mrs. Soames ordered taking charge of the situation.

'Well I must say that it seems hardly worth it' said Dai 'those knickers will have to come off anyway.'

'What? In my house?' his landlady exclaimed shocked to the roots of her carrot red hair. She looked scandalised.

'Now, now, Mrs. Soames don't you go getting the wrong idea. She wants me to take some glamour photos, that's all. It's Norris Parker's orders, and it's strictly business, professional, and above board. That's the truth of it isn't it Doris?'

'Oh! Ye-es, Mrs. Soames. Mr. Parker wants to take them to the Sun and Mayfair and other glossy magazines so that I can become a star, earn tons of money and buy a big house in the country for me mam and dad.'

'Well, I never did! I don't know what the world is coming to' Mrs Soames shook her head. It would never have happened in my day, I can tell you. Fine goings on, and I don't think. Well I suppose it's none of my business. Just you make sure that you behave yourself young Dai, you're not in the valleys now, you know. I expect you to be a proper gentleman. Why, she is little more than a child!' Dai was uncertain as to how to interpret this last remark from his landlady. He thought for a moment and replied 'don't you go worrying your head about Doris Mrs. Soames she really is quite a big girl' (a 35C cup, I would suppose, he thought excitedly to himself.)

He stepped forward and took the tray without another word, and ushered Doris back into the flat leaving Mrs. Soames staring at them from the stairs. When Doris had dried her hair, she entered the studio cup of tea in hand. Looking about her at the white parasols, erected to ensure the best lighting arrangements, she commented 'we could have done with one of those earlier, would've gone nice with my dress too.'

'Er-yes.' responded the now nervous Dai who had done no skinny clipping before this day. 'Would you mind removing your knickers and hands Doris? Then lay on that couch please, and I will arrange you?' Doris suddenly felt shy, and stood around awkwardly not really ready yet to take the plunge. She wandered around the room looking at Dai's past glories. Girls certainly there were many, but mainly in chic fashionable outfits. Models she supposed. Then there were sports shots at football, cricket and tennis matches.

There were one or two grand openings of supermarkets, including one, she noticed, by the Duchess of York. She remembered the occasion, it was the local Tesco outlet opened about six years ago. She had been there and had presented the Duchess with a posy. 'My goodness!' she thought. 'There I am standing a little to the Duchess's right, with my hand in that of my form teacher Miss Goodbody, who had brought the class out from school for the occasion.' Doris had been chosen for the presentation by reason of her stunning looks even at the age of twelve. She decided not to mention the fact to Dai now, perhaps later.

Dai correctly interpreted her general behaviour as indicating her unreadiness for the leap into total nudity. 'Shall I turn round for a minute? If you're feeling a bit shy like?' offered the considerate man from the Rhondda, his soft Welsh accent coming through like a musical overtone.

'That's very sweet of you Dai, but you're going to see me without them anyway. So here goes.'

As she removed her hands, and then the remainder of her clothing, Dai felt his throat contract and go quite dry. She was absolute perfection, beautiful. Her body was pale and smooth, complimenting the ash blonde of her silky hair. Her large blue eyes he had already seen, and they would be stunning on anyone. Her white breasts were pert for all their fullness, and tipped with pink. Her stomach quite flat as it reached down to that little mound of blonde hair beneath. Her legs were long and slim, a dancer's legs he thought.

As she turned slightly away from his gaze, he had to catch his breath at the small pert rump that was situated directly behind her. Unable to take his eyes off her, causing her to become increasingly embarrassed, he reached his hand out for his cup of tea which was to his right but slightly behind him on a side table. By mischance his hand went into the cup instead of finding the handle. He let out an almighty yelp and leapt three feet into the air. Doris misinterpreting his shout as outright disapproval of her display shrieked, grabbed her flimsy bits and bolted back into the bathroom.

Dai seeing Doris's distress was caught between the pain in his poor burned fingers and rushing to reassure her. Unable to stop jumping up and down with pain he nonetheless gradually inched his way toward the bathroom door flinging his hand up and down as if trying to get rid of it or something unspeakable on it. 'Ouch! Ouch! Doris! Listen girl! Don't take it the wrong way girl. I just burned my fingers in the tea. Ouch! Let me in girl so I can put them under the cold tap. Come on Doris please!'

She opened the door a crack. 'I thought you didn't like my bits' she said mournfully.

'Don't be crazy girl. You have the most amazing bits I've seen in all my life. That's why I burnt my fingers. I couldn't take my eyes off you. I was mesmerised I was. Put my hand in the tea 'cos I wasn't watching what I was doing.'

'Well that's all right then, I suppose' she replied opening the door and walking back into the studio now without a trace of her former shyness.

'Well I don't mean it's alright that you burnt your fingers, you understand don't you?'

Dai failed to take in her words immediately, his eyes mesmerised by her winking buttocks. His painful fingers were temporarily forgotten.

'Er don't you concern yourself Doris. I shall survive. I've seen and experienced much worse.'

'You mean much worse bodies than mine?' Doris enquired quizzically.

'No, I meant I've seen and felt much worse pain than mine today. I haven't ever seen a body to compare with yours anywhere.'

This photo session would have to be a thorough one he decided it might well last all day. More even ... He dreamily mused as he ran the cold water over his fingers, the pain now almost a thing of the past.

Returning to his senses and his studio, he started positioning Doris for the shoot. He had her in every position imaginable, with every expression that she could muster on her undeniably pretty face, which had not a trace of a blemish or a wrinkle. When she smiled he was tempted to actually reduce the lighting, so bright did the whole impression appear. He had to agree with the noxious Nosey about one thing, Doris was bound for fame and fortune.

Doris, rather ingenuously and innocently asked him, 'how do I really look Dai?'

'There she is spread out on a deep red velvet chez longue looking for all the world like an original Goya painting, or better really' thought Dai and she asks me how she looks!'

'You're just the best there is Doris. An angel is what you are, no question about it. I will treasure these pictures, because from now on only the really famous photographers will be good enough for you. I hope you won't forget me entirely when you're rich and famous.'

Doris sat up and looked intently at the modest Welshman.

'Dai let me tell you this. Nobody except you is going to take photos of me. Unless it's you, I won't agree. No one else will see me without my clothes on, except when they see the pictures of course.'

A tear appeared in the corner of Dai's eye when he heard this and he moved around the camera set-up to where Doris lay. He took her head in both hands and looked into her eyes.

'You are an angel, and I might as well admit it, I've fallen head over heels for you.'

She reached up and kissed him lightly. Dai grasped her in his arms as his tears ran down onto her exposed nipples.

'You know' she said slyly 'your clothes are very rough against my skin Dai. You'd better take them off if we are to be in such close contact. Otherwise the photos will show red marks.'

Dai was like a man possessed. He ripped his shirt wrenching the buttons off rather than undoing them. As he pranced about trying to remove his trousers he lost his balance and fell headlong onto Doris's knees.

'Slowly, slowly Dai. There's no train to catch.' Doris said softly.

'I can't help myself woman' yelped the happy Welshman 'I'm fair desperate for you. I've got no patience for clothes now.' At last he had everything off and they lay together holding one another tenderly.

'Shouldn't we take some pictures of you too?' said Doris teasingly, eyeing his mighty weapon.

'You must be joking!' ejaculated our Dai. 'That's censored that is. For your eyes only.' 'Hmmm!' responded the girl. 'But not only for my *eyes*, I hope' she giggled.

THE BROOM CUPBOARD AFFAIR

Nosey, meanwhile, had been given a dishonourable discharge from The Seamen's Hospital where he had been caught by the Matron 'handling the goods' in the form of a buxom young redheaded, red-blooded nurse called Marlene Deertish. They had ensconced themselves in the rather incommodious broom cupboard where Norris had sought to remove Marlene's many-buttoned uniform.

Matron Marchford, head of the venerable institution, had been reprimanding a ward orderly, Cynthia, for the spillage of unidentified powder (suspected as being talcum, but who can tell these days) which had been sprinkled liberally on the floor of the corridor. Reaching blindly inside the cupboard to feel for the broom so that she might give it to Cynthia she instead found Parker's personal triumph which was currently homing in upon Marlene. A heated broom handle? That couldn't be. No, the feel of this particular broom handle brought back to her mind a familiar and unhappy experience in her youth. The shock waves hit both Matron and the partially undressed reporter at the same instant. Not letting go of the prize she had collared, she wrenched the door wide with her free hand.

'Ah ha!' she exclaimed. 'Caught red-faced, *in flagrante delicto!* In my hospital. You disgusting people. What behaviour in a broom cupboard indeed! How dare you?' The couple who had not yet coupled offered no excuse.

Finally, returning that upon which her hand had recently alighted to its dejected and unfulfilled owner, in somewhat worse condition than she had received it, she said 'pack your bags both of you, you're terminated.'

She turned on her heel and made for the nearest ladies to wash her hands, against the possibility of catching an unspeakable sexually transmissible disease, and in an attempt to remove the awful experience from her pristine memory.

Poor Marlene was beside herself. Slowly recovering her torn tights she wriggled back into her uniform. Nosey was particularly sad at this development. Tears fell in torrents from Marlene's cornflower blue eyes. 'Ooh! Whatever shall I do now? I am ruined. Ain't that the truth of it.'

'Why you're an Irish girl' smiled Nosey. 'Who'd have thought that a good catholic girl like you would be involved in a situation like this? Never mind Marlene, I have influence with the Matron of St Luke's Hospice. I'll get you another job'.

Marlene turned and smiled brightly through her tears 'Will you really Norris?

Really?'

'Just let me handle you, I mean to say, let's go back to my place and discuss the details right now' he replied.

He bundled her into a cab and gave his address. Thus another young girl found her way into Nosey's untidy knocking shop above the 'Chipperie' in Milk Street, Buttersoft.

ERICH AND SOPHIE AND MORE DIMITRI

Dimitri Loukopoulos, nicknamed by his friends 'the Duke of Athens, or the Bull,' was large and imposing both physically and as a character. Well over six feet and weighing close to three hundred pounds, he was built like an overfed wrestler. Under his huge head of curly black hair (reminiscent of a full size bull's) his eyes, partially hidden by thick eyebrows, which met in the middle, were like large black almonds. They were nearly always squeezed to appear to be half their size by a devilish grin.

Dimitri had been as rich as Croesus, until the oil price crashed recently, when he had eighteen tankers full on the high seas. He had lost millions in one day, but did not bat either of his hefty eyelids. Instead, he'd hailed a taxi to Crockfords and then Aspinalls, and took them for a total of nearly four hundred thousand pounds in a night's roulette, thus ensuring at least three months of continuing revelry.

He collapsed heavily and noisily on to the settee, giving Josephine no choice but either to escape or be smothered. With the agility of a rugby winger, she neatly side-stepped, what might have been excused as an accidental brush of their bodies, which she had correctly read as a precursor to an attempt at embrace.

Sweeping up her Burberry with a flourish, she winked at Henry and said 'Allons y Isabel. OK let's go!'

Henry bowed with pronounced and exaggerated respect and savoir-faire, and said,

'Mesdemoiselles, until tonight. Yes, tonight, Josephine! Er, oh yes, and Isabel! I have been enchanted! I seriously doubt that I shall ever recover.'

This time all eyes together with their associated eyebrows reached for the skies in joint disbelief. Poor Henry, they just did not know how sincere he was on this occasion, as a matter of fact, neither did he.

Henry opened the front door for them, checked that the rain had finally paused in the almost continuous battering that it metes out upon our British Isles, and stepped out gingerly into the street to hail a cab.

'*Au revoir!*' he yelled, as the cab swept them away.

Within minutes of their departure, Dimitri was asleep and snoring blissfully like a champion sow, quite undisturbed by the wetness of the suit that bravely clung on, and valiantly sought to surround him.

Henry took in the view of 'Incredible Heaviness of Being' as a crashing return to earth, shook his head with yet another sigh. He decided there and then that if they were out for yet another night of wine, women in general and Josephine and Isabel in particular, and song, he also ought to grab forty, or even fifty, winks.

He slipped out of the tracksuit and slid painlessly between his crisp new sheets, recently lifted from the overburdened shelves of Messrs Harrods Limited, courtesy of his much abused credit account card.

His mind was instantly enveloped in dreams of streams of blonde hair, blown backwards by the breeze, along a seemingly endless stretch of silver sand, edged by turquoise sea under a faultless blue sky. Only the odd palm tree, the inevitable Gin and Tonic, and a delicious young girl in a grass skirt and chocolate coloured skin complicated the picture. He proceeded to lick that skin only to find that it tasted of chocolate and actually came off in his mouth! These heavenly images, curiously reminiscent of a certain chocolate advertisement, led him softly into a deep and rejuvenating sleep, undisturbed by the rain, which had now resumed its relentless assault on his bedroom window. What a dream! What weather! What a country!

It was the telephone, cunningly and somewhat sadistically placed near to Dimitri's right ear by Henry, prior to his departure into his own bedroom, which awoke them. The Hellenic Giant swept it into his palm without opening his eyes.

'*Nai, pios eisai?* Sorry! Oh you are English! Well, who the devil are you, and why are you phoning at such an hour? I was asleep! Eh? What do you mean it is seven in the evening? Do I have to sleep when it suits you, or may I choose my own time? Hallo? Hallo! Oh! They hung up.'

'Who was it?' called Henry from his bedroom.

He had tried to leap out of bed to rescue the telephone, only to discover that his left leg was still asleep. It refused to co-operate having been slept on awkwardly, and he had collapsed on to the silken Chinese dragons decorating the rug by his bed.

Dimitri yelled back through the doorway 'I dunno. The sonofabitch didn't say. Funny though, his voice was just like your father's.'

'What! You bastard Greek excuse for a Trojan Horse! You spoke like that to my father? I wouldn't leave a patch of pink flesh on your massive torso - it would be all shades of black and blue, if I could only stand up.'

Henry's threatening and warrior like poise was only left unmatched by his pose. Having lifted his body up painfully in attempt to assert himself, but unable to achieve a balance, he fell down again, landing heavily on his rear end. His legs were stuck up in the air, and in that unladylike position, he was not nearly as frightening or imposing as he certainly would have wished.

Dimitri, not perceptibly moved by Henry's bold attempt at simulated aggression, indeed it is not certain that he even registered it, merely interpolated

'Where the blazes is the Johnny Walker? I must have a drink, I have such a hangover!'

Walking to the communicating door he saw Henry in the position just described and murmured,

'Oh sorry I didn't realise you were exercising. What is that position some sort of Yoga?'

This was more than Henry could stand (Henry was having grave difficulty standing in any event) and, though he struggled to his foot, rather than feet, he fell back on to the bed in resignation and unsuppressed laughter when he realised that Dimitri had been in earnest.

'The Panadol are in the cocktail cabinet sensibly parked next to the Scotch. They may be a wiser choice of medicine, in my humble submission, my Duke, I mean my Lord.' Henry had spoken in the time-honoured fashion of all seasoned advocates with appropriate mock solemnity and decorum.

'OK. I will take both the pills and the scotch' compromised His Athenian Largeness.

'How very tasteful and delicate of you, what a wise, poetic and supremely Dimitrian choice if I may say so' conceded Henry.

'Are you by chance related to Lord Byron?' he ventured.

'Not to my knowledge' said Dimitri thoughtfully, 'but I have a large family, and I can't be expected to know everyone, can I? Be reasonable! Of course his being a member of the aristocracy makes it rather likely that we are at least cousins, don't you think?'

'What I think is I'll phone my father and check how his heart condition has responded to the shock treatment *a la Grecque*. I would like just one more chance to make my peace with him before he departs for the Viennese happy hunting ground.'

Henry's father Erich, was of Austrian descent, although he had lived in England since 1939. The Nazi occupation of his native land ended his sojourn in the land of waltzes, schnapps and lederhosen. Erich's father had bribed a ship's captain with solid gold, to take the then young lad, to safety upon British shores.

His English accent was considered by Erich himself to be impeccable, although he had the interesting habit of pronouncing "v" as if it were "w" and vice versa (wice wersa). When asked about the English weather he would often respond

'Vetter than Wienna and vindier, vether I vont the veather or not.'

He would perforce tell all and sundry:

'I vas wolunteer in your Home Guard in ze Vor. Your people made me Intelligence. I vos verking out the qvestions vot ve vonted to ask the German prisoners of var. Wery important verk! Vizout me who knows???' he would advise with an air of candid importance spreading his hands and shrugging his shoulders.

Of course, Henry had learned all of his father's heroic exploits by heart, and when trouble was brewing between them for any reason, he would gently divert his father by asking 'what did you do in the Great War Daddy?' He got this line from an article in the Sunday Times Colour Magazine a few years ago and would bring it out to irritate his father from time to time.

'Not the Great Vor you dolt! The Second Vorld Vor. I may be growing old but I am not zat ancient. In fact warious ladies have told me I don't look a day over sixty.'

'But dad, you are only fifty eight anyway!' Henry would rejoin.

Erich, ignoring the interruption by his progeny, would launch once again into the History of the Second World War. He would dwell upon the particular relevance and heroism of one Erich Rotfeld (now 'Eric Redfield' as he preferred to be known. Having regard to his English accent, and clearly British bearing, it was considered to be much more appropriate as a surname. His fluent German combined with his die-hard English attitude won him acclaim in the back rooms of the military machine even if the front lines never needed, or saw, an appearance by him in person.

Eric, an attractive man who in his younger years had been properly accused of being a dark Latin version of Clark Gable, or Erich as his son privately preferred to think of him, was like so many Viennese, an incurable romantic. Unfortunately he was, with the advancing years, also extremely short sighted. The apparent result of this combination of riches was that he appeared indiscriminate as to the objects of his romantic desire. Charitably, and not unreasonably, it was accepted by all concerned that when he made a pass at a stunningly beautiful girl half his age that he had unfortunately mistaken her for his beloved wife, Sophie.

This, alas, would only be discovered in time if the current target of his romantic darts rebuffed his advances. It is a matter of deep regret that too many such slipped through his wholly inadequate defences, and his innocent 'mistake of identity' was only discovered after the liaison had advanced far beyond ordinary social intercourse.

Stunned into frozen shock at his entirely unprovoked, and unsignalled advances, was, more often than not, the cause of the girls' apparent inactivity. Having not rebuffed his first moves, they would often hesitate to offer a tardy refusal to his second, as they would feel foolish.

Henry had gently suggested spectacles - contact lenses - as an answer to the problem, but his father, being of the 'old school' when it came to matters of expense and expenditure, had, though Henry was certain that it wrung his heart to do it, reluctantly declined.

'Contacts!' Eric had ejaculated with considerable disgust. 'I certainly don't need them, your mother says I am already making far too many contacts!'

He continued wretchedly 'you know, Henry, sometimes I think that your mother doesn't understand me. She says I should be able to tell the difference between her and these other women by touch. Seriously Henry, do you think my hands could be short sighted too?' Erich appeared wery concerned by such a possibility.

Henry had known when he was beaten, but recovered both himself and his good humour greatly, when he realised that he had only inherited one of his father's serious health defects. He had the benefit of 20:20 vision.

Ah! but we digress. Henry dialled the number of his parents' residence in Ascot, which is, as Erich patiently reminds us, situate in Royal Berkshire. It has come as something of a surprise and disappointment to the elder Redfields that they have not yet been invited to 'an occasion'. The Queen's Garden Party or the Royal enclosure are two such 'occasions' and, having proper regard for the situation of the Redfield Country Seat, and the luxurious appointment of the apartments in that household either would be most appropriate.

Sophie, Henry's long suffering mother, believes that the Queen would be delighted with her Sherry Trifle, and she would be happy to contribute one such to the party when the "occasion" finally arose. In the meantime she has attempted to hone it to perfection by thrusting it before, and down, the various members of her family. Following the regularity with which this dish appeared on the dining room, table Erich had become wont to say to her

'Vell Sophie my dear, don't vurry you'll get it perfect ewentually. Remember, darling, If at first you don't succeed, trifle, trifle, again?'

At the third ring of the telephone on this particular morning Erich answered 'Hallo! Who's there?'

Before Henry could speak, another ersatz Erich voice interfered, courtesy of the trusty parental answer-phone message (the answer-phone was on at all times regardless of the presence or absence at home of Henry's parents:

"Hallo, this is Eric and Sophie Redfield. Ve are wery sorry we are not here to take your call, but please leave a note of your name and telephone number and ve phone you back. Goodbye!"

Erich who was a little distracted by his earlier unpleasant experience with Dimitri on the telephone, was disorientated whilst the message was playing. At the same moment, Sophie dragged his attention from the telephone, distracting him yet further, by asking who it was on the line ("perhaps this is another case of mistaken identity!"). Accordingly, when Erich once again pressed the receiver to his ear, all he caught was the tail end of his own message saying "Goodbye." He unthinkingly replied 'Goodbye' and hung up.

Henry could not believe it. When he tried to redial the line was engaged, as his mother was trying to call him for sympathy. This would presumably be about the strange obviously female callers who rang Erich at all times of the day or night with a view to a kill, and who hung up if she or the answer-phone intervened. These predators! Trying to catch a poor, near-blind, old man.

What was the matter with the young men these days? Were they all gay? In her day 'gay' had meant something entirely different, something nice and happy, now it meant that people like Sophie would unfairly deprived of being grandparents. So inconsiderate! Anyway, Henry heard none of this particular repeat, as both lines remained stubbornly engaged.

He decided to send his father a fax instead. He scribbled a quick note. 'Trying to call you - line is permanently engaged there must be a fault on it.' Within seconds he received the reply:

'That's no fault, that's your mother!'

At the next instant the telephone rang, and, sure enough, Sophie was able to recite all her troubles to her beloved son. His attempts to interrupt to explain that the caller was none other than he, himself, and not some "bit of fluff, went entirely unheeded. Before he could say a word, in fact, his mother exclaimed 'oh Henry! I have left something on the light (cooker) must go, bye love!'

Henry shrugged, gave up the ghost and went in search of anything large and Greek that he could find within the confines of his private domain, to pummel to within an inch of its life.

In the event, Dimitri had sought sanctuary within the extremely limited but very secure territory of a water closet. This particular toilet would in any other circumstances have served as a spacious bathroom to the likes of you or I. The admixture of whisky and Panadol had been an adventurous experiment, but regrettably one which, on this occasion, had not met with unqualified success.

Accordingly, Dimitri was adopting the only sensible course in the circumstances. Ergo, the effective and immediate removal of all traces of the offending compound from his body with considerable haste. He achieved this with an accompaniment of various unattractive 'bathroom' or 'restroom' noises, enlarged somewhat in this instance, owing to the Greek's fine bass tonal ability available in stereo surround sound. What pass as decibels to ordinary mortals, are mere squeaks to one such as the Duke of Athens. One should have centibels or better still Bow Bells for the likes of Dimitri.

Knowing that this was not to be his day, Henry sloped off like a wolf, resigned to retreat, into the ensuite bathroom to prepare for the night's action. Following carefully the instructions he had read in the latest James Bond novel he had been reading, he took his shower cold, then piping hot, followed by another cold dousing. After which he felt nothing, if not very wet. His skin was supposed to be tingling fiercely and wide-awake for life's toughest challenge, Instead he felt like a bedraggled half-drowned rat. Drying himself he opened his wardrobe to chose his apparel for the approaching main event of the evening.

Trying to lift his sagging spirits he opted for a black silk polo neck with matching slacks. The black and white check Kenzo sports jacket over the top would round off a meal "with man-appeal" or so he imagined. Also, black hid some of those uncomfortable bulges that he was determined to see off in the very near but rather indefinite future.

Completing the attire with his favourite Cartier Santos cologne, rejecting the Boss, Eau Sauvage, Fahrenheit, Azzarro, and other delicacies at his disposal, he was ready for action. The earlier setbacks forgotten, he slipped into an alter ego, Hyde to his daytime Jekyll. He could almost hear the strains of the John Barry introduction to the major Bond films.

Dimitri sensed the change when Henry entered the room. 'Ah! Ha!' he exclaimed 'that's more like it. But remember Josephine is mine!' Henry nodded reluctantly and then smiled. 'Now, that Isabel is a real sexpot isn't she?' he volunteered.

'Ye-es. She is that's true.' replied the Greek, already reconsidering the arrangements.

'By the way, Dimi, what do you think about her breasts?' Henry asked solicitously.

'What do you mean, what do I think of them? They are superb, of course. She has championship breasts. The children who suckle on those breasts can consider themselves extremely lucky. I hope that I can get there before them!'

Henry suggested 'she may have won trophies for them. Cups. What cups do you think?'

'35D? Maybe even a 36C. What of it?' the Greek looked at Henry wonderingly.

'No nothing' replied the lawyer, noncommittal. 'I just wanted your expert opinion.'

'Now look Henry if this is some ploy ...'

'Not at all, perish the thought' replied Henry. 'Hmmm . . . 'Henry could see Dimitri weighing things (breasts included) in the balance.

'They are certainly both attractive girls' remarked the Greek pawing the ground with his right foot.

'Absolutely! They certainly are. You've hit the nail squarely on the head there, Duke' responded the faithful retainer.

'And I know I could be happy with either were t'other out of the way.' he added asban afterthought.

'Wait a minute! Just a moment! Isn't that a line from that film you like so much, with Alec Guinness and Dennis Price. Now what was it? Come on what was the title of that classic? Dimitri searched his memory bank unsuccessfully.

'Kind hearts and Coronets' supplied Henry

'That's it! That's it! Dennis Price had to choose with which attractive lady to leave prison. They were both seated in their separate carriages waiting for him. The attractive brunette his wife, or the sexy mischievous and dangerous blonde. Then as he reaches the gate of the prison (Newgate wasn't it?) he remembers that he has forgotten his memoirs in his cell on Death Row. Ah yes he quotes that line just before he realises his oversight. Dimitri was lost in thought for a moment.

'We don't now, and didn't then have a Death Row, here in England' advised the lawyer.

Dimitri appeared not to have heard this last remark as he suddenly ejaculated

'Now I see! Yes, yes! Well it is a tough choice between the girls, I agree. OK, OK, Let's be entirely fair. Let's toss for it.'

Henry having privately thought that the girls might decide differently, and even reject them both altogether nonetheless agreed immediately. He said 'right. Heads I win tails you lose. Call Dimitri! Which is it to be?'

Dimitri was still a stranger to these shores and for a moment was confused enough to nod his acceptance. 'Heads' he called. An instant later he relented exclaiming:

"Hey you miserable sonofabitch! You were going to cheat me! That does it! Well I have decided. I choose Isabel, and you'll just have to make do with Josephine. Eat your heart out you scheister lawyer, Old Bailey hack, Docked Briefs!"

"Very well, I accept your decision, kind sir, but I must correct you on a matter of detail, I am a solicitor not a barrister and not entitled to set up my stall inside the Old Bailey. That is the province of your common-a-garden Counsel, and revered Queen's Counsel or bewigged silk. I merely brief, or write some of the script for the old tub-thumpers. Such is the destiny of the Old Bailey Hack. A Dock Brief is, or rather was, a barrister appointed by the Court to defend an impoverished defendant, at a low fixed fee. One might not get the best defence in the world from such a source.

Mind you, if you do manage to get yourself arrested whilst sailing too close to the wind, I could come and visit you in the nick and 'take down your particulars'.

'You leave my particulars right where they are!' shouted Dimitri, hoisting his underpants up from their late position at half-mast. Dimitri had discarded his sodden outer garb at some time during his rest period, and was conducting this conversation in his rather distinctive, not to say, singularly unattractive, underwear. This consisted of a mammoth grandfather's vest and for delightful contrast an elephantine pair of shorts with playing cards, roulette wheels, and dice liberally printed all over them.

'In Greece our lawyers behave very differently, with more respect, I might tell you!' he added morosely, his grumble almost a roar, revealing his true Taurean tendencies.

'Ye-es, I am sure they do. I expect they receive their clients formally dressed, as you are now, too' riposted Henry. He wandered about distractedly as he began to think of the evening ahead and of the enthralling Josephine.

Dimitri pawed the carpet and snorted as though about to charge, but Henry had slid out into the lounge to call his sister.

It was a task allocated to Henry, some minutes later, to push back the evening's entertainment by one hour, to enable the Duke to return to his temporary base in London, briefly to arrange his dress for the forthcoming event. Henry drove him to the Hilton, where Dimitri leapt out, flinging the car door open, and decking the doorman, Bill, who had rushed to open his door. Fortunately that admirable retainer had seen action in the Allied Front line during the war, and was not unconscious for sufficiently long, nor was he miffed enough by the collision, to refuse to guard the coach and horsepower whilst Henry followed in the giant footsteps of the minotaur. Bill regained his feet with remarkable composure and took over the reins and the keys, which were handed to him inside a crisp new twenty.

'Well, well, well' admitted our hero as he entered Greek territory and surveyed the splendour of the Greek's presidential suite. The emperor size bed resplendent with an Arab tent-like roof, was the perfect fit for its incumbent; bowls of fruit and flowers adorned every table. There was, of course, also champagne, Dom Perignon Rosé, Dimitri's favourite tipple at the ready in a colour coded ice bucket.

The paintings and tapestries, which adorned the walls, were originals and valuable. A full size lounge-come-office was at the ready, with computer and fax facilities in the unlikely event that the Duke might feel like a day's work. The decor was tasteful in the extreme. Beautifully carved cornices, an immaculate ceiling-rose, which boasted a huge chandelier, only served to enhance the brilliant impression conveyed upon entering the suite.

'They certainly give you value for your measly six hundred quid a night' Henry breathed breathlessly.

'And the rest!' grunted the bull in a suitably wounded tone from the dressing room as he discovered for the umpteenth time that he had outgrown his latest, in this instance, Valentino, suit.

'What are you wearing tonight darling?' called Henry adopting his best imitation of a caring wife's voice.

This always irritated Dimitri, who found difficulty in appreciating some aspects of British humour, but in the present circumstances, with Valentino refusing absolutely to come to the party, he found Henry's question particularly galling.

'I am wearing that which will put you firmly in the shade you puny, parsimonious, pontificating, pseudo.'

He continued grumblingly 'Τιατί δεν μπορώ να μείνω με αυτόν τον άνθρωπο, ότι είναι τρελός.' A rough translation for the uninitiated is 'Why do I keep company with this man he is mad.'

Despite a magnificent command of the English language, Dimitri would launch into Greek when aggravated (usually by Henry) forgetting that he (Henry) had also acquired the language as part of the package at his boarding school. Indeed, Henry himself, when worse the wear for whisky, often sought commiseration that this doubtful linguistic benefit, was the only thing of value his parents could recognise, for the money they had shelled out during his childhood for his education. Sophie never forgave Henry for abandoning his law practice.

'Listen you overblown Greek buffoon. In England we say it takes one to know one! So if I am mad where does that leave you?'

'Now, now, Henry, you know that all Greeks are mad as a matter of course, so don't complain because you have also become a true Hellenic albeit by conversion or conversation whichever applies here. If you play your cards right you may ascend, by steps, to the full majesty of Greek God-dom and sit by my right hand as my favourite serf.

Henry shook his head in wonder at his friend's exaggerated sense of his own greatness, even if there appeared to be a tip of his tongue in his cheek half the time.

'Let me tell you, my friend, that the only God with which you have anything in common is Dionysus or Bacchus; and if there is a heaven you will be too heavy for the elevator, or the very long staircase, by which the meek and righteous ascend. Also, whilst dealing with this issue, may I ask, how you dare to consider ascending to heaven thus abandoning several of your lifelong friends (now deceased) who will be anxiously awaiting your arrival below?'

'There you go forgetting your own likely destination again', riposted the colossus of Athens. I know that you will be waiting for me in the nether regions cursing the heat, and praying (if that word has any application down there) that I come to join you, bringing with me a case of *Roederer* perfectly chilled.'

The beginnings of his characteristic smile played across Henry's lips, as he considered his next blow, which might prove the outright winner of the current contest between these constant protagonists.

'The only reason that I would arrive first (accident apart) would be the time that you might take descending the staircase through purgatory - and of course your heavy load. You are hardly an athlete up to the regulation *Olympic* standard. You would even be late for your own damnation.'

'And what are you? Ariel? The Will '0' the Wisp? Since when did you qualify as a bantamweight? I admit that I am big, but you would be surprised how much of this is *muscle*' he said, emerging from the dressing room patting flat the stomach held in by an immense effort, part will-power, part corset.

'That is either very *relaxed* muscle, or muscle which has been buried before its time, embalmed in a substantial quantity of a fatty preservative' rejoined Henry. 'And for God's sake breath out before you risk standing Isabel up by having a coronary. For decency's sake, you should at least wait until after you have paid the hotel bill.'

'Come on let's go, the girls will be waiting. I don't want them to wet themselves with anticipation' muttered Dimitri, ignoring Henry's teasing, as he made for the double doors to the room.

As they descended in the mirrored elevator they surveyed each other with considerable satisfaction. Henry was looking a lot smoother and slimmer than he deserved in black, only relieved by the white/black check of his Kenzo blazer.

Dimitri had chosen a smart navy blue suit, cleverly crafted in Savile Row to hide a myriad of unwanted regions. Dimitri had an unusual number of these regions, which together formed areas, and were themselves, in turn, subdivided into districts. The whole was contained in a continent, the continental shelf of which could be accurately defined as the Dimitrial stomach area. A yellow and navy spotted tie (which rose and fell with the contours of the Grecian Front) with matching handkerchief in the best silk, fell in with the yellow silk shirt and navy crocodile shoes to complete the picture.

Bill, the uniformed doorman nodded his recognition and apprehension as they passed through the hotel foyer and the Rolls was at the ready in front of the entrance. Dimitri slid effortlessly into the cockpit and prepared for take-off. The moment Henry's bottom touched the seat, and certainly before the aged retainer had closed the passenger door properly, Dimitri was off. The doorman was still holding the door handle and had been obliged to break into a gallop. Henry for his part shot back into his seat with the effect of the thrust and instantly grasped the safety handle for dear life.

Driving was a passion of Dimitri's although other road users would unfairly hurl epithets such as "Maniac", "Lunatic", and even "Foreigner" at him through their car windows with a sprinkling of ripe old English invective added for good measure. These insults only served as a spur to the Gargantuan Greek lo push on harder still.

'Spare the whip old man!' yelled Henry who was still rolling in the aisle, having been totally unable to secure the aforementioned life belt.

THE CHIPPERIE

Whilst Dimitri was flinging his Rolls around the streets of Mayfair with reckless abandon, back in Buttersoft, Nosey was growing concerned, there had been no word from Dai. A malign cloud had descended upon the normally irrepressible reporter as he realised the potential of the cocktail whipped up, by putting a hotly desirable dessert like Doris with a wistful weasly Welshman like Dai. Remove the clothes and what have you got? Exactly what our Nosey Parker particularly did *not want* to have, a Welsh Rarebit.

Regarding his visage in the hall mirror, his nose was still bandaged to the hilt, Nosey donned his brown Homburg hat, smoothing the brim in the vain, but convincing manner, that he said seen Alain Delon habitually do in a vintage rather juicy murder film some weeks before. For the record there is no physical similarity between Norris Parker and the great French Actor. It was merely the action of standing in front of the mirror and straightening, nay almost stroking, the brim of his hat that had impressed itself upon the mind of our rapacious reporter.

No, Nosey couldn't really claim a physically similarity of any kind with the dashing Delon, his looks being, even in his own rather flattering view, 'rather more rugged'. If anything, he was a taller, balding version of the redoubtable Inspector Clouseau with the regulation French Detective moustache. Of course, at the nose, any remote similarity with the French Star, or anyone else for that matter, other than Cyrano de Bergerac, ended.

Notwithstanding his rather strange appearance, Norris managed by foul means rather than fair, to persuade girls like Nurse Marlene Deertich, more often than not, lo enter his private lair by the clever ruse of appealing to their better nature. Knowing how young girls have a natural fondness for furry and feathered creatures he devised the strategy of suggesting that they join his

"Save the Duck - Share a Pillow" campaign, and encourage them to show their enthusiasm by going into action without delay.

'No need for battle dress, Private Molly, or Susie ...' he would say '...you must be prepared to lay down your clothes in the name of the sacred duck.' He would exclaim vigorously as if on a rostrum, 'Down with down – and feather!'

Animal rights campaigners and sympathisers fell for this quite original approach almost every time. It is true to say that there had been that setback involving the schoolteacher who turned out to be a cardholding member of the Left-wing Lesbian Lassies, a rather militant Scottish Group dedicated to some purpose involving the use of scythes under Kilts? Definitely 'a cut below' in Norris's opinion. He had abandoned her before she could cross swords with him.

Parker was now considering starting a new campaign to save Britain's lambs on the basis that the fewer beds used the fewer blankets would be required. The campaign ran under the title "Keep the Sheep - Be Blanket Buddies"

Nosey had rejected out of hand 'Save the Bo Weevil' - as an excuse for twosomes between cotton sheets, because that particular cotton pest does not rate highly with Animal Preservationists. Furthermore cotton sympathisers were either too thin on the ground or were likely to *bale* out at the last minute. Nosey could think of no good reason to save the cockroach.

Sighing, Norris switched off the hall light closed his personal front door, and made his way down the stairs from his first floor flat, which was situate in a small street which adjoined Lissome Grove, Buttersoft. The naked electric bulb, which normally dimly lit the dusty common staircase, had, alas, ended its natural life and made its passage into light bulb heaven. Nosey gradually felt his way in the pitch-blackness, inching slowly and carefully down the stairs step, by step. His recent and painful experience in the Beauty Parlour had made him much more cautious. He breathed a sigh of relief (through his mouth of course) when he finally realised that he had reached ground floor level.

As luck would have it Costas Kyprianou (known as 'Chippie' to his mates) the owner of the 'Chipperie', had just opened the cellar trap door to fetch some more potatoes. He had been called away to the telephone, for a large take away order of cod, chips and peas for the Buttersoft Women's Institute Meeting at the Town Hall, next week. Ever mindful of the cost of electricity, he had turned off the light in the cellar from the switch near the telephone in his shop, but the trap door remained agape.

The intrepid reporter, having successfully negotiated the staircase now strode purposefully towards the front door which, however, in the murky darkness, he was unable to actually see. Tripping over the sack of potatoes abandoned in front of the trap-door by the careless Chippie, the Daily Spread's top Newshound entered the cellar, and became the first person in its long history so to do, head first. As his poor head and bandaged nose made a crash landing among the unpeeled potatoes, the noise of the unorthodox entry into his premises alerted the brave proprietor. He immediately suspected foul play – a burglar.

Downing the telephone receiver upon the Secretary of the W.I., he picked up the nearest available weapon, an ugly looking frying pan, and, thus armed to the hilt, or in this case handle, he went to investigate. With his blood and his dander firmly up he had completely forgotten not only to switch on the cellar light, but also that he had left the trap door open. It was hardly surprising that he swiftly followed Nosey into the cellar's gloom, but in his case he entered feet first.

His landing, being cushioned somewhat by the ample Parker buttocks which lay directly on his flight path, was proportionately less painful. However the frying pan, which had left his grip during his fall, rebounded off the cellar wall, and was instantly and miraculously transformed into its Chinese counterpart, 'the flying pan'. Achieving a perfect trajectory after the aforementioned ricochet, it returned like a boomerang to the unfortunate Costa, immediately striking a formidable and concussive blow to the side of his head.

The poor Cypriot was knocked clean out, but his suffering was minimal when compared to that of Parker, who having been for some considerable time 'Press', was now firmly 'Pressed'. His current predicament might be compared with that of that curious creature, formerly indigenous in Turkey and the environs, but now found all over Europe these days, now a regular nocturnal visitor to the High Street environs, none other than the *Doner Kebab*. Parker had been unlucky in his landing that had opened up new, as well as old wounds, mainly in his facial region. The swift advent and simultaneous demise of the Flying Costas (not to be confused with any Trapeze or Circus Act of similar name) had assisted Parker with the important discovery of the existence and exact location of his ribs and ribcage. This is not to play down the appearance of boot prints on his buttocks or the painful swelling to his testes which had been forced down firmly into unyielding spuds.

Until they are bruised or broken, ribs, unless they are being consumed in some up market restaurant in the form of rack of lamb, or downtown as 'spare ribs', are really not given very much thought or attention. Parker's ribs, on the other hand, were now of prime importance, constantly on his mind, whenever they could get a mention, in point of fact. Naturally, his nose, head and testes and rump also featured high on the list of priorities similarly clamouring for his immediate attention. Not to be outdone, his right arm had discovered an entirely new angle of poise and adopted it immediately, but this achievement Parker suspected had not been attained without some serious and painful damage to bone and tendon which, upon further consideration, he sincerely regretted.

Using his left arm to separate the unconscious Cypriot from the broken remains of his own body, Norris Parker stumbled painfully to his feet, which, he was relieved to discover, were inexplicably quite undamaged during the recent military type exercises. Stopping only to remove the King Edward's potato that had lodged itself firmly between his jaws (one or two of his beloved teeth choose to remain with the potato), he had cause to remember Shakespeare's poignant oxymoron "Parting is such sweet sorrow".

It was in this much battered state that the fearless, now fragile, factfinder emerged from the Black Hole of Milk Street. Blood dripping from his jaws, he suddenly took on a terrible aspect not unlike the dreaded Count Dracula. Mrs. Chippie, emerging from a busy period serving faggots chips and peas to the local lads from the Dairy, threw up her hands in horror when she saw Nosey, and ran deep fry chipper still in hand out into the road, yelling:

"The Vampires are coming, the Vampires are coming!"

Parker, fearing that he would be seized by an angry mob of milkmen who might drive a stake through his heart, ran back upstairs to his flat, and made straight for the bathroom to survey the full extent of the damage. Twenty minutes later, the familiar siren announced the return of Norris Parker to his favourite hospital, and a doubtful welcome from the Matron.

A NIGHT OUT ON THE TOWN

As it turned out, there was no need for Henry to be unduly concerned about his survival of another bout of Dimitri's stock car driving. They had arrived unscathed, at Shepherd Street, Mayfair, in a trice, where the French Fillies were stabled during their visit to this far-flung region of the European Union. The front door opened and out they trotted. 'What fetlocks!' thought both young stallions in a single whimsy.

'I wonder how many hands she'll stand' Henry mused, looking longingly at the lissom palomino approaching him.

'Oh I should think we'll be alright with these two!' whispered the Duke.

Josephine had chosen a simple white dress by Chanel, which both by its colour and shortness, and by reason of her surprisingly tanned legs, made a stunning impression. Isabel was wearing a yellow Moschino outfit, which blended curiously with Dimitri's dress, especially with its navy blue collar and cuffs, and imitation sun-god motif across its back. The front was far too low-cut, providing a full view of Isabel's considerable charms, and putting Henry in mind of Kim Novak in the lead of the film Nell Gwynn. The vision of the starlet of yesteryear pushing a barrow of suitably large oranges was momentarily distracting, but Dimitri brought him back to the here and now, with an explanation of the apparent coincidence in their dress.

'I sent it over to her tonight, ordered it, from Harrods from my dressing room once I knew which colours I would hoist', Dimitri answered Henry's unasked question.

'She certainly is very well decked out and in full sail too!' quipped the lawyer. 'You never cease to amaze me Dimitri' continued Henry '. One minute you are the impossible road hog, the next the perfect and considerate, gentleman! You actually ordered a new outfit by telephone for Isabel, and to match your knickers perfectly.'

'Just stick with me sonny, and you'll learn things a thousand colleges couldn't teach you' Dimitri responded with an imitation of a perfect American accent reminiscent of Edward G. Robinson. He even lit a cigar to complete the impression. The girls by this time had climbed into the car, legs flashing all over the place.

'Oh no! That's disgusting!' shouted Josephine at the cigar 'put it away! You'll gas us all.'

Dimitri laughed, but threw the hardly lit Havana out of the window 'Litter-lout!' Henry put in his two-penn'orth.

'If you just look back you will see that the cigar was thrown straight into a litter basket' corrected Dimitri over his shoulder. 'I was Greece's own Magic Johnson in my heyday you know.' He puffed himself up with pride with the memory of imagined heroic exploits on the basketball court.

Henry had taken the seat next to Josephine in the back of the Corniche, and was busily searching for her hand, but instead found these seemingly prophetic words,

'Greek causes second fire of London exactly 330 years after the first. What the IRA has failed to do in seventy years of struggle, a one-man Greek Division achieves with a flick of his wrist!' There is your newspaper headline tomorrow!'

Dimitri shrugged his huge shoulders, 'It was an accident, fate intervened *milord*, I throw myself on the mercy of the Court and offer your lordship a new Roller if you find me not guilty!'

'You might get away with that in Greece but not here. Our Courts are the envy of the world for their just and impartial administration of the law. No bribery and corruption here.'

'Oh your system is all very convenient for the rich, perhaps. You have to have a mountain of cash to get a look-in' riposted the Greek.

'We still offer a modicum of legal aid ('Lucozade' to the initiated) to the needy and deserving cases' replied Henry.

To the girls he turned and asked 'Are you hungry yet? We could go for a drink at 'Morton's' around the corner, or go straight to the Elysee. What do you prefer?'

'Oh let's go for a drink, then the Elysee, and then Tramp for dancing. OK?' Josephine completed the itinerary for an evening that Henry saw costing a thousand pounds with consummate ease.

'Wonderful idea' he sighed miserably, praying that his friend would pick up the tab at least on this occasion. They cruised to a halt outside the wine bar, and both men leapt out to watch the girls dismount. Both were happy to taunt the men, by showing a touch more leg than was proper, whilst giggling and whispering all the while.

'Park the car, Henry, there's a good fellow' called the Duke as he threw the keys up in the air.

With a leap, which would almost have qualified as an Olympic dive, Henry, with his right hand outstretched, just prevented the keys entering the drain inconveniently situated next to the kerb where the car was now parked. Dimitri marched the girls into the wine bar, without so much as a glance back at Henry sprawled across the bonnet of his car.

Morton's was characteristically busy, with the *jeune riche*, and a sprinkling of those who had graduated from that class quite some time ago, and had now qualified for the alternative label, *ancien riche*. All eyes turned toward the door as the three quite remarkable new arrivals made good their entrance. It was impossible to tell if the girls or the Greek most attracted attention. Dimitri didn't wait to approach the bar he called out

'Two bottles of your best champagne. How about Perrier Jouet, with the pretty painted flowers on the bottles for the girls, and bring some oysters down from the restaurant -there's an 'R' in the month!'ê

Isabel whispered to him 'but we are eating later. What about our appetite?'

'Oh it's your appetite that I *am* thinking about. That is why I am ordering oysters!'

'*Bête!*' she exclaimed 'Can't you think of anything else?'

'Not much' the Bull responded

Henry slipped in unnoticed, and handed the keys to Dimitri.

'Why is everybody looking at you? What have you done now?' he demanded to know.

'Everyone always notices Dimitri.' Was the rather stiff and offended reply. 'At a bullfight it is the raging bull that is the centre of attraction'.

'Hmmm. Curiously apposite that analogy.' Henry raised his eyebrows. The *maitre d'hotel* had arranged for the oysters which now appeared with the champagne a short cork behind.

'Will you walk a little slower said the oyster to the pail' quipped Henry at the approaching sight 'there's a bottle lodged inside you and it's making me feel frail!'

'Oh how very droll Mr. Lewis! My word, but aren't you a gas when alight!' taunted, his dukeness with more than a touch of burlesque and devilment in his manner and delivery.

The repartit was entirely lost upon the girls who exchanged bemused glances but joined in when neighbouring tables exhibited their amusement at the behaviour of the unlikely lads. They all set about eating and drinking with gusto. Dimitri demonstrated how he could comfortably swallow two oysters at once, provided he had half a bottle of shampoo to wash them down.

'Can you do the same with live frogs?' enquired his friend and lawyer.

'Ugh!' responded the Greek "you are disgusting! Unless ..., of course, by 'frogs', you mean these little French delicacies - our charming companions this evening - for in such case my answer would be - 'bring on the dancing *grenouilles*!' Josephine and Isabel were far from flattered by the reference to them as suitable cases for the 'Reptile Rumba', and the underlying indecent proposal was hardly more enticing. Henry acted to divert them by proposing a hasty toast "to Anglo- French Designs!" he vaunted.

'To what?' asked Isabel.

'Well' Henry recounted 'in the first place my father had a wholesale ladies business by that name. Secondly I am a powerful Common Marketeer. Lastly, both the Greek and the British representatives have plans for mergers with certain French concerns that may become available, mine would certainly come within the description "Anglo French Designs".'

'Ah ha!' said Josephine quickly 'So you, you Anglo-Saxon *Rosbif* have designs upon this leetle French Froggie. Is that what it is?'

'Guilty as charged milord, I mean, my Lady'. Henry threw up his hands in mock despair.

Josephine whispered something to Isabel and the word spread around the room. The furniture was rearranged as much as possible to resemble a Court of Justice.

'Then this Court will retire pour un petit moment to consider what punishment is fit for this *crime terrible.* The prisoner at the bar can order anuzzer bottle of champagne so that the alcohol may deaden the pain of the 'owful' punishment that we are going to inflict.'

Henry bowed solemnly and stepped forward to carry out the Judge's wishes.

'Another flask of your finest, Freddie!' he called. 'It's in the best possible cause, sentence is about to be pronounced upon my unworthy body, as soon as Her Worshipful returns from her deliberations in the Ladies Uncommon room.'

A bottle of vintage Bollinger appeared as if by magic, before him, smoking from its neck like a recently fired pistol. He grasped the thin stem of his champagne flute and tipped the bubbles slowly down his throat.

'Aha! Now I am ready to go to meet my fete.' He declared with stimulating resolve and invigorating bravado. One could not but admire the courage of one, not so young, about to fling himself recklessly into the path of destiny.

Josephine returned from powder paradise, wearing the suitable attire of a black raincoat and cap she had evidently borrowed from another member of the club, and the public parted to make way for her. Henry stood, back ramrod straight, eyes front, waiting.

'Hmmm!' She uttered, clearing her throat. 'This Court has considered its decision in the case of La Belle France-v-Henry Redfield. The Court has heard a lot of irrelevant testimony from the immense Greek Dimitri Loukopoulos. This amounted to a confession by that Giant of his wish to consume two innocent French damsels in one mouthful. From the accused, whose name in French is *Henri Rougechamps*, we heard an admission that he had serious and improper desires on, or regarding the person of the *Juge* - 'Judge' to you infidel Anglais. As I say, having designs upon her, which I cannot bring myself to mention.

I have, however, in reaching my decision had regard to the fine plea in mitigation heard in my chambers and powder room, which was made by Mademoiselle Isabel DuPont. This was to the effect that she believes the prisoner Redfield to be a man of upstanding characteristic, how do you say, he has an upstanding fellow. Non? Oh! *Non, excusez-moi*! I mean he *is* an upstanding fellow! Isabel also mentioned that she believes that this

Redfield was overheard mumbling the name of the Judge in his sleep this afternoon. There is cause to suppose that he may have intentions other than the dishonourable ones that I had thought. I know it seems unlikely, knowing the past 'istory of this infidel, but justice, like love is blind.

Well, I have decided that I want to see more evidence about the dishonourable intentions, and never mind the honourable ones (for those he is forgiven). It is the Judgement of this Court Monsieur Henri *Rougechamps* (*ou* Redfield) that you be taken from this place via the Elysee and Tramp to a place of sexecution, there to be stripped of your rainment. At this point I will personally take that which is hung, and draw a quarter of it into me for starters! Is that not the traditional punishment of this count-try before seven hundred years? *N'est pas?* Voila! Take him down Freddie.'

At this almost impromptu performance, there was clamorous applause from the assembled patrons who all agreed that they had never seen its like. Henry was suitably agog, rather stupefied like one has been told he has won the lottery, even though he didn't purchase a ticket. Recovering his aplomb from where it had buried itself, deep in the recesses of his unconscious, he spoke, and the gathering realised with some relief that, for the time being anyway, he was still of this world. He said, not deterred by the odd cough in the background

'May I, your most Worshipful and Desirable Beauty, be allowed, as a condemned man, to say a few words before I ascend the scaffold of your bounteous execution?' Josephine nodded solemnly.

Dimitri conferred with a couple of drinkers at the bar. 'Lucky to be found guilty. Imagine what he would have missed if he'd been set free!'

Henry cleared his throat for his scaffold speech, which only lost a trifle for not being entirely original. 'Right, well, I will then. Hmmm!

"It is far better thing that I shall shortly do than I have ever done. It is a far better place that I go to than I have ever known."'

At this the other drinkers went wild. Cries of "Brilliant!" and "Superb!" echoed around the building.

Dimitri had to have the last word of course: "Why have a Packet when you can have a Carton" and, "is this a *Tale of two Titties?*"

Freddie intervened at this point. 'Keep it clean Mr. Athens please! No offence like.'

'And none taken I'm sure Freddie!' responded Dimitri mischievously.

Henry approached the bench, and placed his hands on the hips of her honour (which he did not intend to take lightly). He very slowly pulled Josephine towards him until their bodies touched. Sparks must have flown at that moment, because, unbelievably, and coincidentally, the power failed. Probably an overload in the kitchen, no one knew, but before the fuse could be changed or tripped, a kiss had developed which would have put Errol Flynn and Vivien Leigh into the shade. Of course they were not there on this occasion, fortunately for them, and everybody was currently in the shade.

Henry and Josephine were entirely ignorant of the commotion around them. Glasses crashing to the floor, gentlemen colliding gently with ladies and then begging their pardon, waiters' trays became flying saucers almost as deadly as Oddjob's metal bowler hat in the film of that old James Bond thriller Goldfinger.

Dimitri gathered up Isabel as though she were a feather pillow and made for the door. People bounced off Dimitri like tennis balls off a brick wall, he carved a swathe through the thronging populace as though it were so much melted cheese, some of it clung temporarily but then was ripped off, the momentum was too much for it - or them, if you prefer.

Once outside rather dishevelled, and hot and bothered the Greek Giant surveyed his French coup or coups. She was instantly and unaccountably shy, as she slowly lifted her long black eyelashes off her chest and surveyed the man-mountain before her. 'You are just like a bull who has, fortunately, lost his china shop!' she criticised.

He looked at her wonderingly, surprised at her self-possession and English language. 'I most certainly am, and I'm not one bit ashamed of it!' he riposted.

'That's what I like about you' she declared 'you are quite unique. I have never seen anyone quite as piratical and powerful as you are. I bet you are a monster in bed.'

'That's funny' murmured the Greek through her jet-black hair, pressing her to him with his enormous powerful arms. 'I normally win bets but in this case it looks as though you are going to break the bank.'

She shivered with anticipation and then threw back her head and laughed.

'Well we'll just have to see if there is as much substance to you as there appears to be Mr. Loukopoulos, or maybe I should call you Tavros that's Greek for bull isn't it?'

'Why, yes' he replied 'but you see that is already my middle name. When I was born my parents had already chosen Dimitri for me. My second name was to be Stavros. Well like many young children I couldn't say it properly, and it came out as *"Tavros"*. As they, and others in our village outside Athens began to appreciate my size and strength it stuck. At home they do not use Dimitri at all any more - it is just Tavros -the Bull.

But look at you, what a superb woman you are, what fine breasts and slim but strong legs (from *le jogging*)! We would make wonderful healthy, strong children you and I.'

'All right, but let's go and practice first. Eh! And one condition, me on top.' She saw him grimace, and she softened, 'or in front?' Still he offered an uncertain response. 'Oh all right. Well we'll see, but if you are squashing me I'll scream and deafen and frighten the life out of you and all the neighbourhood.'

Dimitri's beaming smile cracked his huge face, and one could see how an ancestor of his might well have been one of the mythical satyrs, that now sell in much reduced size and plaster or china thankfully, to the tasteless tourists who flock to the Aegean in their droves each summer. Isabel had captured a real live one but would she survive the experience?

Dimitri almost sneered 'I know, I know. You'll huff and you'll puff and you'll blow...'

'Enough Dimitri! You must behave. Oh! You are so rude! What shall I do with you?' Isabel expostulated.

'Just wait till after the dancing has to stop, and I am sure that you will know exactly what to do' he replied.

Henry and Josephine emerged from the shambles that had been Morton's, hand in hand, smiling blissfully and almost swaggering with the delight that they had discovered in each others arms. The night air was cool but pleasant and the stars were out. One might have been forgiven for thinking that a nightingale had broken into song in Berkeley Square. The trees made dark weird shapes against the sky, where those stars twinkled their merry messages, unfortunately in a language only understood by other stars.

Was the rest of the evening to be cancelled or postponed? This required a council of war, a meeting of the joint heads of staff. Dimitri immediately feigned sleep and snoring as his contribution to the proceedings. Isabel laughed. Josephine lightly touched Henry's thigh to get his attention, and got it all right.

Henry cleared his throat 'Ladies and sleeping Greek pig. I declare this meeting of the Committee for Private Affairs and Reprehensible Behaviour now open on this fine pavement in Berkeley Square. The Agenda before us tonight is to decide whether:-

1. To go to Elysee, eat, break plates, watch the spectacle of the Duke of Athens dancing and drinking slowly; adjourn to the night-club, Tramp, for disco dancing; and then go home; or

2. To go straight to bed not passing the Elysee not collecting any Tramps.

3. Go to bed for some hours; get up go to the Elysee and then Tramp over to Piccadilly.

4. None of the above.

If there are no speeches from the floor (or the roadside in this instance) then I propose to put the matter to the vote.'

'Point of order Mr. Er! What do we call you? You are not sitting so you are not a chairman. I know, Homo Erectus or Mr. Standing-up' cried the Duke of Athens.

'What is your point of order Mr. Papal Bull?' Henry muttered with pretended irritation.

'Well Mr. Standing Up. It appears to me that the whole agenda is a point of Order. It is a question of the order of doing things. So I would humbly suggest that we sleep on it and reconvene here tomorrow night to discuss this important matter once we have had the opportunity for in-depth research.'

'You do have a major point there Senor Bullock, and I can see that Mam'selle Isabel has already begun to appreciate the significance of it. That's not a dagger I see before me? Perchance is it?'

Henry was always lapsing into inappropriate Shakespeare, as Dickens would say at the 'worst of times'. But then again, really, this was 'the best of times'.

'Just a moment' said Josephine moving her blonde hair from her forehead with a sweep of her hand. 'I wish to speak.'

'She wishes to speak, hush! Quiet! Silence in Court!'

Josephine continued unperturbed by the childish interruptions "To bed or not to bed -that is the question!"

'No, I think that is the answer' interpolated Henry.

'Very well if that is the answer what pray, was the question' quipped Josephine.

Henry sank to his knees painfully and took her hand and said

'Josephine, love of my life, sudden though this may be, I beg of you please give me your hand in lawless bedlock. Consent my winsome, lose none, wench, to be my lawfully unmarried mistress; for better and better; in health and in wealth, till marriage or some swine of a preying mantis of an infidel do us part.'

(Offstage left Dimitri prompted her) Say, 'I will, and right away.'

Josephine responded strongly 'I will and right away!'

Dimitri now intervened (on stage) in solemn imitation of a clergyman: 'I now pronounce you 'Doer' and 'Doee'. Now that you have made the bond of 'Doing' I must ask do have a ring, I mean a thing?'

'Yes' said Josephine 'I have a coil. This, like a ring, turns round and round. It could be said to be a figurative representation of the Mortal Coil.'

'An excellent choice if I may say so' replied the Greek 'use it in good health and safety.'

'Well I don't!' expostulated a petulant Isabel who had been keeping her own counsel for some while.

'Then I shall rely on my friends, or should I say my *Mates*, to help me out of this quandary' responded the beefy Greek Not a word more was said, but the four 'Must-Get-Theirs' mounted their trusty Roller and sped homewards - Henry to Chester Gate with Josephine on his knee, and Dimitri to the Hilton, with Isabel looking carefully at the palm of his huge hand before eating out of it. What a day it had been for the fabulous four! What a future in store! Would they live happily ever after, or would they marry? For the moment a good night's sleep afterwards - was the best they could hope for.

THE FLY IN THE OINTMENT

Nosey, having recovered from his ordeals with Doris, Marlene and Chippie was back, if you'll excuse the term 'on the job'. He had sniffed out a new nurse to attend to his many injuries at Buttersoft General Hospital, and although under the eagle eye of the dreaded Matron, he still managed to whisper the odd word of encouragement to a little waif, Nurse Sarah Paget.

His uninjured hand would pat her on her rear at every opportunity, and he had already suggested a visit to the local cinema as soon as he had recovered sufficiently. He would need a caring girl in case of sudden relapse.

A dental surgeon had been brought in to consider a bridge to replace his missing teeth, and his broken arm had been set in plaster.

Chippie was in the next bed to him out for the count with severe concussion, and sporting a rare example of the "frying pan bruise" on his forehead.

'Serve him right the clumsy idiot, leaving that trap-door open' commented Nosey to Sarah taking the opportunity to stroke her thigh with his good hand. I may have a huge claim against his public liability insurance. My face will never be the same again. His hand in the meantime had travelled to the top of her thigh, and was threatening a further rnore meaningful journey.

'Now behave yourself Mr Parker, we don't want your blood pressure rising do we now?' Sarah replied removing the offending paw from its position just inside the buttons of her tunic skirt.

'Oh! I don't see why. I can afford a little rise' replied Nosey impertinently. 'You should realise just how much comforting I really need Sarah. I'm relying on you to come through for me you know.' Patronising just wasn't the word!

The little nurse looked at him wonderingly. 'I just don't understand how you can even think of it after what you've been through'.

Parker smiled and winked at her knowingly, touching the side of his nose with his index finger, "more to me than meets the eye eh?"

'Under those bandages I imagine there must be quite a lot that does meet the eye too!' Sarah joked. Seeing Nosey exhibit symptoms of hurt pride she relented 'well, I'll see about your suggestion of the cinema when you're properly recovered. Now you just lie down and go to sleep. No! This is something you must do on your own. Behave yourself!' Parker relaxed. Tomorrow would be another day.

Now, whatever had happened to Doris and Dai?

Dai and Doris had finished their photo session and had settled down for a good day's sleep, their unclothed skin reflecting light from the window. A smile could be detected playing across each of their faces, as dreams of the seemingly impossible were engendered by that, which was not only possible, but which they had achieved over the past few hours together. They were enviably exhausted having been mutually, exceptionally entertaining.

Suddenly, the front door opened a crack, Mrs. Soames was on the prowl. 'Dai?' she whispered in a voice that would have been inaudible to someone sitting astride her shoulder. 'I say, Dai, are you there?'

She entered the flat and started tiptoeing towards the bedroom door. The click of the front door had awakened the light sleeping Celt, and, fearing an intruder, he leapt out of bed. Creeping stark naked towards the door he took up a position behind it. The door slowly opened. Mrs. Soames crept in. Closing his eyes against his fear, Dai leapt upon the invader of his realm. Mrs. Soames screamed as she was attacked and pinned, face down, to the floor. When he saw who it was Dai jumped up, but not before Doris had awakened to see her lover, completely nude, apparently forcing himself upon his landlady's rear end.

Both women yelled. Mrs. Soames had sat up sharply, only to find that she was cheek to jowl with Dai's manhood. Doris, seeing a woman in such close proximity to her man's Welsh Rarebit of Leek, threw herself upon the landlady with the ferocity of a tiger. 'What are you doing? He's mine! Hands off!' They struggled with each other. At last our naked Doris sat victorious atop the middle of Mrs. Soames whose skirt had ridden up over her thighs to disclose see-through lacy black knickers, and black stockings with red garters.

Mrs. Soames whimpered 'B-b-b-but I just came for the tea tray. I did knock. I thought maybe that you had gone out.'

Doris wanted to say 'a likely story. You wanted to catch us at it!' but she bit her lip. 'You should have knocked harder, more loudly. We got no clothes on. Dai cover your what's-its-name, don't just stand there!'

Dai, transfixed by the sequence of events, and starting, in spite of himself to become aroused at the sight of a nude Doris spread-eagled on top of his landlady, with her own dress up by her shoulders, looked around wildly for cover. Both Doris and Mrs. Soames had their eyes firmly on his weapon and he could feel their eyes growing in unison with it. He rushed out of the room and into the bathroom where he had left his clothes and pulled on his trousers. His eyes almost watered when he zipped up his fly.

Mrs. Soames was at a loss also. She sat on the floor unable to move. Doris stood up and stepped into her knickers. Her round pert breasts, which trembled with the motion, made Mrs. Soames envious, even though her own bosom was large and firm. She secretly thought, 'I wouldn't mind a piece of that monstrous Dai either.'

Pulling herself to her feet she said, 'Well, no harm done. Would you like a cup of tea love?'

Doris stared at her. She was going to say 'How can you act as though nothing has happened?' but she said instead 'that's a good idea Mrs. Soames. You're right, no harm done.'

She clipped on her bra and pulled her printed dress covered with spring flowers over her head. It was a mini of course.

It was Dai's cry from the bathroom that upset the equilibrium again. Both women rushed there colliding with each other in the doorway. As they entered they saw Dai wrestling with his zipper.

'What on earth is wrong?' demanded Doris.

'I've gone and caught my foreskin in my zip' whimpered the white-faced Welshman. 'I can't release it, and I can't move my legs. Its excruciatingly painful!'

Doris looked at Mrs. Soames 'what are we to do?' Mrs. Soames looked at the afflicted area and said "let me have a try."

Doris was uncertain whether she wanted Mrs. Soames touching Dai's private areas, but the pain on his face reassured her.

'All right' she said 'but be careful'. Mrs. Soames reached down with both hands and delicately felt the tender part. Assuming a crouching position for a better view she saw the difficulty.

'His skin is caught badly in the mechanism of the zip. I think if we try to remove it, the zip I mean he will find it very painful.'

Dai was already in pain, complicated by the sudden and desperate need to discharge the contents of his bladder. Mrs. Soames had grasped the zipper in one hand and inserted her other into his trousers to hold his manhood with her other.

Doris was very unsure about this unorthodox procedure, but saw that Dai was far from aroused by his landlady's touch. When Mrs. Soarnes tried to part the zipper from Dai's person he almost jumped three feet into the air.

'Aaargh!' he yelled 'Stop it! Stop it! You can't jerk it off like that!' Mrs. Soames was not exactly sure what Dai meant, but she let go of the zipper.

'Why are you still holding his thing, Mrs. Soames?' asked Doris pointedly.

'Oh! Well I was thinking about my next move' she replied.

'I'm sure you were, but I think you can safely drop it now. Your next move is out!' said Doris sardonically.

Mrs. Soames reluctantly removed her other hand. 'We'll just have to carry him to the local hospital.'

Doris took his arms and Mrs. Soames his feet as they carried poor Dai to Mrs. Soames Nissan Patrol. He was very heavy, and they had to stop and put him down every few feet. Finally however with a huff, a puff, and a yell of pain from the Welshman he was aboard in the back of the Patrol, with the rear seats folded back to give him more space. Panting and perspiring with the exertion, the two ladies leaped into the wagon and off they went.

At the casualty department at the hospital there was quite a queue of broken arms, cut fingers, and all sorts of sore bits and pieces. Dai's particular affliction was, however, given immediate precedence by all and sundry. He was taken to a room and placed on a bed. After what seemed an interminable wait a white-coated Asian doctor entered the room.

'Got a spot of bother I hear, I am Doctor Anwar' he commented, feeling for Dai's fly.

'Be careful it's very tender' warned the apprehensive photographer. The doctor heedlessly pulled at the zip, thinking a jerk would remove it. Dai thought the doctor certainly was a jerk and kicked out at the pain. His foot caught the Medic amidships and Anwar fell back colliding with the vertical drip, which was on wheels. His hand shot out to steady it and for a second or two they did a strange dance across the room, Anwar's other hand on his own damaged groin.

The doctor returned to the bedside and conceded that he would have to give Dai an anaesthetic so that the zip could be removed without pain. About thirty minutes later Dai was out cold. They wheeled him to the theatre. As the doctor delicately now, sought to gently remove the zip and succeeded, Dai's bladder gave up the struggle. A spray of fresh, warm urine shot up into the poor Anwar's face.

'Oh! No! Oh! No! Please help me!' Anwar screamed his Indian accent coming out more pronouncedly in this unguarded moment, running in crazy circles around the theatre. The masterful staff nurse Sarah Coppitt who was attending the operation, grabbed his arm and with her free hand mopped his brow with a damp cloth.

Dr Anwar moaned 'never in my life have I been so abused and degraded.' His head shook from side to side in that peculiarly Indian manner. 'This is terrible what am I to tell wife? She will not be wanting to come near me. I am become an untouchable. Oh dear me! Oh dear me!'

Sarah Coppitt wondered why her name so aptly described situations in which she often unwittingly found herself. Now she had to console a hysterical doctor who could not come to terms with a simple natural incident in the hospital theatre.

'Now, now, doctor. Urine is sterile you can't catch anything. Why, I have heard people drink it. Mind you I imagine it must be their own urine. You didn't swallow any did you?'

Again she witnessed the incomprehensible wagging of the head from side to side. 'I mean' she continued 'people swim in pools and the sea and we all know what goes on. People urinate all the time in the sea. You see them suddenly stop swimming and women sort of crouch. Men put one hand beneath the waves. Worse still is the dumping of raw sewage, or even the treated stuff in our rivers and seas. Gosh you know, I think you have got off lightly by comparison! You should be pleased.'

Dr Anwar looked wildly at Nurse Coppitt as though she was a reject from a top security Hospital for the Insane.

'You are off your bloody rocker woman! Can't you see I am covered from head to toe in urinal liquid for God sake! Don't blather on to me about women crouching in the sea! I wasn't in the sea I was in the theatre!' He stomped off in search of the miscreant who had so demeaned him, firmly nursing intent to commit murder and have his revenge.

Once the zip was free Dai, the putative victim of Dr Anwar's intended termination, had been removed to a side recovery ward. Doris was waiting by his bedside as he slowly came round. Mrs. Soames looked on anxiously.

'Dai, Dai' Doris murmured gently. His eyes opened. Disorientated, he needed to be told he was in hospital. Remembering everything suddenly, his hand shot beneath the duvet, worry and concern knitting his handsome brow.

'It's alright, don't worry I had a good look and it's as good as new' whispered Doris looking around to make sure she was not overheard. 'I kissed it better as well just to make sure' she whispered.

'She did Dai, I saw her!' exclaimed Mrs. Soames peeking from behind the curtain.

Doris reddened making a delightful colour contrast with her platinum hair. She grimaced at Mrs. Soames who had caused a fair percentage of the trouble directly or indirectly.

'You again! Always putting your head in where it's not wanted. Anyway, Dai, it looks fine'. She then turned to the waiting landlady and hissed beneath her breath 'and it's mine, all mine! So hands off!'

'Well, thank heaven for small mercies, I don't know what I would have done without you, both of you' sighed the weary Welshman, unaware of the tension between the two ladies near his bedside.

Mrs. Soames, ignoring Doris put in her two penn'orth. 'Now Dai Evans I have to tell you that you rather disgraced yourself during the op though. It seems you urinated straight into the Doctor's face. He was in a fine state about it. He ran about the theatre like a headless tandoori chicken! You should have heard the nurses! They were falling about laughing over it.'

Dai looked about him nervously. 'Where are my clothes? I think I had better make myself scarce look you. That doctor may want to tear me off a strip.'

Doris discovered his things in the wardrobe, and he quickly dressed, both women watching him like eagles. Tiptoeing out of the room, they sped to the elevator. Unfortunately as it opened there, in front of them, was the unfortunate Dr Anwar himself.

'Aaargh it's you!' he cried raising his right hand to reveal a scalpel in his grip. 'Stop! I say. Do you know what you have done to me? I want to kill you!'

But they had turned upon their heels and each shown him a clean pair. Down, down the fire escape they dashed, and out into the street. They ran along the High Road, the girls' dresses billowing up in the wind, and causing two entirely distinct collisions involving (all told) five cars, a truck and a milk float. Dai turned his head to see Dr Anwar still in his white but yellowing coat, chasing them threateningly, waving his stethoscope above his wagging head. It was with considerable relief that they flagged down a passing taxi and thus lost their unfortunate pursuer.

A WALK IN THE PARK WITH JOSEPHINE AND THE PHONE.

Down south in Chester Place, Henry awoke to see the sun shining through his net curtains, and turning over in his bed, there she was, his Josephine, her hair spread out in the shape of a golden fan across the adjacent pillow. Lifting the covers just a crack, he could see that she, like he, was totally naked. What a body! Talk about peaches and cream! She stirred at the draught that was now seeping under the bedclothes, and turned around giving Henry a fine view of her rear aspect. Henry slowly slipped his hands over her cheeks and cupped them tenderly, as though they were newly born pups. He kissed her neck and she stirred once more.

'Bonjour' she mumbled from under the duvet.

'Good morning my beauty' Henry replied. 'Coffee will be ready in the twinkle of an eye.'

'Hmmm!' she replied without opening her eyes 'later. Come here first.'

Henry was not one to refuse any lady a reasonable request so he came there first. Later during coffee and croissants in two of Henry's ample, soft towelling, dressing gowns they chatted over plans. The click of the postbox interrupted their discussion, and Henry went to retrieve the letters.

'Just one' he announced to nobody in particular 'and from the envelope it's from a firm of solicitors.' Tearing open the letter he said 'Damn, it's started. Some farmer, a John Thomas, whose farm abuts against my industrial estate in Butter soft is suing me for injury suffered by his pigs. They have been expelling saliva by the gallon and fornicating flat out.'

Josephine looked bemused, 'Why is that a problem for him?'

Henry read on. 'Oh! it seems the pigs were all males, and what's worse, they have started expiring from their excessive excretory exertions.'

71

Six healthy pigs have died of total exhaustion, and others seem certain to follow, He claims damages for their value.'

He reached for the telephone and dialled.

'Hello. This is Henry Redfield. Yes, that's correct. And how are you Michelle? Good, good. Listen Michelle is Mr. Rossitter in please? He's at a conference with counsel? I understand. Listen, Michelle, give him the message that I called, I will fax you a copy of the letter and Writ of Summons that I have received. Yes. Please ensure that he sees it upon his return. He may wish to have a word with Godfrey Hammond QC. Thank you, Michelle. Goodbye.'

Henry sprung straight to his Apple Mac, scanned the letter and copy writ.

And emailed the documents to Mr. Rossitter.

Josephine watched with mild interest. 'Well now that's out of the way, let's see whether the Bull has recovered from last night's goings-on.'

Mr. Loukopoulos is not to be disturbed' answered the hotel receptionist 'he left strict orders.' Henry turned to Josephine and shrugged 'I suppose he's still asleep.' He replaced the receiver. 'OK what shall we do? Barge in on them unannounced, go out for a walk in the park followed by lunch. Or go back to bed?'

At this last, Josephine picked up a cushion from the couch and threw it at him. 'Enough, you English pig! I can't take any more! We go out. We walk to the Hilton, through the parks as the sun is shining, and then we barge in on them and catch them in the act -with the red hands! *N'est-ce pas?'*

So it was decided, and the pair threw on some of Henry's casual clothes (Josephine borrowed a shrunken jogging suit and a pair of ladies trainers which were mysteriously among Henry's collection), and strolled out into the fresh air. The birds had reached the park before them and were in full voice. The flowers and trees seemed to be swaying and saying thank you for the rain and the sun to the gods. The scents of spring filled Regents Park as Henry and Josephine tripped hand in hand through the rose gardens.

'I wonder how many varieties of roses there are here?" Henry murmured quietly. 'Hundreds, I should say' replied Josephine. Wasn't this founded or named after one of your Royals?'

'So I believe. The Queen Mother I think. She was much loved by the people of this country as a caring, gentle and fairy godmother type person' Henry responded to the question with only minimal attention.

The other half of his mind was chewing over the letter before action from Farmer Thomas's solicitors. Suddenly the peace in the park was disturbed by Henry's mobile phone began playing God Save the Queen. He rapidly swung it at his right ear.

"Hallo! Who's that? Oh Norris Parker, the newshound! You've heard then. Yes. They've issued or are issuing a Writ it seems. John Thomas. Is he well hung? I mean, can he afford expensive litigation? You think so. What! I hope there isn't going to be a class action. Pigs marching on the Royal Courts of Justice. I really don't think so Parker. You're not stirring things up too much I hope. Yes of course I'm going to defend, strenuously! Right. Well, I hope to see my solicitor in the next few days, I'll know more afterwards.'

He shut off the mobile and continued the desultory walk through the Park. 'This is a serious business you know, Josephine, I am the target, it seems, of a growing campaign of needy farmers and unemployed or under-employed labourers, and the general public in Buttersoft. I shall have to look for others who should be in the line of fire and put the boot in.'

His solicitor was already working on this theme and burning the proverbial midnight oil. The local council Buttersoft District were an obvious candidate, and the letter before action suggested by Godfrey Hammond QC was already on its way into an in-tray where it would doubtless repose in accordance with true bureaucratic principles for at least three weeks. Another target would be the owner of the Chemical Factory that had gone on to bigger and worse things, Caustic Chemicals Corp. This company was an American Giant that had opened a number of factories and warehouses in England. Several rivers and their small, rather defenceless and unfortunate inhabitants had been affected by this progress.

The Buttersoft factory had closed, as CCC had taken over or overtaken another British Group, Testube Investments that already had an outlet in Sheffield proper. They had moved the staff and some of the equipment that was re-useable across to the Sheffield factory. The Vendor of the land itself to Henry had been an American associate of the chemical giant, Industrial Investments Inc.

Then there was the solicitor who had handled the purchase. Rossitter rapidly removed him from the short-list as he had done his best, and could have done little or no more. However, the callous American Industrial Giant and the local council would both come under fire. The Vendor would have to be investigated to see how much was known, or could be assumed was known by it or its directors, in view of the close connection between the companies in question.

'Shame you can't sue Stateside, Henry, you appreciate, of course, that the cause of action arises in the United Kingdom, that means you can only issue here. I've checked and both CCC and Industrial Investments inc, are big fish, but we can issue new writs or better still third party notices joining them to the proceedings issued by Thomas and his pigs, pretty quickly. Both Hammond and I feel that you cannot be an "End-Loser" here, in view of the shenanigans prior to your purchase when the factory was demolished, and the blank, not to say misleading, replies to your solicitor's Enquiries before Contract. We might even apply to strike out the claim on the basis that you have not committed any tort of misfeasance, any wrongful act.

The problem is that there is authority, as you know, that a landowner can be held responsible for things escaping from his land, such as water, which damage the property of others.

Here, you could not possibly have known the chemicals were ever present under the soil. The plaintiff would have to show that these chemicals were on your land rather than his own or someone else's, and that may not be as simple as it at first seems.

The land originally occupied by the chemical factory included other neighbouring territory. Who knows where all the chemicals are now actually situate? However, Dakers Diggers were excavating your land when the fumes began to be a problem. They can be joined as the actual occupiers and those, whose digging activities inadvertently released the fumes. As you know we really want the big boys who are the villains of the piece.'

Henry was rather reassured by his solicitor's bullish attitude. He responded with a battle cry. 'OK Howard you have my authority to go for them.'

Henry returned from his call to Rossitter to remember Dimitri and their incomplete plans for the day. The moment that Rossitter was off the line, he tried the Hotel again from the park bench, where they had taken up temporary lodging. This time he struck lucky. He asked 'The Duke of All Athens please!'

'Yes, this is himself!' announced the Greek 'which of my unworthy subjects craves an audience with his Wholeness?'

Henry sighed. 'Dimitri! So you are up at last. Do you know what time it is?'

'Here, or in Athens, or New York?' snorted the Bull.

'What are you doing today, do you have any plans?' asked Henry, ignoring the flippant remark.

'I was planning to have lunch and dinner in bed. You could join us, but it's rather early for an orgy, and you have already missed breakfast.' Henry held the earpiece out so that Josephine could also hear the Dionysian drivel being doled out by the dozen.

'If you are now, and are soon going to be decent, then we shall come up and have a delicious luncheon with no expense spared on your account.'

Dimitri considered the offer of marginal interest bearing in mind the rival offer now being made in quite a shameless fashion by Isabel. Quickly reaching a decision he replied to Henry, 'Walk over here very slowly, take your time. Isabel and I have one or two matters to chew over before you arrive. You are, however, invited to lunch, which will be ... (here he looked at Isabel for assistance) taken in the main restaurant downstairs. Yes we'll meet you there in an hour, I'll book a table.'

He dialled reception and told them to reserve a table for four in the restaurant on the rooftop for one thirty. He then conveyed to Isabel, adopting the same sign language that she had utilised that her offer was immediately accepted. Let us leave them to their hors d'oeuvres.

BEARDING JOHN THOMAS IN HIS LAIR

Henry and Josephine strolled slowly down Marylebone High Street, with its many attractive cafes and pubs. They glimpsed at the colourful and diverse shop windows, Josephine making mental notes to return to purchase several chic items of clothing, including a stunning black short silky Mondi dress, and a pair of white slacks by Pierre Cardin in one of the modern boutiques.

Whilst they crossed Oxford Street and entered Grosvenor Square, Nosey was trudging a very different path, up the drive to John Thomas's pig farm, accompanied by Dai who was relating his recent great escape from penile amputation.

No detail was left unamplified. Mrs. Soames's firm grip upon his personal credentials had, on balance, made the whole thing worthwhile. The struggle between the two women had been even better, with Mrs. Soames revealing her skimpy knickers in the heat of battle.

He continued, 'And I am a hunted man Mr. Parker, that's what I am. That Indian doctor has a vendetta against me. I get wild telephone calls from him at all times of the day and night threatening me with amputatory revenge. Imagine him trying to circumcise me at my age!'

Norris Parker found the story rather distasteful. It was clear to him that Dai had claimed Doris as his own. He had little confidence that Dr Anwar would succeed in murdering this damn photographer, and so there was little chance of Nosey getting his hands on Doris's dainty dolly drops. That took much of the excitement of the forthcoming dizzy rise to fame that he had planned for her, which now looked destined to be merely a financial exercise from his point of view.

'Why did you get involved with Doris, Dai? Takes the edge of the professional relationship a bit doesn't it?' he criticised.

'You're right there of course Mr. Parker, but if the truth be known, I couldn't help myself, look you. I mean try to imagine her, in the altogether, putting her arms around me and offering her lips up for a kiss. I could hardly tell her to get dressed could I now? Now would *you* have? I ask you.'

Norris did not say, but he knew that he would not have told Doris to get dressed. His hands would have moved across her body at the speed of light. Yes he thought, sighing, Doris was certainly a cut above and was destined for great things. It just rankled that she would achieve those things without having paid the price of a proper rogering by his truly. Still there were others on the available list, who certainly weren't about to desert him and leave him in the lurch. Nurse Deertish was forever grateful for his help in her job relocation. Nurse Paget had been a success in the cinema in the sense that she had allowed some heavy petting and mild kissing, the latter only suffering slightly from the obstacle presented by Parker's nose which was still rather swollen.

Nosey trudged heavily on through the mud, his thoughts thus occupied, without a reply to his photographer beyond an unintelligible grunt. Both had worn wellington boots for the occasion, now caked with brown, and the smell of the pigsty was heavy on the air. Despite the late hour of the morning, a cock was belting out its call with such vigour that the dead within earshot must have been seriously tempted to awake from their interminable sleep and clobber it. At last the rather downcast pair from the Press reached the front door, which Dai knocked on with considerable force. Within seconds it was flung open by a tall, extremely well built man, thick brown wiry hair forced by brute strength to part on the left. The man was in his early thirties wearing exactly what you would expect of a farmer, all a dull shade of grey to khaki, with professional wellington boots to match.

'Yes, what do you want?' he fairly boomed at them.

'We're the Press sir" answered Nosey with appropriate respect "come to ask you about your Writ against the landowner Redfield'.

'Hmmm. Well, I suppose you'd better come in. No, don't worry about removing your boots. This floor is used by farmers and farm labourers not ballet dancers, mud is good for it.'

He led them into a large kitchen that had the customary Aga Cooking range and numerous cupboards. There was a good old solid looking oak table, with two benches either side of it in a matching grain. A similarly solid farmer's wife was busy at the range creating tempting aromas.

'Sit down. A drink? Coffee perhaps?' He looked at the two men with look of enquiry.

'Coffee would be fine for both us, black without will do nicely.' Dai nodded in agreement not really wishing to impose but looking longingly at what was apparently developing into a famous stew.

'Right then what do you want to know?' Thomas asked with his usual directness, as he slung two mugs down the table with such force that the pressmen had to snatch them up before they dived off the far edge and crashed to the floor. Coffee spattered oak.

With moderately greater decorum, he passed the milk jug that had been sitting on the cooker to Parker who, put it down again, as he had asked for black, and responded 'hmmm, well, I've spoken to Redfield, and he seems determined to defend. He didn't know about the chemicals, and isn't sure that they come from under his land anyway' Nosey summarised.

Thomas stood up suddenly and thrust out his chest.

'Stuff and nonsense!' he thundered. 'The chemical plant was originally built on that land, everybody round here knows that. Where else could the chemicals come from if not from that land. Anyway, on my solicitors advice, I am having an expert do tests on different parts of the property, Redfield has consented, and for good measure we're testing adjoining land too.'

'Including your own land?' enquired the ever-vigilant Parker.

'Including this land' confirmed the farmer. He sat down and took a large swig of his own coffee, the mug was almost buried in his huge right hand.

'What has happened to your pigs, I mean, what is the latest?' asked the irrepressible reporter.

'Ten males dead from utter exhaustion. Some of the females are suffering from the extreme abuse they have had to contend with' Thomas replied morosely. 'I have had to apply a soothing balm to their reproductive organs by hand to cope with the soreness.'

'Ugh!' exclaimed Dai 'rather you than I. That must be a really disgusting chore.'

'Oh it's all in a day's work on the farm, but you get to know the pigs personally, and they recognise you. I couldn't leave the poor sows in pain.'

'Won't you have an increase in the number of piglets born as a result of the non-stop gunfire?' Nosey tried to introduce a more positive note into the proceedings.

Thomas, who had sat down again, banged his huge fist down on the table. 'Now listen here! This whole business has cost me dear. I can't tell if I'll get the odd extra runtish piglet out of this, and I can't tell if the survivors have some sort of infection, which might eventually lead the government to order their destruction. My whole livelihood hangs in the balance, and its there because of that bloody chemical reservoir under Redfield's land.'

'Yes, yes, of course, I quite understand. We do understand, don't we Dai? But Mr. Thomas you do know that Mr. Redfield bought the land from that American company Industrial Investment Inc. with no knowledge of its rather doubtful antecedents, don't you?'

Thomas stood stock-still, hesitating and looking closely for the first time at Parker's face.

'What's happened to you?' he asked. 'You look as though you've just had a collision with a ten-ton truck. Has someone given you a sound beating? Wasn't Redfield by any chance was it?' he asked hopefully.

'Er, no." replied Norris hesitantly. 'An unfortunate accident, two in fact, but I'm a hardy individual. Never say die, you know! In our profession many a reporter has died in the line of duty, covering war ravaged areas like Vietnam, Bosnia and Angola'

'You're not a war correspondent though are you?' asked Thomas.

'N-no, not at the moment' replied Nosey.

'So how did you get these injuries to your face in the line of duty then?'

'Parker put his finger to the side of his nose and said "Top Secret" and winked.'

Farmer Thomas was bemused but brought himself back to the subject of the interview. 'What was it you were asking?'

Dai intervened here to ask John Thomas if he might take a photograph or two of the farmer himself, and more of the farm, especially the pigs.

'Help yourself' the farmer murmured still looking at the enormous bandage on the face of the Newshound.

'Must be something of a record that nose. What did you put on it to have it grow so big? It would probably win third prize in the local marrow competition.' He laughed at his own joke.

Norris Parker failed to find anything remotely funny in this undeserved personal abuse. However, he wanted to complete the interview so he asked: 'Mr. Thomas, if I might return to my unanswered question. Why have you not sued the chemical factory owners, Caustic Chemical Corp., and the former landowner who demolished the factory rather than the hapless innocent, Mr. Redfield?'

Thomas's grin faded faster than the sun on a British summer's afternoon.

'I have accepted the advice of my lawyers on that issue. They expect Redfield to bring in all possible alternative targets at his expense. In fact I understand that they have been told that he is doing as much already. I have no connection with these people. He bought the land from them and therefore has a bigger axe to grind.' Thomas was fast becoming hostile at these undermining questions.

'Let's see the pigs shall we?' said Dai hastily, fearing for the possibility of another devastating attack on the tender extremities of Parker's visage by the irascible Mr. Thomas.

'Right follow me' the farmer ordered and, so saying turned on his massive heels and left the room. Ditching their half-drunk coffee they rushed through the doorway together crashing into one another.

'After you', said Nosey, with restrained enthusiasm, 'after all, you are carrying the equipment.'

Dai bolted through the door in search of John Thomas who was striding across the yard in the direction of a fierce smell and loud hubbub emanating from the outbuildings.

'In here!' he called to them. They fairly hopped it across the yard to catch up with him. Inside the pig sty the sows and piglets were snuffling at their daily bread. The introduction of a camera and flash into the proceedings did not make them pause for a second. Celebrity status was something that they evidently took in their rolling stride.

'Right now Mr. Thomas. A picture of your goodself with the porkers' suggested Nosey. Thomas grunted a reluctant affirmative and stood pointing at the animals.

'That's perfect that is!' commented the clicking Dai. 'Now how about a close up actually in the sty itself?'

'Come on in then.'

They edged their way gingerly into the mucky area.

'Now Mr. Parker can you hold the flash gun please?' Dai requested. 'I think if you stand on that rock over there we will have the best light.'

Before the horrified Farmer Thomas could intervene Nosey had mounted his largest sleeping grey sow. It did sort of resemble a rock, with its head hidden behind another pinker pig and its legs covered with grey-brown muck, facing away from the human intruders, who were tolerated so long as they did not interfere with the smooth running of the sty. However being stood on by a fairly weighty human was something that it was not prepared to tolerate under any circumstances. It shifted its enormous bulk and Nosey began to totter. The rather greasy, and slippery terrain with which he had to contend made his task doubly difficult. The boots he was wearing were not really designed to grip surfaces such as mobile pig.

The sow found her feet against overwhelming odds and Nosey lost his. Turning to savage the attacker who was now lying on her dinner she made for what she assumed was his offensive horn, namely his nose. Tossing and turning in the quagmire he valiantly sought to ward off the ferocious attack. Farmer Thomas stood stock still watching the progress of the skirmish from his vantage point.

'Don't you think we should help Mr. Parker Farmer Thomas?' Dai asked gently.

'Best to stay out of it young man. Might upset the other sows then we'll have a real battle on our hands. No, Mr. Parker seems to be holding his own.'

'It looks to me as if he is holding his own nose. That's all it looks to me as though Mr. Parker is holding' rejoined Dai. Nosey finally regained his feet, but not before receiving a massive bite on his rump from the angry sow.

'Stand on that rock' he mimicked Dai angrily cuffing him around his head. 'And where were you when I needed you? Standing by watching me being mauled by a ferocious animal. I am lucky to be alive!'

'No need to over-dramatise Parker, that sow wouldn't kill you. She just wanted you off her back much as I do now!'

Thomas ended the interview with a wave and a stifled laugh muttering, 'Stand on that rock. Stand on that rock'.

He seemed in a better humour though than at any time during the interview. It was as if the unfortunate pig-rock incident had lifted his spirits.

The pair from the paper thanked him for his time across the increasing distance between them, and began the weary return down the muddy track to their vehicle.

Hoots of laughter followed them from the farmhouse with the oft-repeated words 'Stand on that rock! Stand on that rock, Mr. Parker!'

MEMORIES OF THE VALLEYS

'I wonder if he's selling the dead pigs for streaky bacon', murmured Nosey his injury inciting him to thoughts of vengeance. 'I wonder. I bet he doesn't comply with all that bureaucratic nonsense from Brussels. I'll get the yelping yokel!' He nursed his behind with the occasional furious rub, and adjusted his nose bandage, which had become undone, and a touch muddy, in the affray.

'Rather an imposing figure of a man, if you ask me' offered Dai.

'Thank you Dai. An unexpected compliment from an unusual quarter if I may say so' Parker replied, lifting his nose an inch or two.

'Er, I was actually thinking of Farmer Thomas, though of course that's not to take anything away from your striking profile.'

Nosey scrutinised Dai for any trace of wind up, and after more than a moment's hesitation responded.

'Y-yes there are rumours from where he went to school, about the size of John Thomas' replied Parker, 'according to reports from the boy's changing rooms, he lives up to his name.'

'Well with a name like John Thomas I suppose that he must be Welsh' responded Dai. I might have known. You see Nosey, working down the mines as most Welshmen did in the past, when they had to take a piss, it was all feel and pull, no lights you see. Naturally their John Thomases grew like flowers searching for the light, and also what with being felt and pulled all the time.'

'Oh very droll Dai. I suppose this unfortunate condition afflicted you too?' Parker retorted sardonically.

'Regrettably yes' uttered our Dai with mock despondency. 'I remember as though it were yesterday a chat my mother of blessed memory had with her sister, my Aunt Mary, when I was just a small toddler.

Mother confided to her "You know, Mary, I don't know who the boy takes after but it's certainly not his father. The Good Lord didn't see fit to bless our marriage with such a gift. He'll be getting into all sorts of trouble when he grows up."

Aunt Mary who was never to be outdone replied "It seems to me that he looks pretty grown up already, at least as far as his privates are concerned. Strange how they put me in mind of my Tudor, God rest his soul. You remember Tudor don't you Gwyneth?"

"Er yes" Mary, Dai's mother, had replied reddening somewhat in the cold night air. Everyone remembers Tiger Tudor, his exploits are legend in the valleys."

Aunt Mary who seemed put out at this remark. "My goodness Gwyneth I can't think what you mean. My Tudor was soul of righteousness. I remember his byword and motto was Do unto others as you would have them do unto you."

My mother answered "I never knew what it was that killed your poor Tudor, but I have an idea now. It must have been backs to the wall down there in the valleys. Perhaps some poor husband did unto Tudor as Tudor had done unto his wife."

Aunt Mary was shocked. "Gwyneth are you saying that my Tudor put it about in the valleys, girl?"

Gwyneth replied "I don't think he limited his range to the valleys, Mary. You know I hesitated to tell you before, but we are sisters, and he has been dead ten months now so you are well over him, look you."

"Lucky for him he is dead or by God I'd kill the bugger now!" Aunt Mary spat out with more ferocity than my mother had ever seen before from that quarter.

"Now, now, Mary we shouldn't be speaking ill of the dead, should we? Let bygones be bygones. It's all water under the bridge now."

"I'd bloody throw him off the bridge if he was still alive I can tell you that Gwyneth. Who else knows about these shameful goings-on?"

"Just about everybody Mary, except of course young children not born at the time. The wife is always the last to know. You've got to live for your children now Mary."

"But I don't have any children! You're the one blessed with babies Gwyneth."

"Exactly Mary, exactly."

"What! Are you saying you laid with my Tudor - and you, my own sister?"

"I had no choice Mary. He fairly forced himself on me Mary and you know how strong he was. I tried to resist but it was useless. Then he threatened to tell my husband David ap Morgan unless I continued to submit to his monstrous ways. I was absolutely terrified Mary."

"So little Dai here is Tudor's then? A little bit of Tudor does live on."

"I can see which bit and it is hardly little, sister. Some poor girl is going to suffer just as we did when he grows up."

"Well" replied Mary "I suppose that is some consolation. A problem shared is a problem halved, or so they say"'

Dai sighed. 'I miss my mother you know Nosey, even if there is a lingering doubt about the identity of my other parent.'

'Very touching I'm sure. What possible doubt could there be after what you have just told me?' responded the reporter irritably.

'I don't like to convict a man without a hearing. Tudor never had that opportunity. Perhaps the physical evidence might be considered purely circumstantial. Of course there is my mother's confession too, but what of her husband?'

'Such endowments are not so commonplace. Take it from me. The long and the short of it is, if you will excuse the expression, that Tudor Edwards was your father.'

Next day the papers were full of the Farmer Thomas story, the nationals too. The slant of the story depicted Henry as an innocent caught between the two real antagonists. Norris Parker had been a busy bunny. Even the Financial Times considered in its leader whether the share prices of the two companies might be affected. It was not so much the effect on the pigs, but whether the affected humans were also being driven to a premature demise. Henry was quoted by the Sun in its headline of being:

"PIGGY IN THE MIDDLE"

Henry read this story and initially took the title as being a personal affront, a reference or innuendo about his growing waistline (36 inches and counting). Rossitter told him he didn't need to add a libel case to his troubles, and that he, Rossitter, was sure the paper was not being literal but merely commented upon his unfortunate position, caught between the two real protagonists, the complainants and the chemical company. The practised hand of his lawyer smoothed out Henry's ruffled feathers, and he decided to drop any thoughts of further claims. Rossitter said that they proposed to serve Caustic Chemicals Corp. and Industrial Investments Inc. and they could be served with the legal proceedings here, has they were registered with the Registrar of Companies in the United Kingdom.

Henry reported the developments concerning the geological and scientific surveys that had been commissioned both by him, and the Plaintiff Farmer Thomas. It seems the results would be out within fourteen days of completion of the surveys. These tests were expensive but important. It was impossible to tell how far the scientists would be able to evaluate the reasons for the unusual side effects that the gases were having on the immediate locality.

BEAMISH - COURT - RED HANDED!!!

Certainly indecent assault in Buttersoft was becoming a daily occurrence. A local magistrate, James Beamish, had goosed an off-duty lady police officer, Susan Winsome, whilst shopping in the local "Do-It-All". He was known for being partial to a drop of bourbon, but he apparently thought that the store's purpose (from its name) was other than for the sale of miscellaneous tools and paints. Wpc Winsome whilst bending to consider a pair of pliers and to compare the prices of cans of full gloss paint, experienced considerable pain when her pert bottom was grabbed and pinched very hard by the frolicsome beak.

She showed the budding bruises to Sergeant Spencer who felt that photographs were necessary for the court case, and borrowed the Police Station Pracktica for the purpose. He asked the Wpc to jut her posterior out toward the camera to ensure that the bruises were captured to best effect.

Unfortunately the photographs were not developed in time for the hearing, in view of the enormous size of the enlargements ordered by the zealous officer. Apparently, he has since pinned all the enlargements on his bedroom wall in a bid to stimulate his inspiration. All his colleagues agreed that he must be a workaholic to put in the hours that he generally did of a week, and then go home to still more work. He had even purchased a powerful magnifying glass with the ingenious idea that he might be able to match the bruises to the shape of Beamish's fingers. If he could, it would represent an entirely new advance in forensic science.

He took the Station Superintendent to his house to demonstrate the technique. There seems little doubt that the Sergeant is marked out for promotion, although the Super thought it best that he keep the evidence "under wraps" at his home, in order to avoid unspecified suspected

87

difficulties if they were displayed in the police station. The sergeant has since taken several further shots of the Wpc's rear end so that comparisons may be made, and the recovery period delineated.

The Sergeant's wife on returning home after a trip to her parent's, was apparently unable to share Spencer's enthusiasm for the work, and promptly left home again for an unknown destination. Spencer came to work the next day with a real shiner of a black eye, sustained when, according to his evidence he fell downstairs the previous night.

Several uncharitable detectives spent far too long with the duty officer discussing how it was possible to get a black eye falling downstairs. The inquest was adjourned by the arrival of the Commander for an inspection visit at the station.

The brand new Buttersoft Magistrates Court was crowded as many locals, especially others who had suffered punishment at the hands of Magistrate Beamish, had reserved seats for the occasion. Beamish was brought up before his peers. He stood in the dock in his regular uniform of tweed jacket and cavalry twill trousers, with military tie, and pleaded that the fumes from the Industrial Estate had obviously overcome him. He had helped himself to Winsome's bottom being unable to help himself.

Counsel for the prosecution rose to cross-examine. 'Now Mr. Beamish. Let me see if I have it correctly. You grabbed the behind of the unfortunate Wpc Winsome, whilst she was bent over examining paints and pliers. Is that correct?'

'Yes your Worships that is correct.'

'And you claim that you did this whilst groggy from the effects of pernicious gasses that you had unknowingly breathed in on your way to the shop?'

'Correct again.'

'Isn't it rather strange that you were able to take in the fact that Ms Winsome was examining paints if you were, in effect, intoxicated?'

'I can't answer that. I only know that I had no choice but to grab her bottom and pinch it as hard as I could.' Winsome puffed and spluttered and began to perspire. The prosecutor turned to his supporting solicitor and asked if there were any other questions for the witness. There were none.

The substance of his lawyer's plea in mitigation was effectively that Beamish was helpless in the grip of a force implanted in his body by the gasses. In all the circumstances despite being muddled by some of the lawyer's language, the Magistrates on the bench were minded to be lenient, and gave him an absolute discharge.

They were not amused when a bright spark in the excitable public gallery shouted:

'Discharge? He's already had one of those in "Do-It-All" hasn't he, Done It All, didn't he?'

Another shouted 'Bind him over!' A second yelled 'Bend him over!'

A third replied, 'no that's just what he wants. Probably gets turned on by a bit of bondage. If he's in handcuffs now, he's probably all excited standing in the dock!'

The Court erupted into a furore. The pretty Winsome blushed to her natural brown roots. Unthinkingly, Beamish checked as a reflex to see if his flies were undone, and his lawyer startled in the belief that her Client was about to expose himself, accidentally dropped Stone's Justices Manual, a really heavy volume of the law, upon the foot of the usher. The latter yelping in pain at the weight of the legal authorities contained in the book started hopping wildly all over the Courtroom.

The Justices were very put out at the chaos that had descended upon the Court, and decided to beat a hasty retreat through the side door whence they had entered. As they withdrew, the Chairman, Margaret Fotheringham JP, couldn't help noticing that the Usher in question now had the solicitor by the throat, and that Beamish had once again grabbed hold of Winsome's behind. Winsome had, however, taken retaliatory action in the form of a strangle hold on Beamish's genitalia. A considerable amount of wailing and yelping was heard by all.

The chairperson shut the door firmly behind her thinking 'another day, another bench' as the likely outcome of the uproar. Police whistles sounded and eighteen people were arrested including by some unfortunate error, the winsome Winsome. Bearnish continued to molest the poor officer in the back of the Black Maria. When the back doors were opened at the police station he was firmly astride her, in the saddle and galloping for all he was worth. As the police came to rescue her he shouted *"Tally-ho"* and collapsed on top of her. Winsome had learned from bitter experience what the other half of the proverb containing her name was.

The whole thing reads as the heading next day in one of the lesser tabloids:

"WINSOME LOSE SOME."

The trouble was that this was all coming to rest upon Henry's doorstep. There were rumours of more writs being prepared by local solicitors not least those separately employed to represent Beamish and particularly poor Winsome, and all these seemed destined for Rossiter's in-tray.

MAD JINX AT THE WESTCHESTER HOME FOR THE ELDERLY

It was reported in the Press next day that there were strange goings-on at the local retirement home for the elderly. Weird noises of all-night frolics had been reported.

Henry shook his head and muttered, 'When will this come to an end?'

Josephine soothed him by stroking his head and beckoning to him to lay it in her lap. He willingly consented. Within minutes he was asleep, and on a park bench too. Josephine decided to let him have fifteen minutes shuteye. She looked at the birds, sparrows, pigeons, and the odd robin redbreast, cocking their heads to one side in apparent curiosity at the strange behaviour of a full-grown man. Passers by in the park seemed to emulate them in a most curious manner. Josephine found this particularly amusing and when she giggled the movement awakened the lethargic lawyer.

'Where am I?' he said 'Oh! I can't get up, my neck is stiff!' Slowly he lifted his torso and immediately sought to loosen up his limbs, shaking the cobwebs out of his body and mind.

Consulting his watch he said 'we'd better catch a cab now, or we'll be dreadfully late for lunch with Dimitri and Isabel.'

They found a white one plastered with a newspaper advertisement going their way and jumped in.

'The Hilton, Park Lane' was all Henry said and he fell back into the seat next to Josephine. Minutes later they were entering the suite of Dimitri Loukopoulos.

'At last the young lovers appear! What kept them I wonder?' asked Dimitri to the assembled multitude of three.

'Too long a tale. Let's eat instead' suggested Henry.

They descended to the stunningly presented dining room on the first floor of the Hilton Hotel. A sumptuous buffet of mainly cold seafood including lobster and crab, caviar, oysters and mussels with salads and other complementary side dishes awaited them spread along a special table arranged for the purpose. Champagne was in the bucket. They set to with a will and a fork. Afterwards, as they took coffee, brandy and petit fours, Dimitri asked Henry to describe his problem. As Henry poured out his soul and another cup of filtered caffeine, Dimitri's brows knitted with concentration.

'There seems to be no end to the number of complainants who may come a 'knocking at your door. The bill will be ferocious. Can't you sell, get rid of the land. I know, I'll buy it in the name of an obscure offshore company. How about it?'

Henry pondered. 'It may be too late for that, but I'll consult Rossitter, see what he says. Thanks for the offer anyway.'

Henry, despite the worrying news refused to postpone the frivolities planned for the evening. The four would assemble at the Elysee at ten thirty. The Greek would probably absent himself for an hour or two's gambling beforehand. If they wanted they could stay the night in the lounge, which offered a sofa bed, which Dimitri could order made up by the helpful, well-tipped staff.

Suddenly Henry said, 'Look, after we've digested this meal, I think I'll run down to the gymnasium for a workout to get some of the tension out of my body, OK?'

They all agreed it was a good idea. Two hours later he slipped out. The others had subsided into a comfortable siesta. Henry descended the carpeted hotel stairs into the gym, and changed into the gear, which he kept in a locker there. He managed four kilometres at a fair pace on the treadmill, and had preceded this with a full tour around the various, weighted equipment on offer. Returning to the changing room he slipped off his sweat-soaked vest and shorts, put on one of the proffered towelling coats, and made for the sauna and mixed Turkish bath.

The steam room contained several young fillies cheekily flaunting their sumptuous wares in the hot hazy "Hammam". Henry noticed but said nothing breathing in the Eucalyptus flavoured steam deeply. Emerging from the heat, dripping with sweat, he walked into a running cold shower. From there it was just steps to the icy cold plunge. He then dried off, found a fresh robe and made for the lounge and the Independent.

There it was on the second page. A report with photographs described scenes of unparalleled lust at the Westchester Home for Retired Lady Civil Servants. The blue-rinsed grandmothers who normally took Earl Grey Tea with cucumber sandwiches, had instead taken the under gardener and the one of the male nurses.

On behalf of these gentlemen it must be said that they were not your strapping country lads often encountered in farms and on building sites in the region; furthermore the ladies, who outnumbered them eight to one, had the element of surprise in their favour. There was also an unconfirmed rumour that the ladies had invited the two poor boys to quench their thirst with a 'nice cup of tea' to which had been added a certain soporific. This particular drug whilst relaxing the muscles of the body in general had the opposite effect on the male genitalia. An embarrassing firmness of purpose appears to have occurred to both hapless lads.

It seems that the distressed Matron of the establishment on returning from her rounds of the geriatric ward had found the two boys quite naked flat on their backs being literally swarmed across by a legion of latent Lotharias. Her entreaties to spare the poor boys had fallen upon deaf ears. Alone, she had been unable to restrain the rampant relics of Regents Park

The report continued:

Matron Mannings wrung her hands and moaned, 'If only it hadn't been Sister's night off.'

Reluctantly, having regard to the new ordeal facing her from exposure to the authorities and public of her tale of woe, she had taken up the telephone and dialled the local Police. The sergeant on duty listened to her story with mounting disbelief. When she indicated where she was calling from he decided that she must be an eccentric 'inmate' and tried a rather patronising response:

"Yes madam, I quite understand, there is an orgy going on at the old people's home. Sixteen elderly women have attacked two young men and are having their evil way with them. Tell me madam, are there also pigs flying in your area? Or perhaps the Martians have invaded Buttersoft! Madam, madam, this is a police station. Now, I am sorry that you have this personal problem, but I am sure that the competent staff at the home will do their best to help you. Goodbye!"

Poor Matron Mannings could not believe her ears. She had sat down abruptly on the floor and stared simultaneously at the wall ahead of her and the prospect of defeat. There was nothing to be done. Eventually, however, an idea had come to her. She had rushed to the nearest fire alarm and broken it. It was something she had been tempted to do since she was a child (like pulling the communication cord on a train). The fire bell rang out loud and clear. Suddenly the orgy had come to a grinding halt (but then it would, wouldn't it?) The ladies looked about them in a uniform daze. Just as well really, as it was literally moments later when the uniformed firemen came crashing into the entrance hall.

"Where's the fire?" the Fire Chief demanded

"In their loins," the Matron had replied

The two boys had to be taken to hospital suffering from multiple bites, bruising and utter exhaustion. They had been saved by the bell. The firemen were surprisingly helpful and caring. The old ladies who had quickly resumed both their clothing and their elderly demeanour, and were quietly escorted to their various rooms as though butter would not melt in their mouths.'

The escaping vapours were condemned by the report as the culprit, and the ladies were held up by the article as victims. Once again Henry's name was bandied about carelessly as the owner of the property, with the inevitable innuendo now, that he was in some way to blame. This was the last straw for poor Redfield. He would be tainted stigmatised and pilloried wherever he went. He had almost become an outcast.

Henry put down the newspaper and pondered "I am damned if I am going to be categorised as a an environmental vandal when, in fact, I am quite the opposite. I will fight this to the death if need be. In the meantime I am not going to have it ruin my social life and interfere with my friends enjoyment of theirs."

A SMASHING TIME FOR HENRY!
LADIES IN THE DOCK.

By arrangement they met at the Greek restaurant in Percy Street. One of the three brothers that own that most successful establishment, Michael, a real character, greeted them. 'Good evening Henry, and who have we here? Dimitri Loukopoulos!' They hugged each other in the continental fashion and chatted for a few moments in Greek. Michael was commenting on the beauty of their two French companions. They were given one of the two best table sin the house, and Henry recognised Marios Polydorou, another Greek friend of his and a regular at the Elysee on the next table confronted by a bottle of Black Label and singing along with the band like a good un. Soon they were drinking champagne and joining in with the singing as best as they could. Dimitri knew a song or two and their requests were honoured.

Then as an appropriate song began up leapt Henry. Taught to dance at a farmhouse in Limassol Cyprus by Andreas, a motor mechanic, his fancy had been taken by the "drunkard's dance" or zebekkiko. He swayed and swerved, jumped in the air and touched his heels (a real feat for any sort of drunkard in my experience!) and pranced about the dance floor as if he were in a trance. Dimitri knelt by the edge of the area clapping. A few moments later a huge pile of plates was brought and Marios stood up clasped them to his bosom and with the edge of one began smashing the others. Finally he threw a few remaining dishes on to the dance floor and they smashed into many pieces. The girls put their hands to their mouths in mock surprise. Dimitri ordered another huge pile and they all had a smashing time.

Finally after all the men had danced and pranced, and the floor had been swept for the umpteenth time. A ballad by Yiannos Barios was played. The men took their partners for some real American smooching. Josephine whispered to Henry, 'You're very hot, take off your jacket'. When he did so his shirt was so damp he was concerned that Josephine would recoil. She didn't, she held him tightly and leaned her head on his shoulder. It was a great evening. At about 3am they emerged into the cool night air and wandered a little way into Tottenham Court Road. The traffic was still flowing! They took separate cabs home.

The young under gardener from the Westchester Home for the Retired, Frankie Frobisher and the male nurse Malcolm Mostyn brought an action against both the home and the ladies for indecent assault, battery and a variety of other civil offences. They claimed substantial damages. As an afterthought almost, Henry was joined to these proceedings.

The ladies were also charged, once the police had the fire officers' report, with indecent assault. All sixteen of them were brought before the magistrates next morning. One of their number Minnie Cauldron turned to the lady Wpc standing in the dock next to them and asked, 'When does the train leave? It's so busy in the station this morning. I always tell Oliver (her husband deceased some ten years) you have to leave before seven if you want to avoid the crush. This carriage is really crowded.'

The Magistrates entered the crowded court and were visibly shaken to see so many old respectable ladies in the dock.

'What is this all about?' the Chairlady of the bench asked her clerk. The clerk turned round and whispered an explanation. The Chairlady sighed and wondered how to proceed. 'Yes Mr. Tomkins' she aimed her gaze at the prosecutor in mild despair.

'Madame Chairman, your worships, this is an unusual case where the ladies in the dock, he read out their names, are charged with indecent assault, to wit that they drugged and then physically molested two young employees of the Retirement Home where they are resident. The molestation assumed what was undeniably a sexual connotation. The victims of this extraordinary assault being referred to in the press today as a 'Tea dance gang bang' are presently recovering in Buttersoft General Hospital. You may feel that you wish to commit the Defendants for trial, or possibly sentence to the Crown Court in view of the seriousness of the case. Those are the basic facts.' Tomkins subsided temporarily to allow his opponent a look in.

Jennifer Joyce rose unsteadily and, a trifle nervously. It was her first ever address to any Court following her recent qualification as a solicitor.

'Hmmm! Your worships have heard what appear to be, and what my learned friend Mr. Tomkins chooses to call, "the basic facts". I suggest to you that his description actually omits the most important fact. When these events occurred every one of the Defendants for whom I appear, and I appear for all of them, was suffering from the effects of gasses which had been blown over to the hospital gardens in which they had recently taken their tea. Much has been written about the effects of these gasses upon the men of Buttersoft. It is clear that we ladies are just as susceptible. Look at the Defendants your worships. Is this a gang of vandals, of evil rapists you see before you? No. These are little old retired ladies with long and illustrious service to our country behind them.

Now I am certain that every one of them that is still able to understand what has happened, and that might be as many as eight of them, regret the shock and injury that the young male victims have suffered. There is no question however of their innocence of any intent of the kind required for this offence to be committed. I would ask this Court to try the matter today, if there is time so that it may be disposed of. I have brought experts both scientific and psychiatric to provide clear evidence that these ladies should be set free.'

The Chairlady asked the clerk if the case could be heard that day, and he nodded. 'Very well, if there is no objection from Mr. Tomkins we shall proceed as requested.'

Mr. Tomkins rose. 'Your worships. The facts of this case speak for themselves but I shall bring the evidence of one of the victims the under gardener Frobisher, and the Fire Chief merely to confirm them. Mr. Frankie Frobisher, please. Outside a shout was heard 'Frankie Frobisher!' The solid double wooden doors were flung open and in walked the under gardener dressed in a dark suit. He took a seat in the witness box and took the oath.

'I swear by almighty God that the evidence that I shall give will be the truth the whole truth and nothing but the truth.'

'Now Mr. Frobisher' Mr. Tomkins said after the preliminaries were completed. 'You are employed as an under gardener at the Westchester Home for Retired Lady Civil Servants established by the Government. Is that correct?'

'Yes sir, I mean your worships.'

'Good tell us in your own time about the afternoon of the 23rd February last.'

'Well I had finished my shift and had gorn down to the servants quarters in the basement to shower and change. When I come back upstairs one of the ladies, Mrs. Melrose, asked if I would mind joining them like for a cup of tea and biscuits. I had done so several times before, and I agreed. One of the male nurses was already in the sitting room with about twenty of the other ladies sipping away from the best Doulton China tea set, and stuffing into the scones and cream with strawberry jam that he likes so much. Well I sat down, and the ladies gave me the tea. I had a cucumber sandwich and some biscuits.

Both the male nurse and I began to feel a bit sleepy and groggy, and I was dimly aware of hands removing my clothes. I think I murmured. "No I have already had a shower and changed my clothes" but no one seemed to hear. I then felt hands and mouths all over my body. It was strange, but not unpleasant to begin with. Although I can't rightly be sure as I now realise that I was intoxicated, drugged that is, I believe that several of the ladies mounted me and began riding me in rather a frenzied fashion. Afterwards my private parts were found to be extremely sore. My girlfriend was in a right state about it. Wanted to break it off.'

There was a titter in the well of the Court.

'Oh no, not that! I mean the relationship. She's had a bit of counselling and she understands now that I wasn't a willing participant in the orgy. It was just a bit difficult convincing her. My lawyers have advised me to sue for damages but I know the ladies didn't mean any harm. Still I got to take my solicitors advice haven't I?'

Tomkins interrupted further contributions from Mr. Frobisher. 'Quite We fully understand the ordeal that you and your unfortunate friend suffered. I am sure all parties concerned hope that you will repair your personal relationship with the young lady. I have no further questions of this witness your worships.'

Jennifer Joyce rose and looked steadfastly at Frankie Frobisher. 'My clients wish to apologise profusely for any injury you have suffered. Please convey their heartfelt regret to your lady friend,' Frobisher nodded blushing. 'However, I would like to ask if any of the Defendants has ever, before or since, touched you personally or intimately?'

'No, never! These are real ladies. It was like they been drugged, that's what it was.' Frankie protested.

'Do you know why they attacked you on this occasion?'

'As I was saying it's because they were affected by those gasses ...' Tomkins rose tardily, 'I object to that question your Worships the witness is not qualified to answer it.'

'Objection sustained. Please be careful Ms Joyce in addressing your questions to the correct witness' admonished the Chairlady.

'I apologise your Worships. No further questions.'

The prosecution concluded its evidence in rapid march.

The fire officer confirmed the state of undress of all the Defendants and the two poor victims of the vicious sexual attack. He had obviously found the whole business rather distasteful. Little could be gained from cross-examination as the fireman had just described the scene and not ventured opinions. Jennifer decided to ask nothing of him.

Jennifer Joyce rose to open the defence. 'I call Dr. Magnus Pyetton.'

A short balding gentleman, long curly hair starting to recede, with protruding eyes that disconcertingly looked in different directions took the stand. 'Dr Pyetton please state your qualifications for the benefit of the bench.'

'I am Magnus Pyetton, MD (London University). I also took a postgraduate degree in Psychiatry at Oxford.'

'And can you tell me about your examinations of the sixteen ladies in the dock today?'

'Yes. They are all respectable in essence although half of them are suffering from mild senile dementia. There are more physical ailments too, but I need not dwell on those.' He stared at the bench and the ladies opposite the magistrates simultaneously. 'These ladies are all suffering from depression and allied symptoms about the attack upon the young gentlemen. None of them have the necessary psychiatric make up to warrant their indulging in such an attack singly or together. I am clear that for this to occur they must have been under the influence of strong drugs which left them totally out of control.'

Tomkins could not make any impression on the good doctor in cross-examination, and gave him up. He considered he would comment upon the relevance and accuracy of the evidence in summing up.

Next up was the scientist. He was Geoffrey Johnson MSc.MD. Wearing a good suit of dark green tweed and a yellow shirt and striped matching tie he made a good impression on the bench. After introducing him Jennifer Joyce asked him if he had studied the gasses and their properties.

'I have indeed. The results of my tests were quite remarkable. These compounds do not appear in nature and have resulted from quite a long set of chemical experiments conducted several years ago by former owners or occupiers of the land on which they were found. I have examined the blood samples taken from the ladies at the police station and compared them with those of pigs belonging to an adjacent Farmer. I have also compared samples of the liquefied gasses and gasses in liquid solution with the blood taken. There is no question that the ladies were heavily intoxicated with a dangerously high level of dosage of the chemicals in question.'

'I have conducted tests on monkeys and examined the test results of the Scientific Governmental Group, which have been conducted over a number of months now. I am entirely satisfied that these ladies were simply unable to control their primitive urges which the gasses or drugs had released.'

Again Mr. Tomkins could not shift the scientist and subsided into his seat.

'I move to dismiss this case for lack of evidence and in the alternative on the basis that the defence evidence clearly demonstrates that the defendants could not form the necessary intent or *Mens Rea* to commit the crime. I contend that the scientific evidence has shown that there must, at least, be a clear doubt about the formation of that intent. Without the intent there is no crime.

The magistrates considered their decision following a brave attempt by Tomkins to force the conviction home. 'We find the accused not guilty. You are all free to go.'

The ladies milled around in the corridors many of them confused in strange surroundings. 'Am I going to visit Ellen my daughter?' one said.

'I know when I wear my best-tailored suit from Selfridges Sale that I am going to visit Ellen. Ellen where are you girl?'

Another old lady said to Jennifer Joyce, 'Is it time for tea yet nurse? Why don't we have those nice boys Frankie and Malcolm over. They are such good fun! Now I seem to have lost my way. How do I get to the sitting room?'

It took quite a lot of gentle organisation to herd the ladies back to their bus for the return journey to the home. Mrs. Melrose said 'Oh goody. We are going on a trip. Are we visiting a museum or the seaside?' No on had the heart to answer her. On the other hand those that could appreciate their circumstances felt considerable relief at the outcome.

CAUSTIC CHEMICAL CORP.
ENTER CORPUS GASSMAN

Henry, having read of the worsening crisis, decided that he would seek and find the real villain of the piece! Who was in charge of Caustic Chemical Corp. and Industrial Investments inc. the previous users and owners of the Buttersoft estate? He could not wait for his lawyers to get moving he had to act immediately to eke out a response from these American corporations. He asked the receptionist at the Hotel of which the health club forms part to connect him to the number that he obtained for Caustic Chemicals in London.

A receptionist or secretary answered. She was evidently English and from the sound of things seemed to enunciate her words with her nose in the air with her tongue trying to force them through the roof of her mouth. 'Caustic Chemicals, can I help you please?'

Henry adopted a pleasant and patient tone, 'The managing director please?'

'Oh! That's Mr. Spillar. He's Stateside at the moment I'm afraid. Who's calling please?'

Henry replied 'my name is Redfield, Henry Redfield. Now who is available, because this is a matter of extreme urgency.'

The receptionist pondered deeply. 'Well there's Ariel George Gassman, the Company Secretary, will he do?'

Henry decided that he would have to do.

'Hallo, Gassman here.'

It sounded like a disembodied voice. Mr. Gassman was evidently speaking through one of those telephones designed for people wishing to rest their upper limbs from the vicissitudes of everyday toil.

Henry persevered. 'My name is Redfield and I am the current unfortunate owner of land which you originally owned or leased at Buttersoft Industrial Estate.'

There was a sucking noise at the other end of the line which Henry interpreted either as a sharp intake of breath or evidence that Gassman was talking whilst sucking a drink through a straw.

'I see . . .' volunteered Gassman '...and how can I assist you?'

Henry sighed deeply as he saw the immensity of the task before him. It was going to be, as the saying goes, "like drawing teeth".

'Well, I thought perhaps you might have heard about the problems that have occurred recently due to the emanations of fumes from chemicals which were improperly disposed of by burial just beneath the surface of the site. People and animals have been suffering illness, or unfortunate side effects of the unwitting inhalation of the gasses seeping through the soil.'

'Hmmm, yes, I think I have heard or read something about this. Now where was it? Let me think. No. It has gone I'm afraid. I cannot recall where I saw the report.' Henry paused in case Gassman was going to continue but he had subsided into silence again. 'Look can I come to see you or Mr. Spiller to discuss the serious implications of these developments - serious for us all'

Gassman did not respond immediately then he said, 'it's Spillar not Spiller you know.'

Henry's eyes opened wide and he felt the indignation rising within him.

'Look Mr. Gassman I don't care how it's spelt I want to know if you are going to meet this problem head on, or whether your head has other plans involving something akin to burial in the sands.'

'Steady on, old man' murmured Gassman who appeared to be in some sort of stupor.

'How about a spot of lunch? We could discuss this in a civilised manner and take advantage of the excellent wine cellar that is sported by the Hyde Park Hotel. Do you know it old boy?'

Henry was exasperated at the laissez-faire approach of the Company Secretary, but really there was nothing else to be done.

'Liquid lunch it is. Shall we say one o'clock?'

Gassman uttered a noise indicating that he had shifted some of his bulk slightly in what was probably an extremely commodious armchair.

'Righto Mr. Redfield, Henry did you say it was? See you in the restaurant at one. No need to loiter in the foyer gives the place a bad name what? Ha! Ha!'

Henry put the telephone down with a sense of profound relief. Whether this was due to his having made some doubtful progress in his investigation of the "Origins of the Seepage", or whether it was merely a response to having brought the telephone conversation with Gassman to a close, he knew not. Once he was outside in Piccadilly he flagged down a cab to take him home to change.

He slipped out of his casual clothes and donned his best Savile Row conservative 'three piece suite' (he called it this on account of the similarity in price to such a selection of furniture). Having chosen a tie, which could have easily been mistaken for Eton, he smoothed his hands over his hair. Henry reviewed with some small satisfaction the picture he had created (with some help from his parents and a possible deity) and stepped out into the air, which he immediately sniffed as he looked up at the blue sky mottled with the odd cirrus cloud. Not a bad day as days went in this climate, which some humourist had inexplicably labelled 'temperate'. It was cold. He would dig out the car.

He had rented a garage to protect his pride and joy. An Aston Martin DBS. Although now advanced in years, its recorded mileage belied its years. Colour? It was silver with a faint hint of green. Nothing shabby. The deep bottle green hide was welcoming. He sank gratefully into it. She started first time with that deep bass roar from the exhaust he had come to know and love.

He coursed through Regents Park and into Park Crescent, There was just an odd hint of traffic leading from Portland Place as it evolves into Regent Street by the BBC. Henry decided to avoid it by sweeping right towards Marylebone High Street. The car was responding lustily to his practised footwork. He edged into Baker Street and was soon across Oxford Street and thence into Grosvenor Square. The familiar Irish soft tones of a Radio Two Presenter caressed his inner ear. Henry was advised (in company with an unknown number of other captive audients) to 'go and lie down in a darkened room'. He ignored the invitation.

As always he glanced at the American Embassy with the huge golden Eagle adorning the building, and swung round into South Audley Street.

Curzon Street led him into Park Lane and, having successfully negotiated Hyde Park Corner he merely required a parking space in Knightsbridge. At a suitable moment he swung the car into a 'U' turn and landed abreast of the Doorman, George, of the Hyde Park Hotel in his fine wine coloured livery.

Handing him the keys and a twenty-pound note Henry mounted the steps to the foyer two at a time. He glanced back delighted to see George examining the note by holding it up to the light to check that it was not, "hot off the press". George must have felt Henry's eyes on him because he glanced up. Poor George he was covered in confusion and embarrassment as being caught in the act of examining the note. Finally, however, when he saw Henry's evident amusement he shrugged his shoulders with their golden epaulettes, which swung with the motion, and smiled himself. Off sped the Aston bound for 'free parking'.

Henry pulled down the points of his waistcoat, again smoothed his dark brown curls with his hands, and entered the dining room. The headwaiter was at his side in a flash.

'Yes sir. Good day sir. Can I help you sir, do you have a reservation?'

Henry turned to see a smartly dressed Maitre d'hotel leaning towards him. 'I think your reservation list may contain a Mr. Gassman.'

The headwaiter nodded without consulting his list. 'Ah yes. Mr. Gassrnan's usual table, I think. Francois!' He fired this volley in the general direction of the nearest waiter. 'Francois! Take Mr. Redfield to Mr. Gassman's table. Mr. Gassman is already in residence there, Mr. Redfield.'

Henry glanced back at the headwaiter as he followed Francois to the table. How did his name come into the equation? Gassman must have passed it on. Or, Henry groaned inwardly, his face was becoming a standard household product due to the increasing press coverage about the Buttersoft site. He walked over the thick pile red, gold and blue carpet towards his middle aged host, who appeared to Henry to be a man of considerable proportions.

Gassman rose ever so slightly, and with apparently immense personal effort, to greet Henry as he arrived at the corner table reserved for them today. Henry took in the advantage that this table had, in that Gassman commanded a view of the entire heavily decorated terrain between himself and the entrance doors. No one entered or left unless they first passed beneath the purview of the Gassman gaze. He introduced himself as Ariel George Gassman. His baroque bulk, which was considerable, belied the elfin name of Ariel. He would star in a Midwinter's Nightmare perhaps but nothing lighter. He bore an uncanny resemblance to that actor of old, Sidney Greenstreet. His speech continued and increased that impression. 'Henry is it?' he asked. Henry nodded.

'Well Henry, it is a pleasure indeed to have you join me here for luncheon. Yes a pleasure indeed.' He seemed to fall into a trance or brown study at that point, and he stared at the tablecloth. It was certainly a quality table setting, but surely not worthy of such intense gaze. Henry's eye fell upon the bottle of Margaux in the basket. It appeared to be nearly empty. As if rising to that thought Gassman lifted his fleshy right hand somewhat feebly, and murmured 'Francois, oh I say, Francois, fetch us another bottle of what was it this time? Oh yes Margaux. Or perhaps Mr. Redfield would prefer white. Would you Henry? His eyes finally found Henry's face although the apparently blurry focus seemed to be Henry's chin and two feet either side of it, rather than his eyes.

'Oh white for me please. Puligny Montrachet nicely chilled would be fine. Do you mind Gassman?' Henry could not resist the rather formal and even deprecatory use of the surname and without the title 'Mr.' The slight appeared to have fallen on stony ground or deaf ears however, as the eyes of Ariel Gassman appeared to have wandered elsewhere in the room.

'My goodness!' Gassman whispered. 'Do you see who just came in?' Henry's eyes sought to find the object of Gassman's gaze. 'That's Gerard Boucher one of the captain's of French industry. Rumour has it that he has plans for the ailing car manufacturing giant Caterpault. It seems that Boucher has tied the deal up with one of the car manufacturer's in Korea, It is known as the "Submarine". It seems that they are going to develop the first production line amphibious family car. The idea is to ensure one can get a parking space at the seaside. People will actually park in the sea.'

Henry's eyes travelled up to the vaulted ceiling with its frescos and gilded plaster decoration. The very idea of it. They cannot have done any market research. What game was Boucher playing? He was too smart and seasoned a dealer to go for something as lunatic as the amphibious hatch back.

Gassman was clearly enthusiastic and was attempting to signal to Boucher by various hand and finger signs and some body language, where

Gassman's accent was undoubtedly of the heaviest. Boucher, however, appeared not to notice any of this but the Maitre d'Hotel was becoming increasingly anxious in direct proportion to the wildness of Gassman's gestures. Certainly all the other diners were surveying Gassman with that detached and diffident interest, which one normally associates with the adult attitude toward less attractive children, parents, animals or reptiles encountered during a visit to the zoo. Gassmann finally seemed to appreciate that either Boucher had not noticed him, or was doing his damnedest to ensure that he did not. Gassman subsided in a grunt of disapproval and defeat.

Henry took the opportunity to launch into his prepared speech. 'Now Mr. Gassman, you know why we're here don't you?'

Gassman glanced at him and considered the question with some care. 'Ye-es' he murmured 'we're here to have lunch. Am I right?'

Henry threw up his hands in despair. He was beginning to think that this meeting with Gassman was a large mistake. He lifted his wineglass and took a sip by way both of comforting himself and also steeling his mind for the task ahead.

'We're here to discuss Buttersoft. Mr. Gassman!'

'Butter's soft is it?' ejaculated a suddenly awakened Gassman. 'I say Frederick! He called in the general direction of the headwaiter. Redfield says the butter's soft. Gorn off has it? This is not Joe's Caff you know. We expect better. England expects. Now where have I heard that before?' He scratched his balding head and began nodding into a reverie again.

Henry regarded him with disdain. How would he have any sort of meaningful discussion with this inebriate? 'Mr. Gassman!' he insisted raising his voice an octave or two. Ariel's head performed a three-point turn, and finally the Gassman gaze fell upon Henry's face. Trouble was, it kept falling until Gassman's nose finally made a soft and perfect landing upon the tablecloth. Henry searched the ceiling for some supernatural support, and, as none came, he looked around the room for assistance. Two burly waiters approached the table quietly, avoiding disturbance as much as possible. Putting his index finger to the side of his nose and winking, Henry confided 'Mr. Gassman is a trifle unwell. Perhaps you could assist him to his room.'

The waiters nodded and lifted Ariel's bulk between them.

Gassman stirred at the interruption, and confided in a slurred voice 'Redfield's a little the worse for wear, never could take his drink.' With that he lapsed back into semi-consciousness.

This must have happened before, as the headwaiter returned just as Henry was preparing to leave. 'Oh! Mr. Redfield, please continue to enjoy your meal. Mr. Gassman always wishes his guests to finish their food without pressure even if "ill-health prevents him from remaining with them. Would you like a glass of champagne to ease the tension sir?'

Henry slumped back in his seat resignedly. 'Very well Frederick, a bottle of your best Roederer Cristal and I will take the minted rack of lamb for my main course. Perhaps I'll take Coquilles St Jacques as a starter. Yes.' Frederick bowed and retreated to the safety of the kitchens to relay the order.

"Le champagne est arrivé "thought Henry as the bottle appeared at his table. He took out his mobile telephone and dialled. 'Dimitri where are you?' The Greek was in the Park Tower Casino opposite the Hyde Park Hotel. 'Come over the road and share some Cristal with me.'

Dimitri bellowed, 'What? Have you suddenly come into money Henry?'

Henry looked at the phone as though it had contracted an unspeakable disease 'I am here by invitation but my extraordinary host has passed out before dinner.'

Dimitri did not hesitate. 'I will be there before you can dispose of the glass in your other hand.'

True to his word he arrived in three minutes. Frederick ushered him to the table.

'What's this all about, Henry?' enquired the bull. Henry related the events of the afternoon.

'So you're for the rack of lamb. Well I think the beef on the trolley for me with Yorkshire pudding and all the trimmings Frederick.'

Dirnitri tasted the champagne and took in the other bottles littering the table. 'Quite a drinker your Mr. Gassman. Well what will you do now? He's paying for your lunch (or should I say our lunch) you can't just issue a writ and walk away. Bad form that. You'll have to pay him a visit at his office before the sun leaves the yard arm.'

Henry sighed deeply 'I suppose so'. Dimitri had also noticed the ubiquitous Boucher, who he had met at some party in Cannes during the Film Festival. *'Gerard comment ca va?'* he enquired as he approached the Frenchman's table.

'Why Dimitri, the Greek who dismembers our larders and then ravishes our bedrooms, how are you *mon ami?*'

Dimitri nodded and pointed to Henry who was downing his fourth *verre*. 'That is my friend and lawyer Henry Redfield.' Henry rose and joined the two men.

'Enchanté, Henri.' Boucher offered.

'How do you do?' was the English response.

'Please gentlemen join me. After all the lady who was to have accompanied me is indisposed and I all alone.'

Henry now had the opportunity of a closer look at the famous *homme d'affaires,* Gerard Boucher. Probably about forty five, of average height, and a strong face with a rather thin hard looking mouth. He was worth about thirty million sterling. This was according to reports made mainly in steel trading in North Africa. He was certainly an engaging personality and appeared to be good friends with the Greek.

'Are you in regular practice Henri' he asked.

'No, I am semi-retired. I have been living off the ill-gotten gains made in Africa in the eighties. I do the odd case for a special client that is all.'

'I am looking for a lawyer to handle my acquisition of the French Motor Giant Caterpault. Of course I have French lawyers on the case, but there are assets here and elsewhere, and I need a lawyer to oversee the operation.'

Henry considered the offer. Was this just politeness or was it real. Such a job would pay fees in six figures for six months work or thereabouts. 'I am interested Gerard. Let's meet tomorrow, if you're free, to discuss the fine detail.'

Gerard nodded. 'Dimitri has recommended you and that is praise indeed. Here's my card, visit me at ten a.m. at my home in Mayfair. *D'accord?*'

Henry replied *'D'accord* Gerard.'

The meal passed off without further excitement and Boucher took his leave of them. As it turned out he insisted on paying the entire bill which Henry much preferred. Now he could deal with Gassman without so much gentillesse as would otherwise have been the case. He telephoned Gassman's office and asked for an appointment with the big man.

'Nine a.m. tomorrow will be perfect thank you.' he told Gassman's secretary.

As the two friends descended the steps of the Hotel Henry saw a face he knew climbing towards him. It was Parker of the Press. 'Well, well, well, Mr. Redfield what a surprise. I happen to have an appointment to see Gassman of Caustic for a coffee and a brandy in this delightful resting house. Who do I run into but my old friend Mr. Redfield? Is this a coincidence or does my unerring nose tell me that you have just been with said Gassman, Ariel of that ilk?'

'You have learned to follow your nose Parker, who am I to teach an old dog new tricks?' Henry retailed with a light touch of sardonic scorn.

Parker's eyebrows rose. 'Well then, what did our Ariel have to say for himself and his erring establishment?'

'Not a great deal I am afraid Nosey, he was well over the limit before I could get at him. He is currently sleeping it off in one of the hotel's suites I think.'

Nosey looked disappointed for a second or two, but then brightened and piped up 'and where are you off to now may I ask?'

Henry looked at him for a moment pensively without replying. Nosey got the message. 'I didn't mean to pry, I merely meant to ask, what are your plans regarding the chemicals and the fumes?'

'I am going to see Mr. Gassman tomorrow. I may try to track down Spillar before that. If I get no joy then we will enter the fray in Court with no holds barred. I am not prepared to foot the bill for this. I bought the land in good faith without knowledge of the chemical problem.' With that he ran down the steps to join Dimitri who had wandered ahead.

DIMITRI ON DRUGS???

As they walked back to the Hilton through Hyde Park, Henry was glad of the opportunity to draw breath in the relatively clean air. He surveyed the green vista to the north and felt better in the company of trees than he had the Hotel diners. Dimitri instinctively felt Henry's need for a moment's peace and buried himself in his own thoughts. He had spent time and money on revelry for too long he needed a business challenge. His own field seemed devoid of opportunity at this time, but he sensed that in Henry's peculiar difficulty there might be an angle to make a killing. Maybe Boucher with his thick French moustache and forceful and aggressive approach was another possibility.

Suddenly he broke his silence 'you know Henry I can see a real possibility of a long-term gain with Buttersoft'.

Henry looked at him aghast. 'Really Mimi you know how sensitive I am on that score, please don't try to make it into a joke.'

The shadow of a serious smile crossed Dimitri's lips. 'I do not mean to be facetious, *filemou*. Bear with me a moment and I will summarise my idea. If it is truly ridiculous you may dismiss it out of hand. In the first place, you own the land. In the second place, there are gases or chemicals emanating from that land. In the third place, those gases if inhaled by man or beast cause a frothing at the mouth, and a marked rise in sexual desire and performance. This even affects old people as we see from the report that you showed me about that old people's home. So far do you agree with me?'

Henry nodded.

'Right then, my idea is to send - at my expense - scientists to capture these gasses and contain them for analysis. They will be instructed to reduce the gasses to liquid and/or solid form and commence tests on all three chemical compounds.'

'Is this to help me in specifying exactly what is causing the damage in my claim?' asked Henry.

'That would be, if I may use the term a side effect of their work. No, there are greater possibilities here. Once they have tested the compounds for really serious possible indications, which might cause other harm to persons inhaling or imbibing the chemicals, they can explore the possibility of refining a drug that would act as a sexual stimulant or aphrodisiac. Think of the potential Henry! Impotent men would queue up. Unsatisfied or dissatisfied women would want prescriptions from their doctors for their husbands. What is it you once told me? 'Where there's muck there's brass.' Yes even the brass would want some for their customers! You know the ladies of the lamp, I mean of the street.'

Henry turned to look with utter mystification at his friend's extraordinary face. 'Are you serious Dimitri? Do you really think there might be something in it? I can tell you that this episode is ageing me before my time. Can this chemical be part of the fabulous elixir of life? Surely not? You must be dreaming. I really don't know what to say but you certainly have given me food for thought and lifted my mood.'

The conversation was halted by the temporary risk of their lives as they heroically sought to dodge the speeding traffic and run across Park Lane having passed out of the multi-million dollar gates erected opposite the Hilton at the entrance to the Park.

Dimitri caught up with his fitter and lither friend outside a jewellery shop near the hotel. He fought to catch his breath. Whilst he did so he noticed a beautiful gold watch for sale. 'Henry I am going to buy you a present to cement our deal for the chemicals. Fifty-fifty if it works and I will cover the expenses if it flops. Is it a deal?'

Henry was almost in a swoon.

'Dimitri that watch is ten grand! It's a special Audemars Piquet.' But Dimitri had disappeared inside the shop to make a deal.

He emerged, watch in hand. '*Oriste* - there you are, so the deal is sealed. Put it on and show the girls. Let's wake them up. Should we buy them something? Do you think they'll be peeved if we don't?'

Henry shrugged his shoulders. 'Let's take them out. We have all afternoon if they want new outfits. We can give them a few hundred and let them go shopping. That should keep them happy.'

They walked with a new jauntiness in their gait, Henry stopping every now and then to look at his new watch, as they sauntered through the foyer.

'Any messages Claude?' Dimitri called to the concierge

'Only your wife sir. She insisted that she speak to the lady in your room. I told her that there was no lady in your room, that you were out at a business meeting; that you looked tired, needed a holiday and are missing her enormously.'

'You are a treasure Claude. Here's fifty pounds. Take twenty for yourself and send my wife some flowers by Interflora. The message should read *"Agapi mou* I can't live without you. Home next week. Love to the kids. Missing you all Dimitri." Can you manage that Claude? And remember no calls to the room when I am out - *ever.*'

Henry shook his head 'poor Vicky. She is so beautiful and there are your wonderful kids. Dimitri you're never there for them.'

Dimitri turned to face his friend, 'What are you my mother? To nag me so! You know the way I am and so does my wife. I don't pretend but I try not to expose her to hurt and myself to criticism. As for my kids they will have security financially. I see them every month. I admit I am not a footballing or tennis playing father. I prefer other games that are not for them - yet. Stop trying to convert me. I am a lost cause with no wish to be found.'

Henry stepped back with the force of this onslaught. 'OK, OK sorry I spoke. I was only trying to help.'

They took the lift to the Suite. Josephine and Isabel were not sleeping. 'Where have you been? We thought to phone the police and 'ospitals. Why you didn't at least call us. We didn't want to leave the room in case you phoned, and anyway you took the key. If we left we couldn't get back in.' Josephine finished the first chapter of her complaints and stopped to draw breath.

'Please!' said Dimitri with a mock seriousness that suggested a solemn declaration was in store for them.

'Ladies. Henry and I have been engaged in the most delicate and serious negotiations relating to a new business venture. You don't know how lucky you are to see us at all today. It is a measure of our regard for your minds (not to mention your delectable bodies) that we have appeared back so soon!'

The girls stared at him with open mouths, whether in astonishment at the man's gall or whether they were so impressed by the content of his speech that they were left agog, we know not.

Dimitri continued. 'As perfectly formed specimens of the superior female species you will be well aware of the imperfections which assail most men. I never cease to be impressed with what women are prepared to endure in their menfolk. To add insult to injury, more often than not, the man's main claim to fame his reputedly deadly weapon often fails to aim let alone fire, lacks an impressive barrel, and in performance is often little more than a damp squib. It was to meet the challenge of this serious defect in menkind that Henry and I ourselves addressed this afternoon.

Henry has stumbled across a possibility, and I will not put it any higher than that, at this time, of a momentous discovery that could revolutionise sexual activity as we know it - and many of our future patients do not know, or have forgotten. This gas that percolates through the soil of his Buttersoft land and assails the nostrils of passers-by, or people within a limited radius of the site, has led to a frantic increase in fornication (particularly among the elderly) among inhalers. Statistics hot off the press (Nosey Parker whispered it to me today) indicate that for the first time on eighty-three years the birth rate has begun to rise. Did I say rise? I should have said soar! We want to capture the essence of that sensual emanation before it evaporates. Mankind expects! Womankind demands!'

He sat down to imagined rapturous applause. In fact the girls were shrugging their pretty shoulders and looking to Henry for confirmation of any aspect of what appeared to them to be a wild rant from the Athenian Bull.

Henry, however, nodded his curly head in vague confirmation of the Greek outburst.

'There is certainly merit in pursuing this. If Dimitri should be proved right, we could be on to the greatest money spinner since the National Pottery where potty people pay for a wild chance, or pot luck, to corner a fortune, to take a share of the National Pot. We're sending the best chemical scientist to grab a snort of the 'Rastagas' and see if sniffing is believing.'

Josephine sidled up to Henry and whispered 'you don't need any of this artificial stimulants. God help me if you have some. You'll kill me!' She giggled with delight at the prospect of such an awful demise. Isabel went further she got down on her knees and begged Dimitri not to try the gas.

The Bull lowered his massive head to her and bellowed and howled with laughter. 'Now I have you where I want you. You had better behave or I'll get a bottle of compressed 'Vampire Vapor' which we will market as "Naughty but Nice Nookie Nozzles" and I'II take a Whacking Whiff and then I'II puff and I'll puff and I'll blow your knickers down!'

THE HAIR OF THE DOG?

In the meantime 'Old Boy Gassman' had awakened in the Hyde Park Hotel with a howling hangover. He pressed the button for room service. Actually he pressed all the buttons with his eyes still closed until Room Service answered. 'Bring me the hair of a dog', he demanded.

'Pardon Senor?' was the reply from Maria who had taken the call in the kitchen. She turned to Pedro, the commis chef, with her hand over the receiver, and said 'This man in Suite 249 he want me to bring him a dog's hair. I never had such an order before. Where I going to find it?'

Pedro shook his head 'first you will 'ave to catch the dog. He say which type of dog he prefer?' Maria shrugged. She had no idea where to find a dog.

She spoke into the telephone 'excuse me sir. Perhaps if you ask the Concierge to catch or buy the dog, we can try to cut the hair afterwards.' Despite this seeming to her a helpful suggestion the guest in 249 seemed totally incensed by it.

'Damn foreigners!' he muttered, conveniently forgetting his Teutonic antecedents.

'Now listen my girl. Take a raw egg and cherry brandy a dash of lemon juice and whisk with ice. Bring that and a large pot of black coffee to my suite a.s.a.p. Is that understood? And forget the dog. Last thing I want is a poodle yapping and peeing all over the place!' There was a pause. Then Maria faithfully recounted his order. 'Right away OK?' He dropped the telephone.

Slowly he dragged himself from the bed into the bathroom. He stripped off his now mangled suit and wallowed into the empty bath. The taps were thankfully in the middle of the semi-circular rather grand arrangement and he turned on the cold water. Quite numb with the alcohol he hardly

116

felt the icy stream. He then pressed the button. The shower shot down all over him. Feeling returned to his body with considerable pain and anguish to its owner. The water spattered off his bald pate and ricocheted on to the bathroom floor. He didn't care.

He turned off the water and lay there in a cool half-filled bathtub and fell asleep. The knock on the bedroom door awakened him from the doze. 'Ugh! Just a minute. Just a minute please' he moaned still in a daze and now suffering some hangover effect.

As the bathroom door was closed Maria could not hear his muted objection and entered the suite. 'Your drinks sir!' she shouted, wondering where he had got to. He took hold of each side of the bath with a firm grip and tried lifting himself. Considering his bulk he did well, but not well enough.

When he was half out of the bath the foot that remained within settled precariously upon the Imperial Leather soap bar.

He needed that foot as a fulcrum or pivot point. Suddenly, and at a pace that it had not moved for forty years that foot (his left) shot forward and then as he lost balance upward. His rear was fortunately extremely well padded, as he fell upon the rim of the bath with it. Both his feet pointed towards the recently extinguished showerhead. With one cheek on either side of the rim he achieved a momentary balance. Unfortunately he had not lost all the momentum of the fall and he began to waver from side to side. He fell out of the bath and landed upon the weighing scales. Having received more than they could endure the scales expired.

Maria, who was, to do her justice, a shapely brunette from Southern Spain, hearing the noise of a heavy fall, took her courage in both her beautiful brown hands and entered the bathroom. There she saw the importunate Mr. Gassman from what she would thereafter always refer to as an "Ariel view". The mountainous landscape was far from pretty, although some of it did threaten to turn green or possibly black at any moment.

Gassman could not move he was winded by the double fall, and shocked by the sudden entry of Maria who seemed to be staring at his private parts. The attention aroused him despite his general condition. 'Aarghhh!' shrieked Maria regarding his vital organ with horror. 'It's going to stand up!' and she turned tail and bolted back whence she came.

Gassman relapsed into a stupor after she left. He lay quietly on the bathroom tiles for at least ten minutes. When he came to (again disturbed by an urgent knocking on his door - Maria had returned with reinforcements) he could not move. Was he paralysed? He wondered. He could move his arms although his right elbow hurt. He reached for the face towel hanging nearby and covered his middle section. The knocking now was at the bathroom door.

A man said, 'Mr. Gassman this is the Duty Manager. Maria here tells us that you have had a fall sir. We are coming in with a stretcher to take you to a waiting ambulance thence to hospital in the Fulham Road.' Gassman grunted.

The door was opened gingerly. The stretcher was placed by his side with difficulty in view of the shortage of space around his prone plastered plumpness. Hoisting him up on to it made the ambulance men glad that they did daily weight training. 'Christ he weighs a ton Jim' said one to the other as though Gassman was unconscious or not present. Jim looked at Gassman and said 'twenty four stone if you're a pound sir.'

Gassman lifted his eyebrows and said 'twenty five, if you don't mind young man.' Maria had taken up a secure position well behind the Manager as if she feared that the Incredible Bulk would launch himself from the stretcher directly at her, weapon at the ready. She need not have worried. Gassman had settled down nicely and was snoring in a satisfied sort of way as he was hefted, lifted and shifted out of the suite.

The Duty Manager related Maria's unfortunate experiences with the galloping gourmand Gassman, in unabridged clarity, to his secretary who carefully absorbed every detail. She, in turn, having recovered from the effects of the history, had to telephone Henry to postpone his 9am appointment with the calamitous corpus.

Maria was given the rest of the day off to recover from the least appetising aspects of her experience. 'He never even tasted that horrible drink he had me bring to his room' she complained to the housekeeper Audrey Able. 'He asked me for a dog's hair. I still don't know what terrible things he was going to do with it. And Audrey really! You should have seen his sex. I was shocked. He couldn't stand up but it did. He may be fat now, but he must have been a menace in his day. Put my Jose's in the shade it did. Reminded me of what I once saw on a horse in the Park. It really made me shiver, Audrey.'

The housekeeper put a consoling arm around her and said 'who'd have guessed that he had it in him, or should I say on him. Have a nice cup of tea luv. That will make you feel much better. All got small ones in Spain have they dearie? I don't think I'll be taking me holidays there after all.'

'Oh no Audrey! Spanish men have their fair share, I think. I haven't known many men before my Jose though, so I don't really know. Why you don't try Greece.'

VISIT TO THE BOUCHER

Henry, divested of his morning meeting with Gassman dutifully arrived at the Boucher residence for a discussion, which might directly concern his future. Boucher lived in classy luxury in London's Mayfair. A butler answered Henry's knock at the front door. 'Yes sir, this is M. Boucher's residence. Who may I say sir? Ah! Mr. Redfield. Yes! M. Boucher did warn me that you would be coming. May I take that coat sir? Please wait in the drawing room here sir. M. Boucher will be right along.'

Henry surveyed his surroundings. The staircase had apparently been moved from a stately home in the country. An Ormolu clock of ancient origin marked time on the Adam mantelpiece in the drawing room. Was that a Rembrandt above the fireplace? Surely that green colour was the most exquisite in a Persian Rug that he had ever seen. The dining furniture must owe a great deal to Chippendale. The chez-longue must be original *Louis Quinze*! A chair resting against a wall was surely genuine Hepplewhite? The glass cabinet exhibited a number of jade figures and there! A *Fabergé* egg! A veritable museum of antiques. Priceless. All somehow worked together to demonstrate exquisite taste in their possessor. The huge ancient grandfather clock in the hall sounded the hour with heavy, solid chimes.

Suddenly Boucher appeared, apparently fastening his cuff links. 'Hallo Henry, good of you to arrive on time. How did it go this morning with Ariel? Oh! I see from your face that he again failed to put in an appearance. Well, there will be other opportunities I am sure. Please don't get up. Has Masters offered you coffee? No? Right I'll see to that and we can get started.' He pulled on a tapestry bell.

Masters appeared miraculously with the coffee already on a tray with biscuits and the usual accessories. 'Milk and sugar sir?' Henry declined. Masters withdrew silently.

'Now Henry, as I explained yesterday we are taking over Caterpault. They are aware of our interest, of course. We are already the largest minority shareholder.

We are here to inspect their assets and their books. It is to you that I will look to handle the UK aspect of the transaction. Co-ordinate surveyors and valuers both of realty and plant. Instruct the accountants to check their fiscal and debtor/creditor balances. Draft the agreement for purchase of their English subsidiary, and liaise with Jean-Claud Portier my Advocat of Paris as to the timing and arrangements for acquisition of the French Mother. Here's his card. He will provide you with details of the Italian, German and US attorneys handling the simultaneous arrangements for the local companies.'

'What are your plans M. Boucher? Will you strip the assets out of the giant and sell them. Are you really serious about this amphibious domestic car?' asked Henry.

"Good question Henry. Well, we have to contend with the Unions here and abroad. Caterpault is profitable and expanding. By making a deal with one of the Japanese Computer giants we hope to build the first robot driven vehicle all electric - no fuel required. Computers will constantly update the driver on road conditions. The future we see is without traffic accidents. All drivers will be robots who cannot drink and do not suffer from human errors of judgement and other lapses. The really major advantage will be in the reduction of pollution levels in the air in the major cities of the world. EU grants will be available to assist on the R&D. Now here's our Business Plan - Confidential of course.

As regards the amphibian, that is a possibility for the distant future, but is mainly a red herring for press consumption. I rather enjoy gently misleading them. Any further questions can be answered by Jean-Claud. Your retainer is £100,000 per annum for what will be at best part time work, and, of course, we shall pay all expenses without question.

Now I have to take my car to Heathrow and fly swiftly to New York. We shall be arranging the closing over there next week. Keep in touch.'

With that he was gone again, his coffee virtually untouched. 'Whew!' thought Henry. 'He can't have been in the room more than three and a half minutes! I said hardly a word during the entire meeting. Couldn't. He didn't suppose that I would turn down or negotiate the fee. He realised that it was an offer that I could not refuse. Well he was right of course. He hasn't got where he is today by not being right!'

Having drunk his coffee he rose to leave. Out of nowhere Masters appeared with his coat. 'Goodbye sir!' The carved solid polished wood door, imported from Costa Rica, closed behind Henry and he was out in the street. The whole business had only taken fifteen minutes at the outside. Still he had a spring in his step as he retraced the route homeward.

DAI LIKES PARIS IN THE SPRINGTIME

Dai and Doris had decided to take a romantic weekend in Paris, mixing business with pleasure, as they had a few modelling doors to knock upon just off the Champs Elysées. Doris selected her shortest mini for the trip and Dai commented that instead of tugging at it every time she sat down she should tie weights to it instead. 'You don't understand Dai. I don't want every Tom, Dick or Harry seeing my knickers', she insisted.

'Then why on earth don't you wear a proper skirt instead of that. Why my Welsh Rugby scarf is wider than that, you could wear that if you like. You should show the flag you know, and all that.'

Doris sniffed disparagingly at Dai. 'You're a spoilsport Dai. You like my legs don't you now? Well you can hardly complain if I let the world have a peek too.'

Dai considered this. 'It's just that I don't want men constantly trying to see up your skirt. Is that so wrong Doris? Anyway, I have nothing against your legs. You can wrap them around my waist any time you like!'

Doris sniffed again. 'That's the trouble with you. Randy as rat in a drainpipe you are. Don't you ever think of anything else?'

Dai looked at her with a grin growing on his face by the second. 'To tell the truth Doris when it comes to you my girl, the answer has to be no. I congratulate myself on the strength of my resolve that I don't fling myself upon you right now. You don't know what it's like to walk about with a fully-grown leek inside your trouser leg. Look you Doris, it's not as if you don't ask for it. Look at you. You're a walking rape victim in the making you are. You aren't by any chance in the mood now are you? Because if you are I promise I would do my utmost to satisfy your deepest longings.'

Doris turned from him in a huff. 'Behave yourself Dai, what do you think I am a machine?'

Dai swooned 'if they could build a machine like you my love, the world would be a very happy place let me tell you. You could sell the rights and make a fortune you could.'

Doris sighed and slowly walked those long tapered legs across the room to him. 'All this flattery seems to have worked for you today.' As they clasped their bodies together she felt the difference that she made to his life. Dai lifted her skirt effortlessly and helped himself. She, in turn, gave his leek a long squeeze.

Dai muttered 'I knew that peeling onions could do it, but nobody told me that squeezing leeks would bring tears to your eyes.' Doris rumbled a low sexy laugh.

A few hours later she had put on a more conservative dress and jacket and they made their way to Victoria Station for *Le Shuttle*. The station was noisy and crowded. They found their way to the correct platform and joined the queue to board. Doris had sensibly purchased their tickets from an agent to avoid a last minute crush. The journey was swift but hardly entertaining, that is, if you discount Dai's constant prodding that they should join the "Mile Low Club.

Doris pushed him away. 'Have you forgotten how sore I am since this afternoon. That's no penny whistle you've got there you know. it's not as if you spare me at all. You insist on what the language schools call, 'Total Immersion'. Your family motto is probably, 'Never spare an inch' or 'Give us an inch and we'll take a foot.'

Dai laughed. 'Now I don't remember you complaining when we was at it. Moaning yes, but not complaining!'

Doris kicked him hard and blushed to her roots. 'You're awful. I don't know why I stand for it!'

'But I thought you preferred it standing!' argued Dai with mock indignation, and got another kick for his pains.

Within hours they were walking down the Champs Elysees and Dai insisted they have a petit crème at the Drug Store. They sat outside and watched the traffic and pedestrians and drunk in the Frenchness of it all. The waiters with their inevitable black tight-fitting waistcoats, white shirts and tight black trousers calling for all types of coffees and alcoholic beverages, the passers-by greeting each other and sniffing over their friends costumes to check upon the quality and style.

It is all 'bloody marvellous' thought Dai. To think my life was dull and boring just weeks ago. Doris is the best thing since sliced bread - before it too, come to think of it. He took up his camera and started snapping her, the street everything. She lapped it up and twisted and turned to give him a variety of poses and backdrops.

The waiter appeared. Dai snapped him. *'Msieu. S'il vous plait?'* the waiter inquired.

Dai stared at him. 'Where did he learn to speak like that Doris?'

'He's French silly. They all speak like that. Now what are we going to have, ah yes *un petit crème s'il vous plait'* She beamed at the waiter.

He turned to Dai who nodded furiously in agreement and then remembered 'D'accord, d'accord.' Off went the waiter, bobbing and weaving like a seasoned rugby wing three quarter through the seated populace, tray on hand, napkin over forearm, pen behind ear. There was indeed music, rhythm and dazzling colour and form in this place like none other. As evening drew in the street lit up not just signs for shops as you might find anywhere in England but whole buildings were illuminated. It was breath-taking.

After coffee they strolled looking in the shop windows. Doris could not get enough of the ladies fashion houses. Dai suggested they visit "the Follies Bergère". 'Haven't they closed it?' countered Doris. 'Tomorrow we must see the Louvre and the other Musées. Oh and the *Tour d'Eiffel.'*

Dai held Doris's hand, and felt real warmth in his heart. He, no they, were unconditionally happy. There were no pressures, they could take their time and wander and explore. They weren't staying at the Ritz, but for 40 euros per night for the room their small hotel was surprisingly close to the centre, just moments from where they now wandered.

They selected a restaurant a little off the beaten track which Dai's editor had recommended and had a marvellous fish soup. Doris had remarked that it was really more like a fish medley in sauce there was so much fish in it and remarkably little actual soup. A drop of Sancerre to wash it down completed a tasty picture.

A second bottle was offered by the owner, Marcel Morceau who confided that Dai's editor was a regular visitor '...always bringing a little of thees and a leetle of that with him. One time it is a redhead, the next a blonde. Last time he brought a girl who was half-Jamaican and half-Scottish with him. I asked her how she decided what to drink. It must be *un peu difficile* - a little difficultée - to decide between a dram of whisky and a tot of rum *n'est ce pas?*'

'Ha! Ha!' Doris thought that was very witty of the maitre and simultaneously flashed him a white smile and matching thigh. No contest. The owner eyes went into a sudden steep dive. Dai sighed, life was going to be a series of other men lusting after Doris.

'Oh yes 'ee is quite a playboy zat editor of yours' intoned Marcel. 'Doris told me you stay in the same hotel, Eden, like him. I 'ope you don't have the same room. That bed must be near to collapse! Ha! Ha!'

Doris now regarded him with a stern look and replied primly 'our room is absolutely lovely, with a view over the rooftops of Paris, well, some of them in the next street anyway. I felt the mattress and it is firm and solid, like new. Anyway I thought Paris was for couples in love ...'

'But of course. I apologise ma chèrie. Please don't misunderstand. It is just the editor. He is a rake that one.'

They were treated to a superb cognac, which predated them by fifteen years. Thus warmed they made their way hotelward. The concierge glanced up from his novel as they entered. *'Bonsoir Msieu, madame.'*

'Ooh!' said Doris 'isn't it lovely the way they say that?'

Dai shrugged and mimicked *'bonsoir madame. Voulez-vous coucher avec moi ce soir.* Do you fancy a bit of hanky-panky on ze side mademoiselle? N'est-ce pas?'

Doris stuck up her nose and walked in her high heels and mock high dudgeon across the marble floor clickety-clack, clickety-clack. 'I'm not with him!' she flaunted at the concierge as she passed by. 'He's been following me all night. Such a pest!'

Dai turned up his palms and shrugged at the hotel official. 'My wife always behaves like this. She treats me like dirt and takes every opportunity to chat up strange men. She's a very lusty woman.'

The concierge threw up his hands. 'Les Anglais they are all mad. Zey must have eaten the (*vache anglaise*) English Cow. Zey all have zis Mad Cow Disease. Zat's why we call them *ze Rosbif.* We, the gallant *Françaises*, will 'ave to save Europe, as we did in the War.'

Dai stopped dead in his tracks. 'Eh? Hang on a minute Monsieur Clouseau. It was us British as came and saved you from the Nazis. Us and the Yanks. How do you claim to have saved Europe during the Second World War?'

The Concierge stared at him. 'Monsieur I don't know what type of history they teach at your English schools, but let me tell you it was the brave and *courageux* French Resistance that won the war in Europe. Of course, I admit the allies helped, but so they should. Our girls thanked them well enough. Zere is too much English and American blood running through French veins today. No wonder we 'ave such problems with the Algerians!'

Dai stared at him disbelievingly. 'Now look here Francois or whatever your name is. You may not know but tens of thousands of our boys died here, their blood stains your land, to free you from the Bosch. A bit of gratitude would not go amiss. That's not to say that I denigrate the contribution from the Resistance. Fine men and women they were for sure. I can't understand what you are saying about Algeria. We had nothing to do with that.

Now as it happens I am Welsh (from the Pays de Galles) so I don't eat English beef. Leeks is our national food. I am trying to get Doris to try one. Unfortunately, tonight she seems to be putting up her own Resistance. I don't think I'm going to get anywhere near her knickers.'

'Knickers? What is that?" asked Francois. 'Oh you mean panties, *les slip*, but it is most important that you get near them. How else can you take them off? We French prefer to take off the Knickers before making love. So you British do it with the knickers on? Zat's really strange'

Dai regarded the concierge with a mixture of pity and derision. 'We take the knickers off whenever we can, let me tell you. I'm about to do that right now if you'll excuse me. *Bon nuit.*' He scampered off in Doris's wake.

Once in the room he did not stop touching, stroking and kissing her. She felt as though her body was on fire. Still he made no move to remove her clothing. She clutched at his national pride like a drowning man clutching at a straw. Their loveplay became suddenly more feverish. They had drunk deeply of the romance, not to mention the wine, of La Belle France, and it added a poignancy and fervour to their manipulations and general noisy thrashing about.

The ritual banging on the wall by their next door neighbours went entirely unheeded. Their moans and groans grew, if anything, in their volume and content. Finally, the knickers were off, and they approached the first fence - mutual rubbing with gusto. Whee! They were safely over that and on to the second mouth-to-mouth resuscitation. Up and over that with room to spare now they were pressed to mount in earnest. 'To mount or not to mount that is the question.' They seemed uncertain who would mount whom. They each tried the other in turn, and then appeared to change their minds again. A loud whoop greeted Doris as she passed the finishing line. She had shown a clean pair of heels to Dai in the straight. Though this was not a photo finish she only led him by a short head. He took up the rear quite contentedly. Finally he fell upon her exhausted, yelling his head off as he fell. At last! Their neighbours on either side could get back to sleep.

PARKER'S PARTY

Back in Buttersoft Nosey was not letting the grass grow under his feet. In point of fact this could not happen in Parker's patch as he had crazy-paved his back garden. Parker lived in your commoner garden three bed semi-detached with his wife of twenty-four years, Ethel. This was an entirely separate arrangement from his knocking shop over the Chipperie. His wife, who was entirely unaware of his extra-marital adventures, was late for work, for family or friends for appointments, everything. Nosey called her Ethel the Unready after one of England's ancient Kings who ruled some nine hundred years ago. When they were due anywhere and people rang to ask when they would be arriving, he would always answer "Er, probably in about a thousand years. Ethel is still Unready." Ethel took no notice. Her mother had told her, "Take no notice Ethel." And she did.

Her mother, Gertrude Minns, had realised years before that nothing in this world would induce Ethel to arrive anywhere on time. She promptly stopped trying to force the issue. This removed the stress. She would never wait for Ethel to get dressed for a party or gathering. She would leave the house with dad (and, after he died, without him, of course) and arrive on time. When the hostess asked after Ethel. Gertie would say, 'She'll be along in an hour or two. You know Ethel.'

Nosey had adopted a similar approach. This evening was different however, Nosey was to be given the freedom of Buttersoft by the mayor, for services to the community. Nosey had single-handed, in company with Dye who had disappeared with the proceeds, namely Doris, masterminded the placing of Buttersoft on the National and now the World map. Newspapers everywhere had taken up the story of the strange goings on in the area. CNN had come to shoot the village and the site. Two of their cameramen, overcome by the fumes, had been arrested for molesting a nun and were awaiting trial. All this was down to Nosey and his promulgation of everything Buttersoft. Well perhaps not all of it - but certainly, most of it.

Unabashed and definitely unabated Parker of the Press pressed Ethel to get dressed. He had gone to the trouble of resetting all clocks putting them three hours forward. Imagine his chagrin when it didn't make a blind bit of difference.

Ethel still chugged along at a snail's pace. At last she was ready to leave. He pushed her out of the front door and into their Morris Minor.

They built up a reasonable head of steam down the hill towards Buttersoft Town Hall. Nosey concentrated on the road whilst Ethel mumbled on about the price of vegetables and meat. He was then treated to the latest news about her friend Cheryl Carter and her urine infection.

'Maude Masters tells me Cheryl must have caught it from that Sid Sharpe. Come on you know Nosey, the one that sells those funny brushes that lift the fibres and dandruff from your suit. Not brushes really more pads.'

Parker suffered in silence and continued to watch the road as though his life depended on it - which it probably did. Ethel carried on regardless as contributions from her husband were unwarranted, unwanted and unnecessary.

'Well, you won't believe this but Maude told me that it's NSU or 'Non Sporadic Frights' it is.

'Now you don't get that from sitting on a cold toilet seat - that's piles that is. Maude tells me you can tell if you've got it if you hold your specimen up to the light. You can see bits of stuff like egg white floating in it. Just imagine. Cheryl has had that Sid in her house during the day. Carrie Cormack lives right across the road from her, and she's seen Sid sidling up to the gate, and looking about him warily to ensure that he's not been spotted. Very suspicious. One day Cheryl forgot to close the bedroom curtains. It was in the afternoon. Carrie had just gone to her own bedroom, which faces Cheryl's across the road, to fetch her knitting, she's making little baby socks for her niece you know, when what do you think she saw? Well, they were standing there stark naked. Stark naked! Cheryl's bum was on the windowsill and he was giving it to her with gusto - and the curtains wide open! Carrie's words were, 'In full view of the neighbourhood. What a cheek!'

Nosey turned to her and said 'quite a pair of cheeks from what I've heard in the Three Tuns.'

Thankfully they arrived at this point terminating title tattle, and met with the welcoming committee had braved the elements to usher them into the Town Hall proper. The rotund, ruddy, resplendent Mayor Michael Meecham and his elderly lady wife Maud sat in full regalia at the head of the table. There were aldermen and alderwomen. Then there were younger men and younger women, who were invited from the local polytechnic, the Buttersoft Poly or the 'Unsaturate' as it was known among its inmates.

The room in which the party was being held was originally the main hall or dining hall of an old public school and dated back some three hundred years or more. It had a vaulted wooden ceiling and the room was wood-panelled and covered with various heraldic shields. There was a fine old tapestry, which hung on the North Wall depicting the Battle of Hastings (which, of course, was hundreds of miles south of Buttersoft). The arrow in the eye of the unfortunate Anglo-Saxon chief was graphically detailed.

The Mayor who had partaken of several glasses of good wine beforehand to fortify himself, rose to the occasion.

'Ladies and Gentlemen Lady Deputy Mayoress, Aldermen and women I rise to bid you welcome to this ancient and honourable institution.

We are here today to honour one of our locally born and bred citizens Parker of the Press. Some call him Nosey, but without that quality how would he root out the goodies? In this case it is not just some mere truffle or trifle. Nosey has found such a prize, such a treasure that 'Buttersoft' is today on the lips of the multitude. From Lands End to the Lizard, er, sorry, I mean, John 0' Groats, his praise is lauded.

Now I have written a poem to celebrate Norris Parker's contribution to Buttersoft's development and for putting it and himself firmly on the map.

They seek him here.

They seek him there.

Those Dailies seek him every where.

Is he in heaven, or is he lost?

In that quiet, elusive Buttersoft."

There was a pause for applause. Only a ripple, so he nipped a tipple.

He continued, 'Nosey Parker? We were at school together. He was a model pupil, writing essays that were the envy of the class even then, I remember when the school bully accosted him Nosey shouted:

"The pen is mightier than the sword."

This bold report astounded the audience and there were muted cries of:

"What happened then? Tell us what happened?"

Finally the Mayor gave way and continued. 'The bully gave him a thorough thrashing', the Mayor admitted, engendering a wave of disappointment and anti-climax. 'But he bore his bruises proudly. The bully was made to feel ashamed. At least I think he did. Anyway, from school he went to the 'Unsaturate' and graduated with honours in English Literature. The local newspaper was lucky to get him. We are lucky to have him back amongst us tonight. Ladies and Gentlemen I give you Nosey Parker.'

The applause and general noise went on rather too long and one imagined there might be just a hint of satiric derision from the younger people, who had yet to properly develop a sense of taste and decorum. Nosey rose to the occasion and adjusted his tie.

'Ahem. My Lord Mayor, Mayoress, Aldermen and Alderwomen, Ladies and Gentlemen of Butterfield thank you for your kindness in honouring me here tonight for my modest accomplishments for our important local newspaper. Let me tell you, ladies and gentlemen, the best is yet to come. The story is still at the Genesis Stage. Why whilst I speak, at this very moment, you might say in the words of a famous actor of yesteryear, Arthur Askey "Before your very eyes!" Even as I speak scientists are testing those gasses that have risen from our little sod of earth.'

The lady Mayoress turned herself at this turn of phrase and regarded Nosey with a stern eye muttering almost to herself: 'Tchah, tchah, language, language please be moderate!' Nosey hearing this was halted for a moment in his flow, non-plussed at her unwarranted interruption.

'Ahem! As I was saying. Er- what was I saying?' The younger members raced to his aid in unison. 'Somefing abaut some little sod' they shouted helpfully. The Mayoress was beside herself. 'Please a little decorum there are ladies present!'

Parker having lost his train temporarily was anxious not to miss it altogether. He leaped into the doorway left open by the last exchange.

'Yes brothers and sisters of Buttersoft I trust that you will have further reason to be proud of our heritage, this pleasant land, this corner of England. I believe that the research being conducted by one of these international groups - Greek, I think in this case - will show that there are great medical advantages to be gained from our famous fumes. Cures for serious ailments. Our reputation as lovers on an international scale may yet be salvaged.'

Some of the ladies were heard to murmur, 'Not a moment too soon!'. Unabashed Nosey pressed on '... Paris may soon lose that world title as the focus for lovers that has been theirs for so long. We live in momentous times my friends!'

Nosey sat down to tentative rather than rapturous applause. Many in the audience had failed to understand the finer points of his speech, others wished to be polite. Still others, and by far the largest grouping, were rather the worse for wear. This was due in some measure to the speed and accuracy with which the punch bowl and the port were circumnavigating the tables. The younger group, however, understood perfectly. They stood as a man and, having applauded, left to pay a visit to the Industrial Estate for a breath of those famous malodorous fumes to see if the rumours were true. One of their number could be overheard clearly promising his girl companion, 'I'll whiff and I'll sniff and I'll blow your dress down!' She responded by half dragging him out of the hall towards the waiting Dormobile.

Nosey was rather put out of joint at the sudden exit of a large proportion of the gathered throng.

The Mayoress on the other hand apparently breathed a sigh of relief, at least that was what it seemed to be from a respectful distance. Some less charitable ladies nearby thought they heard a loud report from her general direction, but the acoustics in the hall have never been of the best. One of the waiters kicked the bulldog, the town mascot, who was sleeping peacefully, and was shocked at being treated thus.

The Mayor stood and thanked Nosey once again, whereupon the food and wine were attacked from all sides. So voracious was the general hunger felt by the remnants of the gathered assembly that, upon occasion like fish squabbling and thrashing about over a proffered titbit, the same delicacy was reached for simultaneously by two or more of the participants. This either led to an almost pompous, self-conscious, yet reluctant offering by each to the other of the morsel in question, their hands having been arrested in mid-air as if by the power of second thought. In other instances one perceived a seizing of both the moment and the savoury with a hoot of triumph by the victor. In true British sportsmanlike fashion however, the runner-up did not go away empty handed, as the supply of victuals for such publicly financed dinners was always lavish.

The Mayor remarked to Nosey when his eyebrows shot up at the sight of such a sumptuous feast, 'You know, Parker, the ratepayer funds all this. I am sure he would be only too glad thus to repay the hours of time we put in over and above the call of duty.'

'Have you asked him then?' Parker leaned over so his nose almost reached the Mayoral Chain of Office.

'Well, er, not exactly.' The Mayor leaned backwards a proportionate distance to avoid an unintentional embrace. 'Oh-ho I get it very droll Parker! The ratepayer - as if there were only one! Ha! Ha! Ha!' The Mayor then recovered both his aplomb and his seat somewhat and added deprecatingly on a more serious note, 'We can't go traipsing off for approval for every penny we spend in the taxpayer's name you know. This is a democratically elected government - not rule by Referendum. The electorate, at the last general election, gave a party seeking to govern that way extremely short shrift. The British man-in-the-street doesn't want to be bothered by detail, he appoints us so that he can sit at home, drink his beer, and watch telly'.

Parker surveyed the small red, rotund edifice that was the Mayor of Buttersoft. 'You may have a point there, Lord Mayor. I feel similarly about the position of the press you know. We publish an opinion and the public, more often than not, accept it. Yet what we publish is often accepted as, or reflecting, existing public opinion. Really when it comes down to it you only need Joe Public for the very occasional vote. Most of the time the Government and newspapers take care of the forming and afterwards reporting public opinion. In fact as the newspapers sensibly reflect and even may constitute public opinion, elections would seem to be more and more a waste of time and money.'

They shook hands on that sensible and profound conclusion, and returned to the more serious question of how much of the large quantities of champagne and spirits could be polished off or skilfully concealed under one's coat, and how much would have to be returned to the supplier. Not wishing to seem ungrateful Nosey, with the full Mayoral support (not a reference to the Mayor's surgical appliance despite its undoubted sturdiness), set to with all the gusto he could muster. In the meantime, is dear lady Ethel had unwittingly locked herself in the Ladies lavatory from where she was not rescued until the next morning.

After a most successful evening he was stopped in his somewhat irregular tracks due to the evident presence of a large object evidently concealed beneath a most suspicious-looking raincoat, itself well past its 'sell by date'. 'Excuse me sir!' murmured the security officer from Plus Four sequestered for the occasion. 'May I ask what it is that you have concealed beneath your gabardine?'

Nosey swayed at him belligerently. 'Indeed you may ask! And I may refuse to answer! That my friend is democracy!'

The misleading approach adopted by the inebriated guest rather took the officer by surprise for a moment. He stepped back and Nosey took the opportunity rushing forward past his uniformed presence. The momentum required for the surge forward caused him to relax, ever so slightly, his grip on the Magnum concealed under his Mack. It slithered downwards and landed heavily upon the big toe of Parker's right foot. 'Ouch!' he exclaimed hopping round on the pavement holding his foot in both hands. The huge bottle rolled, miraculously unbroken, into the gutter.

The Plus Four man having recovered both his aplomb and the champers. 'Now what do we have here I wonder? I believe you dropped this sir!'

Nosey relinquished his foot and stood up to face the enquiry. 'What me sir? No sir!' he replied defensively.

'But I saw ...' began the officer.

'But me no buts young man! You may have thought you saw something, but it's my view that you have been drinking young man, and on duty too. What you saw was my foot come into contact with the bottle. I kicked the bottle having failed to see it approaching my foot. Anyway give it to me. Somebody has evidently thrown it away and I found it. Here's fifty pence for your trouble.'

The guard stood there agape at Nosey's cheek, but offered scant resistance to him as he wrenched the bottle from the officer's grasp.

'That must be over a hundred pound's worth, I think I deserve more than 50p!' he complained.

'Oh you do drive a hard bargain, don't you? Very well. Here's two pounds four pence more. Now that's all the change that I have. Goodnight.' Nosey swaggered off clutching his ill-gotten gain and looking in vain for a taxi to take him home to Lissome Grove. The streets of Buttersoft were wet and empty, most of the town's residents were sensibly slippered and dressing-gowned, cushioned firmly in a comfortable armchair, curtains drawn against the weather, watching either the football or latest movie repeat, whilst tipping hot cocoa slowly into their warm and ruddy faces. Nosey's swagger had dropped to a rather sluggish crawl as he dragged his feet and the Magnum of champagne homeward along the cold wet roads of Buttersoft, which reflected the coloured lights from so many windows.

Suddenly, the Chipperie loomed into view, its warm red neon flashing an electric smile at the hack hobbling home. Hoping that Chippie had forgotten or forgiven their encounter in the cellar, and having conjured up an appetite from nowhere in particular, Nosey decided to risk purchasing a small newspaper full of chips. As it turned out Chippie was not in evidence and his young lady assistant Sharon stood on tiptoe to view her customer through the glass counter and take his order. 'Just a bag of chips please Sharon', asked Parker.

'Ooh! Yes Mr. Parker right away. Salt and vinegar?' Nosey nodded. 'Nothing to drink sir?' Nosey lifted the Magnum in silent reply. 'Ooh! What a big one! I never saw anything so big in my life! Wait till I tell my mate Brigitte.' An idea suddenly dawned upon Nosey and he moved closer to the counter looking down at the diminutive Sharon in her little mini-skirt. Her tee shirt was far too small for her chest which had developed out of all proportion to her size.

'Hmmm, Sharon, how would you like to share this huge bottle with me? Now that would be really something to tell Brigitte wouldn't it?' Sharon looked at Nosey and then at the bottle. Her eyes swung back and forth as her little brain worked feverishly to decide whether to go or not to go.

Nosey decided to help her by offering to get her picture in the paper. 'You never know when it might lead to fame and fortune Shar. This could be your big chance. The Chipperie will win the competition for the best

Chip Shop in Buttersoft. It's a doddle. We'll need pictures of the shop and staff for the front page of the Daily Spread.'

That did it for Sharon. She locked up the Chipperie and followed Parker upstairs. The flat was dark and cold when they entered and Nosey put the bottle in the middle of the room on the floor and rushed around to make it more comfortable, even if cosy was going to be impossible. He drew the red velvet curtains and pressed the music button. Strains of musak filled the air and the doused lighting took over from the naked bulb.

"Make yourself comfortable Shar - pull up a chair.'

Sharon giggled at the play on her name. 'Now you've done it, making me laugh like that. Where's the lavatory?' Parker pointed the way and off gambolled Sharon to powder her nose. An extraordinary euphemism when looked at properly. Hopefully, the nose is kept well away from the true function of the lady's visit on these occasions.

She returned saying 'well, Norris, what are you waiting for? Let's get started then!' The reporter looked at her for a moment wondering precisely what she wanted to start, then realised with an internal groan that it would just be the champagne.

'Now Sharon, I am not sure if you know, but opening a bottle of champers is a bit of an art.' As he said this Nosey removed the gold wrapping around the cork and the wire protection which helps keep it tightly in the neck of the bottle. The bottle in this instance was still standing plum in the middle of Nosey's lounge carpet.

Nosey began to wrestle with the cork trying to twist it this and then that, but without any success. 'I see what you mean Mr. Parker. It does look difficult. Can I help?'

Nosey looked at her wondering how on earth she could assist him in this difficult operation. 'You see Sharon, sometimes the cork is wedged in so tightly it can be a real bugger to get out. I just don't see how two people can try at the same time.'

Sharon moved forward with an air of self-confidence that caused Parker to actually stand back. She took hold of the cork in her right hand, whilst her left was employed in gripping the neck of the huge bottle. Her little face screwed up with the effort but slowly it dawned upon Nosey that the cork was moving.

'My goodness, my girl, how do you come to be so strong?'

Not for a minute abandoning the task in hand Sharon replied rather gutturally 'I do weights in my aerobics class Mr. Parker.'

Suddenly the cork flew like a bullet out of the bottle striking the naked bulb in the centre of ceiling, which was directly in its path. There was a second loud report as the bulb shattered and pieces of glass flew in all directions. Then came the champagne. Nosey had somewhat shaken the bottle when it fell (there were, of course no directions on the label suggesting that he do this) and the champagne flew into the air. It caught little Sharon both on the way up when some of it shot straight up her skirt, and on the way down when it landed, for the most part on her taut, tight, tee shirt. Sharon uttered another "Ooh!" or two and bit her underlip at the cold wet feeling she now had both underneath and on top.

She wriggled and jiggled and wiggled at the cold wetness.

'Now look at you! You're soaked through! What a waste of good champagne! Well, never mind. You had better take off those clothes and I'll bring you a towel dressing gown to cover your bits and pieces.' Sharon looked rather apprehensive but she was feeling icy cold and wet through. She shivered. Parker returned with a warm towel coat, and extra bath towel, in hand. 'There you are. Now don't mind me, I have to turn on the central heating from the kitchen boiler so you don't need to be embarrassed Sharon.' Off he went.

Now Nosey was no slouch. He had extensive experience of wet clothes being parted from their owners in his lounge. He had a closed circuit camera and video installed by "Watch It! CCTV Buttersoft's premier security TV installers. He settled down in the kitchen with his pull down screen to watch Sharon go through the motions. He supped his champagne as she parted wet cloth from white skin. Sharon proved to be better equipped than he had guessed. Her firm breasts were nothing if not challenging. Her legs were superbly crafted and would have given Betty Grable a run for her money in her time. As for her behind, cheeky was not the word.

Nosey waited till she had virtually finished drying herself and dispensed with his monitor and walked casually into the lounge as fast as his three legs would carry him. 'Oh sorry, I thought you'd be finished by now. My God but you are beautiful!'

Sharon turned crimson. 'Ooh! Mr. Parker you shouldn't. You've really embarrassed me now.' Nosey sat down to hide his own temporary difficulty.

'Now Sharon you have to learn to show that wonderful body of yours. Page three will kill to have pictures of you, and the glossy mags will be queuing up for your favours. What you need is proper handling. And, my girl, you could not have come to a better place.'

Sharon stopped in mid air with her panties still at her knees. She was bending down to pull them into position when the notion of fame and fortune courtesy of Parker of the Press froze her. She looked up at Nosey as he looked down at her, having risen to his feet and assumed a masterful expression. 'Now you won't be wanting to rush into those knickers Sharon. What we say in enlightened press circles is, "Down with knickers!" You and I should get a little closer to each other and start coming to terms. The knickers fell soundlessly back to earth. Sharon stepped closer to Nosey who was by now positively bursting to add her to his list of conquests, by any chance He found her the most compelling girl he had ever met. Ordinary in terms of academic qualification she might be. Physically he had not seen her like. Doris was sexy and appealing it was true, but Sharon had a sultry animal magnetism reminiscent of Ava Gardner in her hey day.

At last their bodies pressed together and Parker gripped Sharon tightly. His kiss stretched his tongue to its roots as he pressed it inwards and Sharon sucked it downwards. Finally he retrieved it. His clothes were removed by a joint effort and Sharon sank to her knees to view the size of the job now in hand. Nosey peered down at her. 'It's a growing concern of mine', he quipped. Sharon was temporarily unable to find words for a reply. The climax was engulfing. Nosey's head hurt with the evacuation of blood from it to his loins, and his legs were suddenly weak and buckled under him.

Sharon shot out of the room towards the bathroom evidently to powder something. Within moments Nosey had drifted into a comfortable doze.

When Sharon returned he stirred. She was still naked. He grasped her by the buttocks and pulled her towards him. 'Love is always wanting to give as well as receive. He began to kiss her tender areas. She moaned, as girls always do in such circumstances in the lower caste of literature. Initially she had gently tried to pull away, but Nosey was insistent. He used the substantial ridge or bridge of his nose to extremely good effect. In minutes Sharon ascended heights of ecstasy as she never had before.

She joined Nosey on the extremely pretty, if rather tarnished, Chinese carpet which, between questionable stains, boasted a fair array of red pile decorated with fierce gold dragons.

Holding her protectively in the crook of his right arm as they rested their spent cheeks on the oriental design. Parker said. 'I think we could be very good for one another Sharon. I know it's early days but maybe you'd consider moving in here. It's just above your work at the Chipperie, and I would have all the time in the world to prepare you for a stunning career.'

Sharon looked doubtful. 'What's me mam going to say? Never mind me dad. He'll skin me alive!'

Nosey considered these meagre obstacles to a regular sex life of a quality, of which he had only dreamed hitherto and brushed them aside. 'Now Sharon how old are you?''

Sharon replied "I'm just turned nineteen last February 7th"

'Right then. You are old enough to stand on your own two beautiful feet. Being placed as they are at the ends of those stunning legs you should have no problem. Just tell your parents that you are moving into a flat of your own and starting your own life. Don't tell them immediately about me, as that would be like showing a red rag to a bull.' Nosey conveniently forgot to mention her indoors – although currently in the ladies lavatory - namely Ethel. In fact he had decided that it was well nigh time that Ethel packed his bags.

So it came to pass. Sharon left home and moved in with Parker who was now pressed at home as well as at work. Sharon proved to be insatiable. Parker's face began to show the strain of being kept awake until dawn. He would often sit down suddenly as he felt groin strain coming on cupping his aching testicles in his hand. 'What am I to do?' he moaned.

He visited the doctor complaining of soreness in the general area of his manhood. Dr. Theresa Blunt held the limp object in her hand and regarded it through her pince-nez with considerable disdain. 'Been burning the candle at both ends have you Parker?'. Nosey winced at the unintended pun. 'Well I'll give you some soothing cream. Now do you need a note to take home with you excusing you ... er, homework?'

Nosey weighed up the considerations. 'Er - I think I'll take you up on the note, doctor, I really need to sleep, I am utterly exhausted.'

The doctor found no humour in Parker's wretched state. Nor was she the slightest sympathetic toward him. He was evidently one of these dirty old men who lusted after young innocent maidens, and then found that the pace was to too fast for them. She dismissed him without another word in favour of Mrs. Briggs, the vicar's daily woman, and her lumbago, whose large posterior was comfortably spread across two chairs in the surgery waiting room, where she waited with bated breath and all the village scandal, which now would include the exchange she had just overheard through the door of the doctor's surgery. Mrs. Brigg's substantial arms were folded beneath a fulsome bosom, which had seen considerable action during the last war.

THE GIRLS ARE TESTED, AND FOUND WANTING.

Back in London, grass had given up the struggle of growing under Dimitri's pounding feet, or hooves if you prefer. He was collating scientific reports from Buttersoft and poring over the results of clinical tests being carried out by his newly appointed team of researchers.

'Henry!' he called to the lawyer who was polishing the captain's chair with the seat of his trousers in the Greek's office.

'Henry, we are making progress. The clinical tests have reproduced the slaver effect in our volunteer gentlemen. They are poring over nude magazines to a man, reduced to masturbation as an outlet for their frustrations. No harmful side effects have been found. Several formerly impotent men have responded to the call to arms, and are straining at the leash waiting to get home to their anxious wives.'

'I think, to adopt the words of Margaret Thatcher when she saw victory in the 1979 general election inevitably in her sights. She said I am 'cautiously optimistic.' She was referring to the likely outcome of the General Election. I am talking about the results of our tests, "The General Erection!"'

Henry shrugged. 'It seems like light years since we've seen the girls' he uttered morosely. 'They might have been kidnapped, returned to La Belle France, or chosen other, more attentive suitors for all you know.'

Dimitri shook his huge head ruffling his curls in the process, 'I know precisely what they're up to. As a matter of fact they are on their way over here. I have persuaded them to act as our first female guinea pigs!'

Henry blanched. 'Steady on old man!' he said. 'You can't take risks with the girls you know. They're much too precious.'

Dimitri sneered lifting one eyebrow in a menacing manner, 'I know what this is all about. You're terrified you won't be able to accommodate a demanding, insatiable, Josephine.'

Henry looked scandalised and retorted not over convincingly 'er, not at all. I have had no complaints so far. My concern is for the safety of both of them. This product is untried.'

At this very moment in waltzed the French fillies their mini-skirts swishing in the air evidently dying to start the process of inhalation. Henry regarded them with conservative disbelief.

'This way my beauties!' Dimitri led them without more ado into the testing chamber.

'Are you quite sure that you want to do this?' Henry called after them.

'Poof! This is just a bit of fun' returned Josephine 'get ready for me, because when I come out I am going to be hunting you!

Merde, I have caught my tights on this damn table. Dimitri why are there just girlie magazines here? Don't you have the ones with naked men in them? Sexist pig!'

Dimitri entranced by the form of his own ladylove stroked her bottom lovingly as she entered the chamber. 'See you soon my love, and don't worry. I will be here to 'grant your every wish and satisfy your every desire" Dimitri promised.

Isabel shot him an insolent look dark with mystery, and then laughed, 'You had better do some exercise if you hope to escape. As it is I could catch you with one leg tied behind my back!'

With that parting shot the girls were gone and the gasses started to filter through the vents constructed for the purpose into the chamber. As they breathed in the fumes the girls felt their skin start to tingle. Within minutes they were aware of a tightening of their abdominal area. They felt the beginnings of pure unadulterated lust rising within them. Josephine run her tongue lightly over her lips. Isabel found her hands rising gently over her ribs to her breasts. Seconds later they were each stroking the mounds between their legs.

'This is amazing!' Josephine exclaimed.

'Wonderful!' echoed Isabel. 'Where are you men? We need you NOW!' they shouted almost in unison.

Henry looked at Dimitri and after a second's pause they opened the door.

Inevitably some of the gas swept out of the chamber and was fully inhaled by the men.

'Right!' said Dimitri. 'Take my assistant's office - he's away on a trip. I am taking Isabel into my office. Each room has a couch and curtains. Champagne in the fridge. Goodbye!'

His office door slammed shut behind Dimitri and Isabel. Rude noises could be heard as Isabel had negligently perched her bottom upon the intercom button. Henry after raising his eyebrows at some of the language being used disconnected the machine from the wall. Josephine had removed her panties and lay provocatively on the desk eschewing the couch for the time being anyway.

Henry gently parted her legs and they joined together in a song of unison which, although it has never reached the top twenty in the hit parade, is nonetheless the most popular ditty ever written. The whispered wooing, the muffled moans, the excited excesses, all conspired to create the nearest thing to paradise that we have on this mortal coil. If Henry's rendition of the song of love was an excellent baritone then Dimitri's was a deep and resonant bass, Interspersed with heavy grunts and snorts the duet between bass and Isabel's alto worked its way up to a powerful crescendo. The bull's single horn pierced Isabel to the quick and she surged upwards to an earth-shattering conclusion. The bull collapsed as though finally brought to earth by the matador, save only that in this instance, the final thrust was his own.

Henry reconnected the intercom. He pressed the inevitable button. 'Hallo numberone. Earth to Starship Bullock! Come in please.'

'Hrrumph!' Grunted the fallen boeuf.

'Ha! Ha! Is that the sound of the bull in the ring rolling in the red dust, as it utters its last? Is there a proud upright matador standing with his (or her) foot on your chest savouring the triumph of the ultimate conquest? Where is that fiery barrel-chested colossus that once I knew?'

A series of loud grunts, reminiscent of a straight through exhaust finding its deep bass voice, wafted through from the other end of the intercom and caused Henry to pause in his ironic soliloquy. 'Is that a lark or starling, whose melodious tune enhances the break of day?' Henry smirked at Josephine.

'You called?' Dimitri had thrust open the interconnecting door between the two offices. Henry was shocked. He sought to cover his embarrassment and his rod and tackle with a handy file. Josephine merely stretched and arched her back as if oblivious to the intrusion. 'Quite a sight the two of you. Venus and a somewhat shy Adonis. Really Henry you don't need a file, a fig leaf, or a credit card 'would do nicely!' Seriously though, neither of you have anything to be ashamed of from where I'm standing but Josephine seems to know this already, Isabel joined him giggling wearing only her minuscule underwear. Henry was so shocked at the advanced state of development of her chestal region that he almost dropped the file.

'Eyes back in sockets Henry!' Josephine warned him in a tone that would clearly brook no opposition. Accordingly his eyes and any other relevant body parts shrunk back into their boltholes.

'Right!' said Dimitri 'well we have sampled the stimulants first hand now. Is there any doubt about the strength and effectiveness of the chemicals?'

'No.' they chorused.

'Then we must move ahead quickly to corner the market and protect our interests.'

Without more ado he made for the telephone and dialled. 'Is that the lab?' he asked. 'Loukopolous here. OK. What progress has been made in reducing this gas to its constituents? Right. I see. And how long do you think before we have it in liquid and or tablet or powder form? Really! Excellent! Work overtime all of you, you'll be handsomely compensated.' Putting down the receiver he turned to Henry.

'We'll have this finalised within a week. I must have the patent agents working together with the laboratory so that we get worldwide rights over this. Alright partner?' Henry nodded vigorously and lay back dreaming of what had just been and what was going to be.

Josephine now more properly clad plumped slimly down beside him on the leather sofa. She stroked his unshaven cheek in an affectionate manner and looked at his eyes. The natural green colour appeared to best effect in the bright sunlight streaking through the office windows and the vertical blinds which are standard office uniform these days. The sun amplified the hint of turquoise and the tan around the iris seemed almost orange. 'What extraordinary eyes you have young man!' she whispered in her seductive earthy tone. Kittenish now, her attitude, if not her colouring, was reminiscent of Eartha Kitt, a distinctive and captivating black singer of the sixties.

'There is nothing about you which is even faintly ordinary, young lady' was Henry's immediate response. Then the kissing started again.

'Whoa there cowboy! Enough is enough!' Dimitri reminded them of his presence. Let's get moving! We've got a billion to earn this year and the sooner we start the better!' So they did.

DRAMA AT SPAGHETTI JUNCTION...

Ariel Gassman was released from Fulham General hospital on Tuesday the fifteenth of October. A midnight blue Rolls Silver Cloud collected him and a uniformed chauffeur ushered him into the rear of the vehicle. He surveyed the crowded streets of London on a relatively dry and sunny, if rather blustery day, as people braved the bracing breeze to proffer their custom freely to the shopkeepers who, in turn, depended upon them for the payment of their exorbitant rents.

The odd mini skirt sailed down the Kings Road in search of a briefer replacement. 'Now I know what that bemusing poster meant when it stated 'Less is more" mused Gassman, as yet another potent and potential model stretched her long legs in the direction of Peter Jones and an Arab Potentate. 'I think I'll stop for a coffee at this coffee-house James.'

The Rolls drew to a gradual halt.

'Ah yes! Gianetto's. Just what the doctor ordered!' Gassman exclaimed. In point of fact the doctor had ordered nothing of the sort. A diet of Spartan proportions had been his directive. Gassman ignored him as he had every 'quack' he'd met in his long and varied existence.

'Table for one sir?' exclaimed the sprightly young waitress with peaches and cream complexion and an ensemble to match.

'Better make it for two - I shall need the room' Ariel laughed at his own expense.

'Will this do sir?' Her nametag affixed on the pretty pink dress gave her name as Crystal.

Gassman surveyed this pensively. 'Are you by chance licensed, Crystal?'

The girl looked at him and her watch in one movement. 'Certainly sir. What is your pleasure?'

Gassman smiled 'what indeed? A bottle of your namesake my dear.' Pausing only for a moment, Crystal went off in search of the nearest Roederer. Moments later, waiters and waitresses swarmed around Gassman like workers around their queen.

'Some hors d'oevres or canapés sir?' a waiter suggested

Gassman jerked his head around swilling his jowls from side to side in a most unattractive manner as he did so. 'Where's Crystal? She's my waitress.'

As if by magic, she was there, by his side, brushing the back of his hand accidentally, or so it appeared, in the process of pouring his champagne.

'Taste it for me will you Crystal?' She looked around. The manager nodded in a manner reminiscent of a Casino Inspector giving mute authority to a dealer. She lifted the glass and the bubbles slid playfully down her perfect throat. Gassman gazed at her immaculate lines with a wistful sigh from his thick red lips.

'Good is it?' queried the bulky customer recovering a proportion of his considerable aplomb.

'Perfect' she replied.

'Here's my card young lady. I need someone to serve me at home in Belgravia. Give me a call.'

This time she did not look around for approval but rather to see if the manager was fixing her with his beady eye. To her relief he was looking at the incredible slight of hand of Julie Wong a new waitress.

Miss Wong, having taken on more plates full of a variety of dishes than her hands could properly hold, was doing an unusual variation of the juggler's act. She managed, having dropped a plate full of beef stroganoff with her right hand, to catch it with her left; having edged a tottering plate of steak Diane and 2 veg on to the rim of the nearest table. Balanced on the crook of her right arm was a third plate of spaghetti bolognaise. However, this was made unsteady by her dropping movement to catch the falling stroganoff. Try as she might, she was torn between steadying it and dropping a bottle of Chateauneuf du Pape, which was squeezed between her left arm and her thigh. Deciding that the loss of the spaghetti was the lesser of the two evils (the wine being of an elderly vintage) she wrote it off.

Regrettably the plate did not miss the table as she had judged it would. Falling almost vertically but slightly tilted to ensure no loss of the food it rolled like a wheel around the table. The eyes of the dinner guests watched it as if transfixed. Finally a collision with a substantial beer mug caused it to change course, and make a beeline for the lap of a willowy blonde top fashion model aptly named Golde Lox. It might not have mattered had it landed food upwards. This was not to be. Golde tried to open her legs to allow the meat and the heat to pass through without damage to her person.

As luck would have it, however, she was wearing a tight mini-skirt, which though short, forced her long, slim legs to remain virtually touching each other. The panic that seized her gave her the strength to force them further apart than would normally have been possible, in the process yanking her skirt up over her thighs. Notwithstanding her Herculean efforts in this regard, she received the full force of the hot spaghetti with its generous portion of red meat sauce in her crotch.

She yelled, as those about her calculated the damages that she might be awarded if her sex life was irretrievably cut short.

The head waiter, Harding, a man of considerable intelligence and renowned for his practical good common sense, grabbed the jug of iced water and poured it over her scalded abdomen and legs. The shock of the cold water caused her to scream again. Harding seized a handful of ice cubes and pressed them tenderly to the affected area. Golde's eyes grew wide with shock and terror as one of the cubes slid underneath her flimsy knickers and entered her. However, the sensation was not entirely disagreeable, especially having regard to the numbing of the burning sensation that was achieved.

Harding, having put out the fire, began to clear up the debris. Gently, strand by strand, no doubt employing the First Aid principles he had learned as an adjunct to his induction course, he removed the spaghetti that now clung to her loins with the sticky adhesion only achieved as it dries. Golde did not interfere with his delicate work, although his feather-like touch unexpectedly, began to arouse her. She could not avoid a gentle movement of her hips and a flutter of her long eyelashes.

Her fellow diners watched with fascination at the task that the headwaiter had undertaken. Golde was unconcerned and unaffected by their gaze. Harding's fingertips touched her now in a more meaningful manner. Was this intentional? Was he taking advantage of situation, or was this an inevitable side effect of his neo-medical ministrations to an injured customer.

Finally, and it appeared, with considerable reluctance, he removed his hands, having no more spaghetti to recover. Slowly, Golde adjusted her knickers and pulled down her skirt an inch or two.

'Are you able to make it to the Ladies Powder Room by yourself madam?'

Harding asked solicitously.

'I might need a helping ... hand' Golde whispered, her unlined face creased with affected anguish, still in apparent pain.

'Certainly madam!' Harding took her elbow and led her to the Ladies Restroom. Seizing the "Out of Order" sign from its storage compartment he affixed it to the door and entered with Golde.

Once inside Golde appeared to have a further painful attack. 'Where does it hurt Madam?' Harding asked solicitously.

'There, between my legs' Golde pointed as she drew up her mini. Harding opened the first-aid cupboard and drew out some salving balm.

'Will you apply it Madam?' Harding suggested

Golde whinnied, 'Would you do sit for me, Harding please, you have such a tender touch?'

Harding plunged his fingers into the cream and surveyed the affected area with mounting enthusiasm. Golde helpfully proposed the removal of her knickers to enable him to have full scope. What a feast lay before him - and, no spaghetti! He started to apply the cream around the tops of her legs, but within thirty seconds his fingers had moved in upon her private areas. She moaned and only a connoisseur could tell whether from pain or pleasure. Harding progressed, now massaging her clitoral area.

Finally, and all of a sudden, she screamed, 'Yes! For Chrissake yes!' and subsided into a heap on the floor.

Harding was by now nursing a formidable erection. She opened her eyes to see it towering over her. 'Come on big boy, come home to mama!' she coaxed. Harding was unable to contain either his delight or his erection and willingly obliged. Golde partook of both with renewed vigour making much of the headway herself.

'Amazing!' thought Harding and all this on what was previously a nodding acquaintance. What would one call it now? A rodding acquaintance? Well Golde was nodding like a good 'un. Harding swivelled round and gave as good as he got. Nodding still more furiously Golde forced her long fingernails into Harding's bare bucking buttocks. More of a painful distraction than the encouragement intended, Harding was hard put to maintain his concentration. Nonetheless, they reached a crescendo together this time with unabated, unabashed vocal accompaniment.

The adjustment of their clothing was achieved in minutes and, with an air of assumed decorum, they opened the door to leave the rest room. A crowd of thirty diners had massed to form an audience at the door of the Powder Room. They might have preferred that description on this occasion having regard to the explosive nature of recent events. Knowing looks were cast vigorously, like rigorous stones at adulterers in biblical times. Harding raised his eyebrows in mock question at such implied accusations, and marched on triumphantly to the kitchen. Golde returned to her table wreathed in smiles (not all her own) but first concealing Harding's private telephone number safely within her purse.

Crystal and Gassman had watched the cameo with considerable interest. 'Are you by chance fond of spaghetti Crystal?' Gassman asked with a smirk.

'Well not usually, but I can see that there may be circumstances when it might be worth trying.'

Gassman's hefty thigh touched her own as he turned toward her. 'Come to serve me spaghetti, lapside, at home tonight. Be there at seven.' She nodded and went about her duties. Gassman thought dreamily of the feast to come.

A waiter appeared at his side and announced that there was a telephone message for him. 'What? Who knows I am here?' he asked nobody in particular. 'Very well I am coming. No! Wait! Better still bring the phone to my table.'

'Yes. Hallo! Who's there? Rossiter? I don't know any Rossiter. Oh! You're the solicitor for that fellow Henry Redfield. Right. Yes Mr. Rossiter what can I do for you. You're instructed to defend proceedings for Redfield in regard to claims from supposed injured parties. You've had a writ from Farmer Thomas and other locals. It's all about this chemical effusion. Hmmm. You want to join my company as a third party or second defendant. Well I can't stop you can I? Our solicitors are Happliss Boundar & Whelke 42 Boundary Crescent London EC3. Mr. Happliss Junior is, surprisingly, the senior partner now and well into his seventies. He'll probably assign some new-born babe straight down from university to the case, but call him, tell him I said so. I'll drop him a line this afternoon.' He cradled the handset and mused 'I'd better call Ponsonby of Mercantile Equity Insurance to put them on notice of this claim or the boss will have my considerable guts for garters, braces, belts - and a noose to hang me with!'

He dialled the insurance company from the table but Ponsonby was lunching also. A Miss Standforth took the telephone. 'Ye-es Standforth here!'

Gassman was amazed. 'Stand where?' he asked.

'No. Standforth is my name. What do you want?'

'Ah! I see. Yes. Well I am Gassman, normally deal with Ponsonby. It's about that industrial estate that we sold a while ago - the Buttersoft Industrial Estate. We had a policy with you or I should say it was covered on our block policy. Well it looks like we are going to have a claim. So tighten your braces.'

'I do not wear braces Mr. Gassman!' was the severe reply.

'Figuratively woman! I was speaking figuratively. We must prepare for a substantial claim or claims.'

Miss Standforth paused for thought and to allow the second half of her brie and tomato roll to lodge itself finally in her digestive tract. I have checked the computer file Mr. Gassman. You sold it ages ago haven't you - the land I mean?' She swiftly took a draught of her coffee to assist the descent of the cheese roll.

Gassman frowned seeing the problem approaching like a gathering storm upon the horizon. 'Yes, but the claim will be for negligence which occurred during the time that we were on cover.'

Another pause whilst she downed the dregs. 'Please send in your claim and we shall review it with our own legal advisors.'

Now Gassman was worried. It was his view that many insurance companies were notorious for seeking to avoid liability once they have consumed your premiums with disgusting relish. 'Not on my Nelly!' he thought. 'M.E. can pay up and with good grace!' However much he blustered, he could not dismiss that sinking feeling from his substantial belly -which had nothing to do with digestion - that a painful war of attrition was about to begin.

JOHN THOMAS DISCOVERS THAT WHERE THERE'S A WILL THERE'S A MAY.

Farmer Thomas was not a happy man. His lawyers were coining it in asking for all sorts of advances of the financial kind, but the Court hearing against Redfield and the Chemical Company and its cronies seemed light years away. His pigs of the male gender were still dying of exhaustion. A silver lining was however making itself apparent in the form of pregnant sows. No sooner did they drop one litter of piglets than the males were bursting to provide them with another. It would be months before he would feel the benefits however. The pigs had to be grown and fattened properly before he could pack them up in a truck and ship them to market for sale, or the slaughter house for pork and bacon.

The bank manager whom he had approached for support in this his time of need seemed singularly unforthcoming. The Buttersoft branch of the Agricultural Regional Mutual Society ("ARMS for Farms" was the declaration in the advert on TV) seemed very limited in its approach even though that word did not appear in its name or title. Mr. Meekers was the local manager in question, a man who appeared old before his time. He had a pronounced stoop and was thin and pale. Unusually for a bank manager he wore his wispy red hair rather long and looked more like a failed hippy than a successful commercial man. He presented quite a contrast to the strongly built handsome Thomas, who radiated a positively bursting personality and barrel-chested physique.

Meekers murmured 'I'll have to put the matter in the hands of the Area Manager.'

Thomas had been beside himself. 'Look Meekers! I need cash flow. I've lost some pigs, which have died of exhaustion, but their meat still sells. it will take time for payment to filter through. Birth rate is up as you would expect, but up 100% on last year. I shall soon be up to my ears in piglets. What is a bank for if it won't help in these circumstances?'

'Hmmm! Yes Farmer Thomas. I quite understand your predicament. Well I'm sure Mr. Knowles of head office will want to help, but you must understand I don't have the discretion, the power you know, to give you what you're looking for.'

'Then get him on the phone and let me speak to him!' growled Thomas aggravated beyond endurance.

'It doesn't work that way sir. I have to put in a report and then Mr. Knowles will consider it.'

Farmer Thomas stood up legs apart in a manner reminiscent of the legendary Colossus of Rhodes. 'You may lose this account to the Northern Mutual (the 'Notmuch' for short) so I wouldn't hang about if I were you Meekers!'

With that Thomas stormed out. His tremendous strides took him through the typist pool and his right foot snagged upon the chair of May Westerman who had recently won the Bank Beauty Contest (BBC). The chair with its occupant was sent flying across the room spinning as it went. It came to rest by colliding with the water dispenser, which began to wobble violently. The bottle atop the dispenser worked loose through the force of the collision and in falling groundwards sprayed its contents liberally over several of the secretaries, but poor May took the full force of the blast. She was quite soaked.

John Thomas came to a grinding halt. 'Ugh! I am sorry. What have I done to you? I was in a furious temper and caught my foot on your chair.' He rushed to help her looking around for a towel or something to mop up the water.

She looked at him and said, 'Don't worry it was an accident, no real harm done.' One of the other secretaries brought some strips of kitchen roll and she proceeded to pad at the damp areas. Her nipples were hard through the thin white cotton material of her blouse. John saw this, May saw his eyes widen, and they both blushed.

'Look' he said 'please come to dinner with me at the "Dolce Vita" tonight to make up for this I really wish you would.'

May was staggered by the invitation and initially thought of turning it down flat, but Thomas was quite a figure of a man and, evidently, unexpectedly not conceited. 'Tomorrow 'she said. 'Tonight I shall try to repair the damage. Here's my home number and address you can pick me up at 8.00pm. Is that OK.'

Thomas smiled broadly 'you've made my day. I shall really look forward to our dinner . . . May'. He saw her name on the note in his hand.

HENRY TAKES STOCK...

Henry in the meantime was not in such high spirits. His solicitors were hard at work defending the Farmer's Writ. His barrister had drafted a defence claiming that Henry was blameless and totally unaware of the chemicals in the ground. The Farmer would retort that the owner of any land is responsible for damage caused by emissions of any kind from it whether he was negligent in allowing the emissions or not. He would claim that Henry had done nothing since the problem was uncovered to stop the fumes from rising from the soil. Henry would say that he had let the land and had no right to interfere with the land. The tenants, Dakers Diggers were also going to be in the frame, or so it seemed.

Now joining Gassman's mob to the action added another headache for the lawyers and Henry had to dig deeper into his pockets to fund it all. He sat in his flat leaning heavily on the armrest of his leather swing/swivel high-backed chair. He stared at the computer screen. His lawyer had asked him to trace all relevant offices of the Caustic Chemical Corps. and Industrial Investments Inc. he surfed the net for information. Having had a modicum of success he penned some EMAIL to them seeking annual accounts and brochures. He used a nom de plume (Dimitri) to ensure that they responded. Dimitri had taken the precaution of buying a block of the shares of both companies to ensure that they would reply.

The telephone disturbed his labours. It was Rossiter. "Hallo Henry. Now listen. I don't want you to worry but there are further Writs against you on the way. A beak by the Name of Beamish apparently assaulted a WPC, a Susan Winsome. He claims he acted whilst under the influence of these fumes. She is nursing a bruised behind and reputation. The old biddies at the home are up in arms and the two men they assaulted are recovering in hospital. The male nurse is suffering from terrible nightmares.

One bit of joy though, we never did hear from Doris Freebody. It seems that she may have taken the damage in her stride - for the time being anyway. There is talk of combining these claims in a class action, but the difficulty for the plaintiffs is that they are at each others throats too.

'Look Howard let's get the Local Council into the litigation too. We should have the entire motley crew at the receiving end.'

'OK. OK. We are now ready to join the two companies you have fully researched (thanks for the fax) as co-defendants. Counsel thinks we should serve them with the proceedings in the United States as well as at their London offices. It happens tomorrow and the press will jump straight on it. You have to be ready to talk to them at length, although we would normally recommend against it. In this case stating your case could cause the Plaintiffs to get cold feet about your involvement. Caustic are the real villains of the piece, although it is unclear what knowledge Industrial Investments had of the chemical burial at the time.'

'When do you suppose this is going to come to trial Rossitter? I have to try to plan for the costs and my own availability.'

'Well, it is such an involved case, not just the unusual set of facts, but also on the legal issues. Caustic are bound to involve their insurers, and if they are responsible then settlement offers might be squeezed out of them. Perhaps interim payments. Otherwise I can't see this seeing the light of day before 2020.'

'Whew! I don't know whether to feel relief or concern at the fact that this will hang over my head for years to come.'

Rossitter continued 'Counsel sees the issues coming down to this. Caustic Chemicals Corp, buried harmful chemicals possibly it seems without license or authority to do so, Industrial Investments Inc. owned the land at the time and may have known and even authorised the burial. Dakers Diggers unwittingly unearthed them. You now own the land. People and animals have suffered injury and damage from inadvertent inhalation of the resultant fumes. In our view there is a clear claim against C.C.C. and a reasonable prospect against I.I.I. You are, unfortunately Piggy in the Middle, and claimants have found it convenient to issue against you.

Now we're joining the two real Defendants and we shall try to demonstrate the connection between them and the Plaintiffs. It is even possible that we could get an order a little way down the road consenting to our being relieved of being a party to the proceedings, i.e, a summary judgement in your favour. I personally don't think that is too likely, so don't raise your hopes at this stage. However, I shall keep a weather eye upon the situation and if a suitable moment and opportunity appears I shall apply to the Court. We have to see how the pleadings take shape, and what evidence and documentation is disclosed.'

'Thank you for your careful and detailed approach. Please keep me informed.'

With that Henry said goodbye and replaced the receiver. 'How do I feel now?' he asked himself. 'I have a fairly well protected position in the litigation, and a major chance of making a fortune manufacturing and producing aphrodisiacs for worldwide sale. Not bad, not bad at all'.

He lit up a cigar and lay back in his recliner. He puffed away happily for a while turning his options over in his mind. It really was time to reassess his whole attitude to life in general, to return to firstprinciples.

Now what was first? Should he review the basic quality of life in general, or perhaps its direction or purpose? His past life had been lived on rather a superficial material level. Was it enough to simply throw money at his problems and continue as before? No. He knew that he needed a spiritual lift. He was not specifically religious. His attitude to God was rather ambivalent. He could not justify the deity's existence in pure rational terms, but at times he would find himself, half-consciously, almost in conversation with the almighty. He had had a meaningful brush with Buddhism and felt that it had a great deal to offer him, but after a while he had drifted away from any sort of observance of the ritual. That he had mislaid his book of chants in a move was true, but he had disobeyed the self-prompting that had often autosuggested that he contact one of the other Buddhists in his group for a replacement copy. He did feel its loss, but not enough it seemed.

So spiritually Henry needed a boost. Despite the superficially satisfying lift that Josephine gave him, not merely physically but arising from the bonding that was developing between them on a deeper level, he needed more. 'Doesn't everyone?' he wondered. Perhaps he should go back to Buddhism. It was then it came to him. The only real satisfaction that one could find was from helping others. He made a bond there and then with himself or his God or whoever was out there, that if and when he made a killing, he would not immerse himself in partying and skin deep playing. Some at least of his time and much of his money would be employed in serving others, particularly the needy. Disadvantaged children appealed to him as a worthy cause.

What else did he have to address on this important red-letter day? Josephine? Should he consider changes in his private life? He would certainly entertain the idea of marriage if she would have him, but he needed to get beneath her outer skin and know more of her essence before that commitment would be made. He suddenly realised how little he knew of her past life and family, her aims and desires. He would see her tonight and keep her at arms length for once, discussing these and other matters of concern.

What else was there? The case was a major factor in his immediate future. However, it would take its course. He felt he could rely on Rossitter, he was a capable fellow. It would take time and looked as though it would not have an unhappy ending for him. The business possibility that Dimitri was developing promised real future benefits and Dimitri had the bit between his teeth. Nothing would stop the Bull of Athens charging forward with this project. He could see his Aston Martin gleaming in the rays of sunlight, which had filtered through the clouds. A relaxing drive through rolling green fields and fresh air in the country? Perhaps, Hertfordshire and Buckinghamshire?. They could drive north or west and find a pub or restaurant for a quiet and pleasant lunch. Perhaps Henley would appeal.

...AND JOSEPHINE TO THE COUNTRY

He dialled her number. *'Allo.'* It was Isabel. He asked for Josephine. 'Oh Henri! *Un petit moment s'il vous plait.'* Josephine was on the line. *'Oui?* Oh! Henri it is you. You want to go for a drive in the country and lunch? It will be just the two of us? Why of course! What should I wear? Casual. Hmmm. OK. I'll be ready in half an hour. Thirty minutes OK. You pick me up."

The afternoon was glorious. The car purred happily westward towards High Wycombe. He took the road for Henley passing along country lanes where the foliage of trees on either side met above their heads and formed a magical leafy canopy. They arrived at the restaurant just after one. He had chosen an ideal place for lunch.

The Pied Piper, a restored Tudor Inn, was distinguished particularly by the whitewashed walls and starkly blackened beams supporting both walls and ceilings. Outside, Ivy was making progress up and across the walls. One looked out onto established English country gardens, alive with colour and form, with peonies, dahlias and rhododendrons intermingled with a variety of roses. Marigolds had replaced the daffodils of early spring. Huge, thick-trunked and aged oaks and plane trees shared the wooded areas with beech and silver birch. Another area was set aside as an orchard, where the Inn found an adequate supply of Cox's Pippins and Cherry for its pies. Among the bramble thickets, raspberries and gooseberries flourished. Climbing honeysuckle and even jasmine fought bravely to ascend the fences. At night, in season, the scents that assailed one's senses, were strong sweet and entrancing.

The kitchen garden supplied potatoes, tomatoes, cucumbers, sweet pea, cabbage, lettuce and a variety of root vegetables. The lake within the perimeter boasted both fish and duck, though whether these were culled for the platter no one knows. Deer reputedly used to roam through the woods but regular visits in past centuries by hungry patrons had decimated their number. Even then it was a capital offence to hunt the King's Deer without proper authority. Unfortunately this was a rule more observed in the breach, as the venison appealed particularly to the appetite of those who should have enforced it.

Inside the Pied Piper, heraldic emblems were displayed recording the rich and famous barons and earls and knights who had stopped their horse or carriage in order to take rest and refreshment. Their lazier passant and gardant kindred watched lions, and dragons rampant and salient take up their menacing stances.

Bezants of gules and torteaux were emblazoned upon and around the various escutcheons. Mottoes in Latin and French from *Dieu et mon droit*, Per ardua ad alfa, of *Honi soit qui mal y pense*, *Cheris l'espoir* and many others graced the various heraldic emblems which adorned the walls.

The Inn was reputed to serve the best duck this side of London. They ordered and complimented it with a bottle of light Bordeaux. Josephine whispered, 'Well Henry this is un peu, a bit out of character. I mean, it's very nice and all that, but what prompted it?'

Henry looked into her soft brown eyes and moved closer. 'I want to dig beneath the surface and discover the real Josephine. I need to know what you want out of our relationship. I want to know your family and history.'

Josephine eyed him warily. 'Reasonable. But why now, suddenly?'

He took her hand trying to avoid clichéd overtones. 'We are getting close, dammit we are intimate with one another. It's about time we decided if we want to take this further maybe live together.'

'Well I want that' she said simply. 'You are a good person, I feel it. I know we haven't spoken about our past in great detail but we feel one another's pain and joy.

You know where I live, near Versailles. My father, Georges, has dealt in paper pulp for years. He has money. My mother, Claire, is a wonderful cook and a lovely person. You will fall madly in love with her. Her guinea fowl is unparalleled, and she makes a mean salmon and asparagus tart. My grandmother is a sweet old lady who loves me to bits. I have a brother, Jean-Paul, who is studying to become a doctor, and a young sister, Claudine, still at school. She is nine years old. She will flirt with you shamelessly. I have a University degree from Nanterre where I studied English and Spanish Literature. That is Josephine in a nutshell. Oh, no, one other thing, I think I love you Henry Redfield.'

Henry reddened and his eyes moistened. 'Well I love you too, you wonderful funny person.'

'Right now that that is out of the way, can we finish our lunch?' Josephine joked tartly. The *'Canard a l'orange* was superb, tender and tasty. Josephine was tempted to try the zabaglione for desert, whilst Henry eschewed his standby apple pie and custard in an attempt to ward off further waistline development. He glanced out of the leaded light window as Josephine toyed with a teaspoon of Italian delight. The gardens were superb, and beyond them the hills rose and fell the green interspersed with browns and the bright distinctive yellow of rape-seed which was an amazing contrast to the adjacent field of lavender. A blaze of yellow contrasted with startling purple. Wasn't it just a perfectly memorable day?

His ruminations were disturbed by the classical tones of his mobile telephone whose very existence had been temporarily forgotten. Reluctantly, and with an embarrassed glance at other lunchers who had turned toward the source of the alien sound, he pressed the connect button. It was Dimitri.

'Hello Dimitri please hold on for a moment.' Henry rose and nodded to Josephine he made his way outside to take the call privately.

'Where are you?' asked the Greek

'In the country with my fiancée having a quiet superb meal to discuss our future life together' replied the lawyer with a faint hint of irony.

'What?' yelled Dimitri. 'But that's fantastic news! We must have a party. I'll organise it. Don't even think about it. I only wish it could be a double wedding but I am already married.'

'You mean that you were last time that you checked. That must have been at least a month ago. Dimitri you treat Vicki abominably. I mean I understand what you see in Isabel, but for God's sake you have three kids!'

From somewhere connected with his own new situation Henry suddenly found new courage to remonstrate with his friend. There was a pause.

Dimitri sighed, 'You are quite right Henry. I must make my own decisions for the future. I provide for Vicki and the kids, but I am an absentee father."

'You are missing so much, but not as much as they are', said Henry as a final clincher. Dimitri's conscience would trouble him now at least for the rest of the day.

'You bastard, you know how I am going to suffer now especially because I am at least a little in love with Isabel. I know, I know, I am being unfair to her too. Damn, damn, damn, why is life so complicated. I have the strength of four ordinary men why can't I have their wives too?'

Henry laughed at this brazen admixture of vanity and frustration. 'We have a saying in English 'You only need one bull in a field.' It seems, that although you are Greek, that you have adopted it as your family motto!'

'Well, I am going to have words with Isabel, and then I'll talk to Vicki. I will sort this out today - one way or the other. Will I see you later? Oh! By the way there is good news about the project. My men have passed the gases into liquid and have now reduced the liquid to a crystalline form. As a powder it can be dissolved and taken in water. Tests have shown that it loses none of its potency following the processing. We are now in contact with both the patent office and the Public Health people here and the Food and Drug Authority in the States to get the administrative end attended to. We are on the way partner! Bye, bye.'

Henry put his mobile back into his inside pocket and re-entered the Inn.

Josephine had been powdering her nose and they collided gently in the corridor.

The accidental physical contact was used shamelessly as an excuse for a lingering kiss. 'What shall we do now? Josephine whispered coyly.

Henry murmured 'hmmm. I think it would be wise to rest after our meal. I mean all that wine. I really couldn't drive now. I'll ask about a room at reception.'

He wandered off to the desk where the receptionist was talking on the telephone to her nearest and dearest friend, 'Hold on Julie, I'm wanted, just hold the line a minute dear. Yes sir what can I do for you?'

Henry looked at her and said, 'Have you by chance a room vacant, we've just eaten a glorious meal in the restaurant and I for one could do with a sleep, a rest anyway?'

The girl's name was declared on a breast tag as being Sheila. She nodded, comprehending, evidently inured to this sort of request from luncheon guests. 'You won't be wanting the room for the night then? We make a special day rate if you only want it for the afternoon. Check out time is 6pm. The price is sixty pounds. One hundred for the night.'

Henry pondered. 'It's two thirty now - I think the day rate will be fine. If I decide to stay the night I'll call down . . .'

Sheila cut him off '...before five o'clock please'.

Henry raised his eyebrows 'Oh! Right-o. Sobeit. I'll call you at five either way unless I am fast asleep. Call me if you don't hear from me please.'

She nodded and made a note. Henry wandered back to Josephine grasping the key to Suite number 1 in his hand and waving it for Josephine to see. 'Oh great!' she said 'And so ... to bed.' They showered together despite the narrowness of the unit washing each other with lingering care. Henry exited first and fetched a huge Turkish bath towel in which he tenderly wrapped his lady. He then set about briskly drying his own body, which was exhibiting signs of coming to life. The mahogany four-poster bed with its deep wine-red velvet drapes was perfect for the purpose. After lovemaking they drew the drapes to shut out the world and the light. Five then six came and went. Josephine had taken the precaution of unplugging the telephone. They slept till eleven p.m.

Henry yawned and stretched confused by the pitch-blackness around him. Slowly a dim recollection of his whereabouts returned to him and he drew aside the bed curtain. 'Christ it's eleven o'clock!' he whispered to himself. Not wishing to disturb his sleeping beauty he withdrew to the lounge area. He saw the telephone was off the hook and instantly understood. He replaced it and then lifted the receiver to dial reception. 'Sheila?' he whispered.

'No sir this is Damien the night porter. Sheila's shift has ended. You are Mr. Redfield?'

'Hmmm, hmmm,' Henry cleared his throat. 'Yes, I'm Redfield. Changed our minds, we'll stay the night. Is that OK?'

'Why of course sir. Will you be wanting any food though? I ask because the kitchen is about to close, as is the bar.'

Henry considered this. 'Very well send up something maybe a warm Chicken Salad. Oh and a bottle of your best Chardonnay. Thanks Damien.'

Henry had to clean his teeth to remove the taste of sleep from his mouth. He then searched for the mini-bar for cold bottled water. In the lounge he quietly turned on the TV and skipped to CNN. It was the usual admixture of Northern Ireland, the Middle East, and adjustments to the Bank Rate. He waited for the sports results and noted that his favourite team had won a local football derby. He grunted with satisfaction particularly at the spectacular winning goal a twenty five-yard drive into the top corner.

He tiptoed back into the bedroom and drew back the curtain. Josephine still slept. He brushed her lips with his softly as a summer breeze. She stirred mouthing words from some current dream. He saw her eyes moving under their lids. 'I wonder what adventure is going on inside that beautiful head' he whispered.

Josephine sighed and turned toward him. Her eyes fluttered open 'I was dreaming that I was on a sailing yacht, a ketch I think, and it was rolling in high seas. You were in the water with your arm outstretched. Holding the mast with one hand I stretched the other out to you. The next wave actually flung you back toward the boat and you grasped its rim with one hand. After several tries your other hand found mine and you were safe.'

Henry regarded her with concern tinged with slight amusement. 'Are you alright now?' he asked.

'I'm fine, just fine' she replied.

'I've ordered a light supper and some wine as you evidently planned to stay.'

Josephine looked sheepishly at him. 'I knew you really would not want to drive back, and that you needed a good sleep. So I made a call downstairs to Sheila and told her that we'd stay, you were already sleeping.'

'Fine but what are we going to do now?' he asked. 'We have the whole night ahead of us.' She smiled at him mischievously and he knew.

THOMAS VISITS HIS LAWYER...

Farmer Thomas sat in his solicitor's office waiting room. He was to see the senior partner of Braithwaite & Edes, Mr.Trevor Edes. These were Cambridgeshire solicitors who had advised the Thomas family for generations from the times when the farm had been situated in that County. Farmer Thomas now had made the train journey down to Cambridge and had entered a world of long ago with formally dressed clerks, crusty libraries, and a not unpleasant odour of musty, dusty but hopefully not rusty law tomes. Miss Peake the efficient secretary had brought him tea in a china cup that resembled a large thimble in the farmer's massive paw, but he drank it thankfully.

'Mr. Edes will not keep you long he is just collecting his emails,' she said.

'Does he have to go to the post office himself then? Don't you have deliveries down here?' asked the suddenly interested Client.

'Oh No! I don't mean the post, letters and the like, of course the postman delivers those. No, what I meant was the Electronic Mail, which he collects by logging in on his computer.'

John Thomas was little the wiser being unable to understand why one would have to place logs on a calculator to make it work, or how letters could be sent electronically. From her expression Miss Peake gathered that he was still in a fog, but decided that discretion would be the better part of valour, and that she should let the dogs she had awakened return swiftly to their slumber.

All of a sudden the elderly Mr. Edes appeared. Mr. Edes was a traditionalist through and through. He wore formal dress to his office as his fathers and more remote forebears had done in years past. He was a tall ramrod straight man with a military bearing. His face was lined providing a map to his extensive experience, and his wiry hair was almost entirely white. At a guess he must have been in his early seventies.

'Good afternoon Thomas' he said with a warm smile and a Scots inflection. '...and how are the pigs today?'

'Those that are still with us are holding up. I have followed your advice and kept them inside. A friend has helped me install a complicated arrangement for pumping oxygen into the sty. So the pigs are breathing less of the fumes coming from Dakers Diggers development. Although I can't tell myself, I am told that it also makes the place smell less too. Certainly the pigs don't complain. The piglets are growing and will be ready for market in a three-month or so.'

'Well I am sure that you are here to hear how we are getting on with your case. Proceedings have got under away and now there are several other parties involved, brought in by the Defendant Henry Redfield. Caustic Chemicals Corporation who actually ran the Chemical Factory at the site and who allegedly buried the chemicals that have caused the problems. Also brought in is Industrial Investments Incorporated. They owned the land at the time and had leased it to CCC. There is an ownership connection between the two companies it seems. My opposite number Howard Rossitter tells me that Redfield tried to see the directors of CCC but has had no luck so far. In the meantime, other Plaintiffs have joined the fray. Beamish and Winsome you will have read about. There are also some hospitalised ladies of advanced years and some workers at the institution.

The paperwork, which we call the pleadings, is now proceeding quickly and we can expect some fireworks from Redfield pretty soon. His solicitor, Rossitter has said they propose to apply to the Court for a preliminary ruling on a point of law. What I suspect is that he is going to ask to be excused from the case on the grounds that he cannot be in any way at fault and that just owning the land is not enough to make him liable to you. If he succeeds you may have to pay his costs so far, but I think it probable that the Court would hold over a decision upon that until the final hearing against the other parties involved.'

Although Thomas bridled at the thought of having to pay costs he had too much respect for Edes to say so. The idea was to find the true culprit and make he or it or them pay. He ruminated upon the possibilities as Edes took a call from the switchboard.

He motioned to Thomas to stay, and wrote a note to him indicating that it was actually Rossitter on the telephone. 'What is that you say? They want a joint meeting to negotiate? It's rather early days for that. What are they playing at? They want to buy the land back. Ah ha! The plot thickens! Are you proceeding with your application to the High Court? I see. You refuse to be delayed by these possible smokescreens being thrown up by CCC and Industrial Investments. Very good, well thank you for keeping me informed and I shall naturally wish to attend the proposed meeting. Goodbye Rossitter.'

'Well I think you got most of that didn't you?' Thomas nodded. 'Basically, a meeting is proposed to discuss a possible early settlement. However, I do not recommend that you raise your hopes at this stage as both Rossitter and I see it merely as a fishing expedition on the part of the American corporations. Apart from anything else they have got wind of the fact that perhaps these chemicals have some positive value and they are looking to buy back the land. I don't think Redfield will sell now though. But we shall see. I will keep you informed. You have nothing to worry about just now. I suggest you get back to the piglets and do what we lawyers call mitigating your loss.

You must make the best of the situation and seek to limit your financial exposure. All right? If you can limit the amount of your actual loss by way of increased numbers of piglets you will be seen in the best possible light by the Court. It was good to have seen you. Take care now.' Mr Edes left the room.

Farmer Thomas left his solicitors in better spirits. His dinner date with May Westerman was this evening and he just had time to catch the train back to Buttersoft from Kings Cross, change into more casual attire and collect her from the address that she had given him. He caught a London taxi to the main line railway station enduring traffic in and around Holborn but Grays Inn Road was relatively straightforward and he alighted dashing straight for the ticket office. 'A first class single to Buttersoft please,' he asked the lady at the counter. She produced the ticket and he the money. He put his money in the security tray and his ticket appeared within seconds. Which platform and what time please?

'Platform 12 change at Crewe. You have three minutes before the 4.50 departs.' He sprinted over the station lobby colliding with a drunk who resumed his recent prone position in the middle of the station. Thomas fairly flew past the ticket collector who was waiting to check passengers prior to boarding and still running turned to flash the ticket at the Railway Employee. He had made it. He clambered aboard and asked the first passenger he saw, an old lady in a brown tweed suit and good solid Irish brogues reading an Agatha Christie novel, 'I say, excuse me, but this is the 4.50 for Crewe?'

'Oh yes young man, and this she said, holding up her novel, by coincidence is entitled "4.50 from Paddington".'

'How extraordinary' he replied smiling weakly.

'Don't you think that it is life's coincidences that make it so very interesting young man?'

He was about to try to manufacture a suitable reply when she hurtled on. 'Why, it was only yesterday that my niece described to me how she had met a young man through a mild collision that he had with a water dispenser in her office.'

John Thomas could only stare.

'Then from this very window I observe you colliding with that unfortunate drunk, and following that collision we meet. You see had you not collided with him, at the pace you were travelling you might have reached the carriage in front of this one and chosen a compartment in which you could be entirely alone.'

'My niece described the man she met with incredible precision, as I always taught her.

I brought her up you see, following the unfortunate premature death of her mother. The man in question is a trifle over six feet three inches, weighing about two hundred and twenty pounds. He has really thick wiry brown hair and exceptional features, his facial bones appear to have been carved out of solid wood, she said. Very attractive, he conveys the impression of physical power and strength above all. He is a farmer and owns a farm in Buttersoft. Add to that clear description, this photograph in the Evening Standard courtesy of one Dai Evans and it is clear that you are indeed John Thomas, gentleman farmer lately become a litigant extraordinary.'

'Well I'll be blowed he said. You must be Miss Marple, you certainly look like her! So you are May Westerman's Aunt. Pleased to meet you.'

'How do you do Farmer Thomas. My name is Margaret Rushton?' They shook hands and resumed their comfortable well-padded seats in the first class carriage.

'Tell me about May, Mrs. Rushton, I mean her experiences as a child.' 'Ah, May was a lovely well-behaved child. She excelled in school and had we been better placed she would have been sent to a proper finishing school in Switzerland. As it was she obtained a good second class honours degree in law at Manchester University and decided to go into the bank.'

'My goodness I thought she was just a secretary! Whew I nearly made another costly mistake. What does she do in the Bank then?'

'She reviews correspondence and files acting as a watchdog. There are allegations regarding promises made by the bank almost every day. The bank might be giving advice to customers that have far-reaching effects. May reviews all these papers and advises on any necessary changes or adjustments that are required. Naturally if a matter becomes too heated outside solicitors will be employed.'

They took tea together and Mrs. Rushton described the cottage where May spent her childhood. 'I still live in it. It is a 16th Century pink-walled house, with thick brown wooden beams both inside and out. I have a thatched roof, which is very pretty but takes some maintenance. An unusual feature is the stained glass windows in certain rooms that add character. There is one of those Inglenook fireplaces in the lounge. Being an old lady I rather tend towards chintz in the soft furniture and drapery. I like tea served from a silver teapot and poured into the best china.

The cottage has a lovely warm atmosphere. Outside there is a veritable explosion of colour. I have countless types of flowers. I suppose I am rather a silly collector, everything from bluebells to tulips. I buy seeds of anything I can find and seek out a place for it. Climbing wild roses give my home its name, 'Wild Rose Cottage. The gardens are mature and have carefully manicured lawns, and at the rear I have a cherry orchard. Naturally there apples and pears too. May was happy there despite the tragic loss of her mother at a very early age. We would play endlessly on the grass with her dolls and toys. She still loves the cottage.

Goodness how I prattle on! I hope May won't mind my having told you her secrets.'

'Oh I am sure that it will be all right. I shall love hearing it all over again from her own lips. Well, here we are in Crewe. Are you travelling on to Buttersoft?'

'Oh no. My cottage is in Borsham so I take a different train. It has been such a pleasure meeting you Mr. Thomas. I hope we shall see you again soon.' Mrs. Rushton positively beamed at him.

John felt her approval and thought how important it might be one day. He stared out of the window at the passing flashes of green, brown, red and gold of the English countryside, and patiently awaited the arrival of the residential and industrial intrusions into it, which marked the approach of Buttersoft.

Arriving back in Buttersoft he drove his Range Rover from the station back to the farm. He telephoned May to confirm the time of their rendezvous and jumped in the shower. In half an hour he was dressed in blazer open neck shirt and extravagantly a cravat, and grey flannel trousers. He then leaped into his light blue metallic Austin Healey 3000 convertible, an old car he had restored himself. It gleamed with the polish and elbow grease that had been fondly applied. He arrived bang on time to see May's front door opening in welcome. She smiled and said shyly, 'Hallo John. How nice to see you. What a really lovely car!'

'Thanks,' he said gruffly clearing his throat. 'Here let me open the door for you. I have the top down, so do you have a scarf or shawl or something for your hair?'

In answer she produced a silk scarf from her handbag and placed it carefully over her attractive head. 'I have just had a call from a mutual friend of ours.'

'Oh?' he said. 'Ah, you mean your aunt. Yes I met her on the train back from London. I had been visiting my solicitor Mr. Edes. She really is a charming old lady. You are very lucky. Wild Rose Cottage sounds absolutely superb.'

'It is. You must visit. She has invited us for tea at 4pm sharp on Sunday, the day after tomorrow. Can you make it?'

'Wild horses wouldn't keep me away!'

...AND SAMPLES LA DOLCE VITA

May looked at him in peak physical condition and thought 'I bet they wouldn't.' She said 'please dress casually, my aunt doesn't stand on ceremony. She will probably be wearing her gardening boots and a pinafore. Now where was it we were going for dinner?'

'The Dolce Vita if that's all right. Do you like Italian food? If not there is a choice of Indian, Chinese or Turkish. Or, if you prefer we could try the Midland Hotel I understand their three course dinner is well thought of.'

'Italian will be fine' May laughed. Anyway I fancy some Italian red wine Brunello or Bardelino, even a good Chianti.'

'Your wish is my command beautiful princess. Heigh-ho Silver my trusty steed carry us to La Dolce Vita!'

The Austin Healey's engine purred and the car leapt forward. It swung around the country lanes to a beautiful but unusual destination. La Dolce Vita was a white walled house with green shutters on the windows and a green tiled roof. It was situated on its own against the backdrop of evergreen trees in the countryside on the outskirts of Buttersoft.

The sports car pulled off the road into the parking area. With the roof down as Thomas switched of the engine the air was still and quiet. The evening country scents assailed their nostrils and they relaxed breathing it all in for a few moments.

'I suppose we should make a move,' May hinted softly. 'I am afraid my tummy will start rumbling if we don't eat soon. I must admit though that the countryside is beautiful and even at night it has its own special charm.

John opened the door for her and they went in. John had to duck to avoid hitting his head on the door lintel evidently designed with the shorter Italian in mind.

Paolo Ventura, the owner/manager rushed up to greet them wreathed in smiles and almost singing, 'Welcome Signore, Signorina, *buona sera*. 'Ow lovely to see you. Can I offer you this table by the window? It has its own little romantic alcove.'

'Tonight you are very lucky we 'ave an Italian group that usually plays in Bayswater, London come up to visit us. The guitarist is my nephew. I told him. "You want to come for 'olidays in Buttersoft? S'all right, but you gotta play some nice Italian music in my restaurant specially if you want me to put up with your friends as well."

So they all agree. But *mama mia!* They don't stop eating and drinking all day long. I'm thinking to change the name of the restaurant to "Costa Fortune"!' May and John could not but laugh at Paolo's comical delivery when he spoke. He was quite a character.

'Now what will you 'ave to drink for aperitif? Can I suggest a Campari and Soda? Alright Signorina, and for Signore Thomaso? A gin and tonic ice and lemon. *Naturelmente, bene, bene.*' Off he went to arrange the drinks. John looked across the table with its green red and white tablecloth at May's gentle brown eyes. His hand stretched at and enclosed her much smaller version gently within it. She did not pull back or flinch, but smiled warmly revealing a beautiful set of gleaming white teeth.

Suddenly they were surrounded! Young men in gypsy type colourful dress with red bandanas on their heads began to serenade the couple. South American guitar and Italian violin alternated and combined in Latin harmony. The drinks arrived, followed hotfoot by the Brunello.

'What a superb wine!' commented Thomas. 'Where did you discover it?'

'I spent several holidays in Tuscany where flowers abound that my Aunt would love to have grown. I had a car and drove from village to village and town to town trying out their restaurants and hotels. I had my Aunt with me and she has read so much she was able to nudge me in the right direction. These paperback sleuths always seem to be wine buffs (among many other things) in their spare time! So I must have tasted forty or fifty different types of Italian wine in my time. Problem is I can't drink much, neither can Auntie, so we always ended up giving away at least half a bottle to the grateful restaurant staff.'

'I don't think we'll have a problem tonight. If necessary I can leave the car in Paolo's garage if push comes to shove, and we can take a cab. Or perhaps his nephew could drive us although it would be a bit of a crush.'

'*Antipasto Italiano!*' cried Paolo as he wheeled a trolley covered with delicacies including giant marinated shrimps, Parma Ham, avocado, artichoke, anchovies, sardines, asparagus, shell fish and many other tasty bits to their table. ''elp yourselves Signori. 'ave as much as you like. While you eatin' I should tell you for main course we got a wonderful Dover Sole *al Limone* or *alla Griglia*, if you like fish. Or Entrecote *a la Dolce Vita* is special if you prefer meat. Pasta we gotta linguine, spaghetti, tortellini, and of course lasagne al verde. The Spaghetti *a la Vongole* is a favourite of mine but you getta quite a bitta garlic with your clams.' The couple looked at one another. May said 'Although the Vongole sounds tempting it's our first date. I think I'll have the grilled Sole with spinach and cauliflower if you have it, perhaps *gratinée*.'

'Certainly Signorina! And per Signore?'

'Well I have only been to Italy once as a child and I had a veal cutlet in breadcrumbs with spaghetti bolognaise on the side. You don't have anything like that, by chance, do you?'

'I have it ezactly! *Vitello con spaghetti va bene!*' shouted Paolo to no-one in particular.' The couple looked round for evidence of a chef or other waiter but there was no answering call. Off went Paolo perhaps to prepare the meal, whilst the couple dug deeply into the hors d'oevres. The Brunello began to disappear and the music became merrier. Two other couples had tables in the small but charming restaurant. The guests were encouraged to join in the singing, which proved a little difficult, as they knew neither the language nor the words. May was the exception. She appeared to know half the songs off by heart, and had a really outstanding voice. Paolo's nephew Giovanni insisted that they sing at the microphone together. They did so with startling success. The group begged her to join them on the road promising that they would make a fortune. She laughed and thanked them agreeing only to join them on a record if they ever made one.'

John watched his wine intake carefully, having only taken a sip of the gin and tonic. He considered he was fit to drive her home after the meal and they set off.

'It's been really lovely John, I haven't enjoyed myself so much for years. Now you aren't going to let Auntie down on Sunday are you?' He shook his head. 'Good. Well here we are at my gate.'

John leapt over the car door and was around at the passenger door like a flash. May's eyebrows shot up in surprise. '*Signorina piacere*' he mimicked Paolo.

'Well, *grazie Signore*' smiled May. He kissed he forehead and bid her a fond '*Ciao*' and was off. She stood and watched him drive off waving his cravat in the air merrily as he sped across town. What an evening? What a girl? These were his thoughts as he drove up the unmade road to the farm. Locking away the Healey he wandered into the house. The phone was ringing he pounced upon it.

'Somehow I knew it was you' he said.

DAI ASKS THE QUESTION.

Dai and Doris had returned from France some days ago and professional snaps had been taken and a portfolio created. Dai and Norris Parker had shown this to a number of publications and had immediate and positive response. Contracts flew around like confetti. Doris's likeness began to appear in both glamour and fashion magazines. One of the famous model agencies contacted Norris and offered to have her trained for modelling on the catwalk. They were in the money. Norris Parker was to be her agent, Dai the fashion photographer, and Doris the model. Other models were asking for Dai now and Doris encouraged him.

'So long as you don't let them seduce you it's OK.' Of course that was just what some of the models did want. They lay temptation before Dai's eyes a hundred times. They undressed in front of him, brushed against him, one even grabbed his leek which was fighting the good fight with enormous difficulty. But Dai was steadfast. He put the naughty girls in their place, which to their surprise was not his bed. Norris had advised him, 'if you so much as touch one of them the word will fly like wildfire to Doris's ears. They just want to cause problems because they are jealous of her not of you.'

This made a lot of sense to Dai and he listened hard. Two months passed and he asked Doris to marry him. She literally jumped on him. 'There's nothing I want more. If we save now I will be able to retire in a couple of years with good money behind me and we can have some beautiful children. I do want to have your children Dai, you know.' He hugged her tightly. She continued, 'Do you realise if it wasn't for the fumes leaking from that old Chemical Plant I might never have met you?'

BEAMISH BACK IN COURT

So someone had benefited directly from the pollution of the atmosphere and they do say, 'it is an ill wind that blows nobody any good'.

Ex-magistrate Beamish was not in such a happy condition. He was at this minute standing in the High Court of Justice in the Strand in London. Wpc Winsome's counsel was cross-examining him on the detail of his handling of her bottom.

'Now let me see if I have this correctly from your evidence in chief, Mr. Beamish you claim that when, on 3rd May last, you seized my client's buttocks you were under the influence of gasses which had emanated from the land occupied by Dakers Diggers?'

'That's correct' Beamish was pleased to confirm.

'What period of time elapsed between your sniffing these gasses and your assault upon Ms Winsome?'

'Objection my lord' Beamish's counsel was on his hind legs.

'Yes' Mr. er Tadpole said the learned Mr. Justice Wigfield reading old Tadder's name from the slip of paper in front of him. 'What can you possibly find objectionable in Mr. Davenport's question.'

'The use of the word assault in a prejudicial manner milord and further more the implication that my client perhaps deliberately 'sniffed' the gasses.'

'Now Mr. Tadpole we do not have the benefit of a jury in this case so that little figurative descriptions delivered gently in his time honoured fashion by Mr. Davenport need not cause your dander to rise. I am hardly going to be easily taken in or swayed by colourful language, am I Mr Tadpole? No, I am going to overrule your objection. Please continue Mr. Davenport.'

'I thank you My Lord. Now Mr. Beamish please answer the question.' Beamish looked rather lost. 'You've forgotten have you. Well let me repeat it for you. What period of time elapsed between your sniffing these gasses and your attack upon Ms Winsome?' Mr. Tadpole began to rise to object to the word 'attack' but a stern look from the Judge made him think better of it.

Mr. Beamish looked about for assistance but there was none. He thought carefully. 'I don't know. Just a minute! How on earth would I know? These gasses were in the air I was breathing all the time...'

'Come, come, Mr. Beamish the question is not a difficult one. The gasses are not everywhere are they?'

'They only affect the immediate vicinity of approximately one hundred yards in any direction from the site of the works. At what time did you pass the site? It is directly on your route from your house to the Do-It-All store where the assault took place. When did you leave home?

'At about eleven a.m.'

'Very good Mr. Beamish, well done. We are making progress at last. At what time did you reach the store in question.' Mr. Beamish once again looked around for inspiration.

'May I help you? In your evidence in chief you admitted to having assaulted the Plaintiff at 11.17am. Now how long does it take you to reach the store from your house. The distance is some 973 yards.' Mr. Beamish still looked lost. 'Well I suggest to you Mr. Beamish that that journey could have taken you no more than fifteen minutes. Do you accept that?' Mr. Beamish nodded mutely.

'Good more progress! Now the works are just under half way say 400 yards and that we estimate took you five minutes. So can we agree that you had sniffed the gasses, if at all, at or about 11.05am?'

'Yes that seems reasonable, I'll accept that Mr. Davenport', offered Beamish wanting to be helpful.

'Good. Now it is clear isn't it Mr. Beamish that you could well be under the influence, as it were, less than ten minutes later? We have scientific evidence which you have heard and seen in the evidence produced in your defence that the gasses may affect a man for as much as an hour after breathing them in the concentration accepted to exist at or near the site.'

'Oh yes!' Beamish was enjoying himself now. Silly old Davenport had handed him a clear defence to the charges and the injunction Ms Winsome was seeking.

'Very good Mr. Beamish, I can see you are pleased, positively beaming. No one is sorrier than I to destroy such a happy mood, but I fear I must. Help me with this. You were arrested at 11.35am and taken to the police station. Is that correct?' Beamish nodded still not seeing where this was all leading.

'You were kept in all day for questioning and overnight until the magistrates hearing next day. Is that right?'

'Absolutely! And if you've got the record of that hearing I was let off! This hearing is like double jeopardy it shouldn't be allowed!' Beamish pouted.

'Oh yes Mr. Beamish you were let off, very lightly too, and at 11.17am the following day, the fourth of May, you assaulted my Client the Plaintiff again in precisely the same manner. Is that not correct?

'Oh well, yes I suppose so.'

'You suppose so. You suppose so. Is it not also true that you assaulted her again some half an hour later in the police van itself whilst being driven to Buttersoft police station? That you forced yourself upon her in an indecent assault, which clearly amounts to gross indecency?'

'Eh? Gross indecency? Steady on old man! It was only a bit of fun. Winsome enjoyed it I'm sure. I've never had any complaints you know.'

'Mr. Beamish I have to tell you that the Director of Public Prosecutions has authorised the issue of a warrant for your arrest in that connection. These current proceedings however are, as you know, civil proceedings for an injunction and damages. Do you understand that?' Beamish nodded his smile now gone completely.

'Can you see any reason why an injunction should not issue from his Lordship against you this morning? There I am giving you an opportunity to speak up in your defence.' Beamish was struck mute.

'No further questions My Lord'.

'Thank you Mr. Davenport. You can step down from the witness box now Mr. Beamish. I don't think I need to trouble you for a final address Mr. Davenport. Mr. er Tadpole, can you, of all people, see any way that your Client is going to wriggle out of this?'

Tadpole tottered to his feet. 'Milord,' he began. 'It is the Plaintiff's duty to prove his or her case on the balance of probabilities. The Plaintiff's counsel has conceded that the noxious gasses emanating from the Dakers Dig affected the Defendant. He has conceded that the first assault occurred entirely as a result of the effect of the fumes. It is true that the scientific evidence did suggest that the effects would wear off within a short time but the view expressed was pure speculation...'

'It is not my habit to interrupt Counsel's address' said the Judge 'but may I remind Mr. Tadpole that the scientist in question was a defence witness.'

'Thank you Milord. I am aware of that and indeed it should highlight the sparse nature of the evidence produced by the Plaintiff in this case. It is our case that at all material times poor Mr. Beamish acted entirely under the influence of gasses which he unknowingly breathed in prior to the assaults which are the subject of these proceedings. Thank you Milord.'

The Judge took a long hard look at Tadpole over the top of his pince-nez and adjusted his wig. He began his judgement:

'This is a case where both parties agree upon the basic facts. The Defendant, until recently a Magistrate, dear me, assaulted the Plaintiff on two distinct occasions. The first of these occasions was whilst she was shopping for a pair of pliers or pincers and paint in the DIY shop called Do-It-All. I have been to the shop in question myself and seen the vast array of merchandise on offer and can't imagine anybody possibly doing it all. That is by the bye.

At 11.17am the Plaintiff admits she bent over to examine a likely pair, of pliers that is, and some cans of paint, whereupon the Defendant came up behind her and grabbed hold of both cheeks of her buttocks. In that instance there is no suggestion that the Defendant sought to put his hands under her clothing, nor is there any claim of rape. Furthermore, Mr. Davenport for the Plaintiff has graciously, and if I may say so sensibly, made a concession. He concedes that the assault took place at a time when, on the balance of probabilities, Mr. Beamish, the Defendant, was acting under the strong influence of noxious gasses breathed in by him unbeknown to himself, moments earlier.'

'I have heard expert evidence that the gasses in question are, and were at all material times, seeping from the spot identified on a map by Mr.

Beamish's counsel, Mr. Tadpole, and that they cause men and women to have uncontrollable sexual urges.

The judge turned away for a moment and muttered to his clerk, 'Don't you dare tell Mrs. Wigfield about this, or she'll have me on the first train up there!'

'So although she was undoubtedly assaulted in a grossly sexual manner in public, the Judge continued, she has no recourse against the Defendant. She may well have recourse against others, and indeed I understand that separate proceedings have already been issued in that regard.

'Now we come to the second and much more serious assault which took place actually in the Magistrates Court in where?'

His clerk stood up from his position directly in front of the Judge and turned to whisper to his Lordship, 'Buttersoft, my Lord'

'Really? Oh right. Well, this attack took place in Buttersoft Magistrates Court. Mr. Davenport points out that more than 24 hours had elapsed since the gasses were inhaled, and that the effects - as stated by the defence witness, Mr. Cheapside MSc (Chem.) could not have affected the Defendant over such a long period.'

'Mr. Tadpole rose to address me on the balance of probabilities. He pointed out that his own witness could not be categorical in his judgement about how long the effects would last. The witness had said, "About an hour". I must say I cannot see how the leeway of doubt could change his opinion from one hour to one day. I am not here today to consider the question of damages but in response to a plea from this poor woman for an injunction to prevent further similar attacks from the Defendant. My conscience would not allow me to refuse her and the evidence happily does not lead me to consider such a course.'

'Accordingly I hereby grant an injunction against the Defendant in these proceedings, James Beamish, former Magistrate, ('Good God!' he thought) from approaching the Plaintiff or coming within three hundred metres of her, and from assaulting her in any manner whatsoever.

I realise that the Defendant would find it difficult to assault the Plaintiff from three hundred metres but just in case he is a champion javelin thrower I am covering the possibility. Now I warn you Mr. Beamish that if you disobey this injunction you will be arrested and imprisoned for contempt of this Court. Now do you understand that?'

'Yes your honour, I mean my Lord.'

'And I award the Plaintiff two thousand pounds damages and costs on an indemnity basis. Is there anything else gentlemen? Nothing? Good. I order that there be a certificate for Counsel's appearance. Good morning.'

Everyone stood to allow the Judge to retire. Beamish was speechless. Tadpole said weakly, 'Of course you can appeal, but personally...' As they left the Court Beamish was approached by two policemen. One of them held a piece of paper in his hand.

'James Beamish I have a warrant for your arrest on a charge of indecent assault and gross indecency upon the person of one Winona Winsome on 4th May 1997 in the Buttersoft Magistrates Court, and again in a Police van travelling from the Magistrates Court to Buttersoft Police Station. I must warn you that anything you say will be taken down in writing and may be used in evidence.

Have you anything to say?'

Beamish almost burst into tears. 'I thought she wanted it. I couldn't help myself'.

Wpc Winsome passed by the small group which moved slightly to the left to allow her free passage. Davenport followed her and might be forgiven for sneaking a view of the target of Beamish's recent exploits. 'I'll be damned' he thought 'if that wouldn't be his best defence. Look at her stern, she is superbly crafted.'

Chasing after his Client and her solicitor who were exchanging pleasantries prior to parting he shouted 'Winona may I have a word?' Off tripped the solicitor. 'Yes Michael what is it?'

'I just wondered if you mightn't like to go for a sail sometime, get some fresh air and put all this behind you'. Inside his head he was imagining exactly what was behind her. Having run after her to catch her up, he was panting slightly and perspiring. Breathless both from his exertions and with anticipation he looked at her straight in the eyes. She appeared to hesitate. Smoothing a lock of her straight auburn hair from her forehead she considered his proposal.

'Don't you think it is a little soon after my ordeal to be thinking of dating? I mean I know that you did an excellent job for me in there but I am still emotionally shaken up.'

'I realise that, and that is exactly why I am offering you an opportunity for peace and fresh air, freedom from stress and I would emphasise that there are no strings attached.'

'No ulterior motives?' she rejoined sharply.

'None for the moment. Listen of course I like you and find you intensely attractive, but I am human, and I understand the terrible experience that you have just been through. I would like to show you that not all men are like the dishonourable Mr. Beamish.'

'I will take it under advisement, counsellor. I need time to recover and give yourproposal some thought, I have your number I will call you. One way or the other.'

With that she turned upon her heels and walked briskly up Chancery Lane in the direction of the central line underground station. Davenport watched her amazing form in retreat.

'Heigh-ho' he sighed 'We shall have to wait and see old man, we shall have to just wait and see.' He returned to his chambers in the Temple and the room allocated to him.

His clerk Stan looked round the door. 'Mr Davenport sir!' Davenport looked up at him. 'Yes Stanley?'

'I thought you would like to know that Mr. Beamish has been carted off to the cells. The Crown Prosecution Service wondered if you would like to handle the criminal case for them as you know so much about the facts of the case.'

'An interesting proposition Stan, I am not sure if I can you know. I have to consider whether there might be a conflict of interest. Let me ask the Bar Council if it would be all right.'

HAM REVISITED

Matters were moving pace in the other side of the litigation.

A date had been set for the hearing of Henry's preliminary application for summary judgement against Farmer Thomas. Counsel were briefed for 30th of June and Mr. Justice Wigfield who was already familiar with some aspects of the case was appointed to hear it in court 13 in the Royal Courts of Justice in the Strand, London WC2.

Just prior to the case Henry visited Godfrey Hammond QC in his chambers in company with Howard Rossitter his solicitor. Once again they clambered up the well-trodden almost sagging steps in the centuries old building. Delia was there to meet them her amazing legs topped with a saucy frill which was a mere excuse for a skirt.

'Tea or coffee gentlemen?' she asked.

They were both so absorbed in Delia and her sartorial arrangements they simultaneously answered, 'Yes'.

'Which would you prefer gentlemen? Tea or coffee.'

'Hmmm' murmured Howard in Henry's ear. 'Which would be on the higher shelf tea or coffee? We don't want to make this easy for her do we now?'

Henry giggled. 'I think high tea is appropriate Delia.'

This turned out to be a good guess, as Delia had to stand on tiptoe to reach the tea out of the cupboard. Her skirt began to creep even further up her legs. Both men shrank down in their seats to afford them a better view. Then she had the tea in her fingertips and the game was over. At this moment the Ham made an entrance.

'Gentlemen! Welcome! I see that Delia is keeping up appearances. Why, you've chosen tea. A very wise choice, if I may say so, given your position. If you also take sugar things will definitely be looking up.'

They glanced at the top shelf and saw the tell-tale Tate & Lyle wrapper at the very back.

'Have you any sugar for the gentlemen Delia please' smirked Godfrey Hammond.

He did not hang about when there was fish to fry. Delia gave him a look that clearly indicated that she knew what he was cooking. She pulled her typist's tilt/swivel chair over to the cupboard and with a swift leap was on it. There was an inevitable revelation of pretty pink panties involved in this operation, but she had acted very quickly keeping the damage to a minimum.

The problem lay in the nature of the chair on to which she had made her leap. Tilt/swivel. She was wearing fairly high heels and this made her centre of gravity even higher than it would normally have been. Once she landed upon it, the chair began to swivel furiously round and round and even threatened to go into tilt mode. Delia wavered from side to side lifting her leg up, showing tantalising glimpses of her tiny knick-knacks in the process, in a vain attempt to find her balance.

She flushed and blushed and the gentlemen gushed. Delia then tottered and wavered, attempting valiantly to keep her balance. Had she not instantly reached up for the sugar as she came to rest upon the chair's surface, she might have retained her balance. In the event she wobbled the seat swivelled and she fell backwards. From the point of view of propriety, this was the better direction as she fell head towards the two seated onlookers. The swivel had turned her body round so that in falling she also negotiated a superb twist. The upshot of all this was that she fell facedown. Her landing was softened by the location of the redoubtable retainer, Henry, who was sitting directly in her landing path. Although his reactions are pretty quick in normal circumstances, Delia's twists and turns made evasive action a difficult proposition. Delia landed smack in his lap, head down.

Both Counsel and solicitor looked agape at Delia's face buried between Henry's thighs. As she had landed with some force Henry experienced pain rather than the pleasure that might have been imagined at such intimate contact. Shock prevented her from rising immediately, but she slowly lifted her head and assumed a hangdog expression.

'I am so sorry Mr. Redfield. I can see that this was more painful for you than it was for me. You broke my fall.' Henry bit his lip to avoid giving the natural reply

As she lifted one knee to rise, Henry had a full view of her see through frillies. He groaned as the pain returned with force. She couldn't really offer to massage the affected area, and even he felt constrained not to do so. Howard who had also benefited from the close up of Delia's delicate delights had turned a darker shade of his usual pale, and was already making plans to ask Delia out for dinner.

'If the Chamber Games are now over perhaps you would care to follow me into my room for the consultation,' remarked a more sober Hammond. 'You may bring up the rear with the tea Delia' was his spicy afterthought.

Delia was not amused by the thought of bringing up her rear for Hammond or anyone after her recent nerve racking experience, but she made the tea nonetheless and brought it intothe meeting.

'I hope you are feeling better Mr. Redfield' she said with genuine concern as she set down the tea things.

'A little tender perhaps. I may need a doctor's certificate to keep me off games for a day or two, but I shall be all right, thank you Delia.'

She marched out on those long slender legs of hers watched by all three. They dragged their attention back to the case in point. Hammond opened the batting.

'Now gentlemen. We are before the Judge in Chambers, the Chancery Master having referred the case to him as one containing or referring to matters which may be of particular legal significance, and the hearing is almost upon us. I, together with my supporting junior counsel, Miss Tayke, have sketched out a skeleton argument for the learned Judge to consider. As you may know Wigfield is sitting and I take that as a slight advantage for us. He can understand the finer points of the law, and his judgements are bold when necessary with a liberal sprinkling of the essence of justice always perceptible in his reasoning.

Our argument will be that Henry has done nothing, and can do nothing in relation to the land as it is let to Dakers Diggers (Duncan Sands QC has been retained for them incidentally). Dakers actually did the acts that released the gasses. The Buttersoft Council (represented by Harvey Price) allowed the works to start and had stood by whilst CCC (represented by DP Underwood QC) buried the stuff. Industrial Investments Inc. (counsel will be I. Newett) have not admitted knowledge of the burial but we are suspicious.

So Henry, we say, is faultless, and was powerless to intervene at any time. I shall seek dismissal of the claim against him or judgement in his favour. I shall also seek an order for costs. If we should fail in this application then we shall want discovery of all documents relating to the Chemical Factory and its history, and its relationship with its landlord, Industrial Investments. I shall be asking questions (interrogatories regarding their relationship) which are designed to make them feel uncomfortable. I hope that will all be unnecessary if the Court accedes to our preliminary application. Does that all make sense to you Henry?'

'Yes, I understand perfectly Godfrey. Why should our application fail though? What can the other parties say to keep me in the game?'

'They will quote a well-known case, Rylands-v-Fletcher, old authority for the proposition that if something (such as water) escapes from your land on to the land of others causing damage, then you, as landowner, are liable regardless of fault. Now in that case land and property suffered from the escape of water. No such damage occurred here. There the owner knew about the existence of the Water. Here you did not know of the chemicals. As I have stressed previously, the land was in the exclusive possession of Dakers Diggers and they carried out the acts that released the fumes.

Then of course there is the principle of Public Interest. Cases of pollution of our water and seas are becoming of greater and greater concern today. Too many factories, sewage treatment farms, oil tankers and the like have run roughshod over our land and environment for too long. The public, and perhaps the government, is looking for cases like this to highlight the problem and create a groundswell of motivated opinion for change and the legislation that can bring it about. There is a considerable case for such change.'

Henry digested the escape of fluids, pollution of British waterways and sewage treatment. Having done so, he commented 'OK. Well you seem to be ready for the fray I shall see you on the day appointed. Is there anything else Howard?'

'I don't think so Henry. I will stay behind for a chat with Godfrey about one or two other matters. If you have five minutes Godfrey?'

'Certainly. Goodbye Henry. Delia will see you out.'

Henry left Hammond's room and saw Delia sitting, holding something bandage-like against her knee. 'What's wrong Delia? Did you hurt it during your fall?'

'It's just a bruise Mr. Redfield. How is, are your . . . 'she was unable to find a suitable word.

'Fine, right as rain. I believe that I am already in full working order again. Any way I must get back now, thank you for the tea. I know what hard work it was!'

Henry took the steps down two by two and bounded out into the street. Finding his way out into Chancery Lane, having negotiated the well-kept Gardens of the Inns of Court, he decided to pop into the Law Society for coffee and a club biscuit. This he found in the grand drawing room set-aside for this purpose. He watched his brothers and sisters-in-law congregating in twos and threes discussing some case or other.

An old gentleman sitting next to him in a comfortable leather armchair suddenly jerked out of what was obviously an afternoon doze. 'Hey! What! Oh! Sorry I was sleeping,' he offered to Henry 'Must have dozed off. What is the time now?' he asked the fob watch that he removed from his waistcoat pocket. Hmmm. It's four thirty. Just time for a coffee and I will have to catch my train. Oh sorry to prattle on.'

This last remark was addressed to Henry and looked properly in his direction for the first time since waking from his snooze.

'Just a moment. You're *whatshisname* aren't you? You know that fellow with the chemicals.' Henry sighed and thought, 'What a way to be known or recognised'. Aloud he said 'yes I am *whatshisname* all right.'

'That Farmer is suing you because his pigs are reproducing too fast or something like that. Can't for the life of me see what his problem is. Should be shaking you by the hand. Fellow must have taken leave of his senses to sue you. Is he one of these modern crackpot's that wear a ring in their nose and listen to that loud banging that passes for music these days?'

'Not exactly. He is, from what I have heard, quite a traditional farming type from a long line of farmers. He is upset because some his choice pigs have overexerted themselves and died from their labours.'

The old man screwed up his eyes thoughtfully and shook his head. 'How can you be responsible for that? Didn't steal into his farm at the dead of night and egg them on did you?'

'No!' laughed Henry. 'His complaint is that these chemicals you mention, gasses uncovered by excavations, and buried there by a former occupier of the land, have emanated from my land and directly affected his pigs in the way I have described.'

'Well for my money he hasn't got a hope in hell against you. Load of rubbish. That's the trouble people will start an action against their neighbour for the every little thing nowadays. It's the American disease starting to infect our legal system. People want to get rich at the expense of others, rather than the way I did with the honest oil and sweat of my brow. Anyway what's his loss? He has to provide an account of the benefit that all these additional piglets have provided. I tell you it's a non-starter.'

'Well there are others making claims now. A policewoman attacked by a magistrate, the *beak himself*, and some people from an old people's home.' Henry realised that all of these people would oppose his clearing out of the proceedings.

'I am sorry for the Wpc. The beak deserves a sharp rap across the knuckles and a prison term of a goodish length. His only way out is to show that the second, and more serious attack, occurred whilst he was still under the influence so to speak. The retirement home story is less serious but they do have a point. In my view the Chemical Company must pay you all damages and costs.'

'I am sorry' said Henry 'I haven't formally introduced myself 'my name is Henry Redfield, that is when I am not using my alias of *whatshisname*.'

'I know your name young feller. How do you do? I am Warburton. For my pains when I am not sleeping it off here I do a bit of judging as a Deputy County Court Judge. Not that you will be able to use my opinions as authority before Mr. Justice Wigfield, but your able counsel should be able to manage without them.'

'Well Judge I am heartened by your straightforward, no nonsense approach. I hope those sentiments are echoed in the High Court. It has been a real pleasure. Good day.' Henry walked out feeling better still. He was concerned about the Wpc too. He wished he could do something for her particularly. He couldn't even contact her it would be improper.

TO SLEEP PERCHANCE TO DREAM...

Out in Chancery Lane again he stopped a passing cab and gave Chester Gate as the destination. He called Josephine who had partly moved in with him now. 'Hallo darling I am on my way home. Anything you need particularly? I'm to buy some eggs, bread, water and a bottle of bubbly. Is that it? Fine, I'll see you in a jiffy.'

Within ten minutes the taxi drew up outside the Redfield residence. He jumped out and tossed a fiver to the driver. 'Thanks' he said. He pressed the newly fitted entryphone button.

'Oui?' Josephine demanded. 'Oh Henry! I can see you on this little screen you look rather strange. I don't know if I should let you in.'

Nonetheless the buzzer sounded and the door clicked open. She raced toward him and leapt into his arms, causing him to take a step backwards. They held each other and whispered those things that such lucky people do. Henry led her into the lounge and sat her down on the deep green leather couch. They sank into it and he related the events of the day and gave his opinion as to the likely further developments.

Josephine looked at him. 'You need a rest Henry enough is enough. Get undressed and go to bed. I'll put the shopping in the refrigerator and go out to meet Isabel.' I'll be back to fix something for dinner. OK?'

He nodded and started to take off his clothes. Within minutes he was in bed fast asleep. It was only 6pm. He dreamed of taking a cruise with Josephine. It was a wonderful liner and their cabin was a stateroom, really quite superb.

Henry and Josephine walked along the deck to the first class dining room. Extraordinarily the judge he had met at the Law Society was dressed up as the Captain. He had a stuffed parrot fixed to his left shoulder, and a pipe dangling from the right side of his mouth. He approached as they entered the room. 'Hallo me hearties!' he said to Henry and Josephine. 'Join me at my table tonight as Captain's treat. We got a special dish on the menu tonight. *Pigs trotter* a *la* Thom.'

Henry looked aghast, but Josephine giggled and said 'can I have fish instead?'

'Why certainly my dear! Have all you want!' He winked at the piratical looking able-bodied first mate. 'Do the honours Jim.'

The sturdy strapping sailor seized a shocked Josephine and swung her over his shoulder. He stomped out of the dining room doors on to the deck. Henry rushed after him shouting 'hey you! Stop!'

The sailor appeared not to have heard him, and to Henry's horror and dismay the sailor hefted Josephine over the ship's rail and down she went into the dark and heaving sea. 'Eat as many as you like, lady!' he shouted after her. Henry rushed up, grabbed the handrail and frantically looked overboard. There was no sign of the hapless demoiselle. He seized the front of the tunic of the sailor and shouted

'She'll drown! You've killed her. At least throw her a lifeline or a life belt!'

The sailor seemed impervious to Henry's cries. Taking off his shoes Henry dived into the briny. It was cold and unwelcoming and overwhelming. He opened his eyes and despite the pain of the salt looked urgently in every direction for his lost ladylove. He thrashed about hunting high and low, diving and surfacing. Then he saw her sitting like a Lorelei on a rock which protruded from the foaming sea actually eating raw fish! He swam for the rock in a daze of incomprehension.

Mounting its slippery surface with extraordinary difficulty, and dripping from all orifices, he made good his seat upon the rock. He grabbed hold of Josephine. 'What on earth are you doing? You had me worried sick. Why are you sitting here in grave danger eating raw fish? How did you catch them anyway?' He removed his outer clothing, which felt like cold lead against his skin.

Josephine turned to him removing as she did so a fish bone from her lips. As she turned her body shifted on the rock and a gigantic fish tail appeared where her lovely legs used to be. 'Josephine a mermaid!' Henry thought? How?' At that moment a huge wave swept him off the rock and she also was gone again. 'Josephine' he called. He shouted her name between gulps of seawater. Through a mist he heard her calling 'Henri wake up. Henri! Henri!!!'

He awoke still calling her name. Josephine sat on his bed.

'My goodness that was one heck of a dream you were having. You kept calling my name. What happened? Can you remember it?'

Henry could, and related it all to her.

She was astonished. 'I will ask my medium friend who lives in Versailles to interpret it for you. Mais c'est extraordinaire quel reve!'

PARKER OF THE PRESS

Norris Parker was putting the finishing touches to an editorial he was doing for one of the broadsheet national daily newspapers. He had covered the history of *the Buttersoft Experience* from its inception to the present day. He had used the unusual circumstances to put out a warning to Chemical and Industrial Polluters everywhere about the damage being done to the environment, to people and animals. He exhorted governments to take stringent action to inspect and curb violators. He extended his warning to nuclear pollution.

He said, 'Let us learn from the relatively painless experience here in Buttersoft, that humans, and animals alike, can be seriously affected by careless or wanton polluters. These chemical and industrial giants are motivated by the profit factor alone in many cases, and take the easy way out when disposing of their waste. The convenient river or seacoast, the simple landfill burial, are ways of passing the problem on to a future unsuspecting generation. Now is the time for action to be taken to stop this sort of criminal activity, and to legislate for heavier penalties for the perpetrators, imprisonment should be the norm, and long sentences should not be ruled out.

We cannot leave a polluted legacy to our children with hidden dangers round every nasty corner. We have a duty to rise up and challenge our governments to make them take decisive and necessary action today. The dangers that we must address are everywhere from our own River Thames via the jungles of Africa and the open sewers of India to the rain forests of Brazil.

Rise up! March now! Organise! Go to your Houses of Parliament and Rulers Palaces in force. Let them know that enough is enough. The callous chemical cowboys can be cornered and castrated. There is no time to waste and waste must be dealt with in time. Trees, forests, fields of grass and corn, flora and fauna, our animals and we, frail human beings are at enormous risk. Nuclear waste millionaires and billionaires are the worst of the cult of wastrels and vandals. Prepared for a quick buck to callously to risk even their own future existence.

In quiet remote areas where ignorance and poverty prevent or overrule objection they dump their dreadful and awful waste product. They must be stopped and words alone will not be enough.

Legislate and make these people arrestable now. Put them in prison and seize their assets. We do this to drug lords and dealers who kill but allow these criminals to carry on as 'successful businessmen. Let us open our eyes and awake in time to prevent the future tragedies that are now in the making. Stop pollution and polluters. They are public enemy No. 1'

Response to Norris's publications of which this is the choice item was overwhelming he was in demand for chat shows and interviews all over the world. He was making a fortune. He divested himself of much of it in favour of charities and organisations who either cared for victims of pollution or who sought to ban it from our planet. CND's banner now was just that:

"BAN IT FROM OUR PLANET."

Nosey was feted and asked to become honorary President of that and half a dozen other similar organisations. He visited the victims and those especially the children made him cry buckets of angry tears. This was now his fight and he would see it to the bitter end.

AND SO TO COURT...

Talking about fights Henry was about to enter round 1 of the fight proper. The date was set for the hearing of his application. That day dawned at last and the impatience that had begun to seep to the surface of his consciousness waiting for a possible resolution of his problem was assuaged. He trotted out of his flat at 8.30am and decided to try to walk at least part of the way. He turned into the Park and strode across the grass.

All the smells and sights and sounds of nature came to massage his heightened senses. The flowers flung their fragrances at him challenging him to approach them nose to petal. The ducks crackled out their morning greeting which appeared quite indistinguishable from their afternoon rendering. The colour and form of the Park was the most dramatic of all the experiences presented to his senses that morning. A mass of variegated colour from the flower beds, the soothing shades of green from the grass up into bushes and the trees, and the sun breaking through soft white clouds surrounded by sky of deep blue hue.

Henry was invigorated and drunk in the perfumed air. Immediately that he left the Park for the dusty atmosphere of the Marylebone Road, he chose to flag down a taxi. Traffic was heavy and he held his breath to avoid the murkier fumes exhausted by the buses and trucks. The driver had turned into Marylebone High Street, and Henry could watch the shops and cafes wearily opening their eyes, soon to surge into life and wakefulness waiting to pounce upon the unwary customer who might wander carelessly within their reach.

He stopped, having time, at one of those cafés for a cappuccino. He sat outside despite the coolness of the air in the shadow that still hung over that side of the street. Businessmen and secretaries hurried along anxious to reach their offices and the coffee or tea that awaited them there, impervious to his stare. A dog kicked out early by his local owner sniffed the parking meters that had replaced trees at the edge of the street, as unhappy with the substitution as his counterpart human. The meters too had awakened and required an immediate and substantial feed. Their wardens were already on the loose, fiercely alert for careless drivers who had not provided their charges with their daily bread. Henry drank his coffee aware that a thin film of froth remained on his upper lip. He took a serviette and dabbed at it. Impressions, everything is impressions, particularly the first of that genre. He rose, leaving coins on the table and signalled to another cab. 'The Royal Courts of Justice in the Strand please,' he shouted over the steady rumble of traffic.

'Jump in sir,' said the cabby and off they went.

Winding through the side streets in deference to the rush hour, good progress was made. At 9.15am Henry arrived at the huge gothic building and stared at the tall doors he must pass through to reach the Court.

The huge gothic entrance was swarming with berobed and bewigged counsel, standing and chatting to their instructing solicitors, or giving last minute advice to a nervous client. The press stood around making rather a dejected group clearly sad at having to be in such a place at such an early hour, carrying their drooping microphones and hefting heavy cameras on their aching shoulders, whilst standing rather than lying in wait for their prey. Henry thought suddenly of this as a photographic safari really. The litigants were the hunted animals, their advocates providing in the final analysis only scant protection from the newspapermen and finally the big game hunter, the judge, he, who is dressed to kill.

Henry sallied forth not expecting acquaintances to recognise him at this hour. Suddenly he turned as he heard a voice calling, 'I say Mr. Redfield, could we have a word please?' He recognised nobody and wondered if he had imagined it. But no, there was the voice again closer. 'Mr. Redfield, could you tell us how you think your application will go this morning?'

'My God!' thought Henry it's television and they've captured me already. Sure enough the interviewer had just finished opening the topic of Henry's case to the public, and now turned to the man himself for an in-depth analysis no doubt. 'Mr. Redfield how confident are you of success this morning? We understand that today you are applying to be cleared of any liability in the case before it proceeds further.'

'Ahem! I cannot and would not be advised to speak at length about a matter that is still *sub judice*. I will say that my lawyers and I are hopeful of a reasonable result whichever way our application goes this morning.' He swung away from the reporter looking for an avenue of escape.

'Mr. Redfield can you not be more specific than that about why you are seeking exoneration from the consequences of the inhalation of gasses coming out of land which clearly belongs to you.'

The clever wording of the question effectively prevented Henry's immediate departure. 'I have done nothing more than buy the land as an Industrial Investment. I have not dug in the land, buried or exposed chemicals within it, nor did I have the slightest idea that chemicals were buried there. I am seeking compensation, as are all the complainants from the real villain of the piece Caustic Chemicals. I really can't and won't say more until after the application.'

With that he made good his escape and found his way to the long corridor, which led him on a lengthy walk to the Court. His solicitor, Rossitter was already there, and he saw Miss Tayke, junior supporting Counsel for Godfrey Hammond QC. The familiar face of Duncan Sands for Dakers Diggers hove into view and he boomed a hearty 'Good morning to one and all.'

Henry imagined that bearing in mind the likely brief fee for a queen's counsel for what might be little more than a couple of hours, the morning would take on a very benevolent appearance from the point of view of a QC at any rate.

Harvey Price rounded the corner and walked toward the growing group in company with the Buttersoft Town Clerk and his solicitors. I Newett and DP Underwood QC, counsel respectively for Industrial Investments and Caustic Chemicals wandered in, last of the major contenders. They were chatting to each other as though they were about to watch a cricket match rather than take up weapons, against Henry, and each other in what could prove to be a very expensive battle indeed. A watching brief was held for the other Plaintiffs by agreement and Jennifer Joyce had instructed Mr. Davenport, a senior junior of good reputation, who had previously represented Ms Winsome. he would not appear for Beamish though, as the ex-magistrate's interest conflicted with that of Wpc Winsome. Beamish was represented by a new counsel Carstairs-Carruthers an unknown entity.

The usher took all the names of parties and Counsel representing them and disappeared into Court. He re-appeared some minutes later to ask if everyone was ready. A general nodding was the response.

'Right would you please come into Court then and take your places gentlemen.'

The doors opened and they entered the Court, which had not changed in appearance much in fifty or more years. The old seasoned wood worn with the years gave the room character which the library of available law books added manifold. The judge was seated upon high, and the rows of wooden benches and desks in the well of the court for counsel and solicitors, were broken up by the lecterns provided for Queen's Counsel to rest their papers on. When everyone was seated, and Henry noticed that Farmer Thomas and his retinue had arrived rather late, the clerk retired to fetch Mr. Justice Wigfield.

Everyone stood and bowed with the conventional respect shown to Her Majesty's Judges. The Judge returned the bow, his long wig and purple gown a contrast to the subdued colours otherwise filling the courtroom. His clerk whispered to him having to twist around to face him. The Clerk then stood and announced the case of Thomas-v-Redfield and others no 973 of 2016. The judge took up his pen and shifted his notepad into position.

'Yes Mr. Hammond, I believe this is your application.'

'It is my Lord' bellowed the Ham. 'If I might crave your Lordship's indulgence I will briefly summarise the background to the case and the reason for the present application.'

His Lordship nodded and poured himself a glass of water.

'My Lord, to assist the Court, I have had my junior draw up a plan of the Town of Buttersoft and its environs. Paper rustled and a colourful map emerged and was placed on an easel provided for the purpose. The Ham took up a long pointy stick.

'Hmmm!' he cleared his considerable throat. A movement at the back of the Court disturbed his beginning. Dimitri, Josephine and Isabel slid down the row next to Henry who winced at the interruption being watched by Mr. Justice Wigfield very carefully. Sliding into the press row was none other than the redoubtable Norris Parker and the inevitable Dai Evans (even though photographs were not allowed and his equipment had been left outside).

'Is everybody now sitting comfortably?' Justice Wigfield asked rhetorically. 'Right Mr. Hammond pray continue.'

'Thank you my Lord. My Lord may I draw your attention first to the land in question which is outlined in red on the master plan, I think your Lordship has a smaller version in front of you now.' His Lordship nodded. 'Good. Then the land outlined in red is the land now belonging to Mr. Redfield, coincidental that the field is outlined in red My Lord, quite coincidental. On that land coloured blue are the areas where chemicals have been found to have been buried. You will see that in two instances part of the blue area crosses a neighbour's boundaries. We are not concerned with that complication today, it may have relevance later. Farmer Thomas, the Plaintiff has his land edged green, and your Lordship will note that one of the overlapping blue areas straddles the border between the red and green edged land. The green land is to the south of Mr. Redfield's hereditament.

Now Dakers Diggers occupy the whole of the relevant portion of the red land as no blue areas impinge upon parcels of land which are let to Mr. Redfield's other tenants. The Civil Service Retirement Home for Ladies is on the yellow edged land on the north side of Mr. Redfield's land. Now the road makes the third boundary to the west. A group of houses comprising a small estate including at its furthest reach, the house of a Mr. Beamish is to the East. All parties use the road anyway, which is accessed through adjacent minor roads or pathways.

Now prior to Mr. Redfield's acquisition of the land on January 27'h 1996, the land was owned by Industrial Investments Incorporated, an American Company. They are represented today by Mr. Newett who leased the red sector to Caustic Chemicals Corp, again from across the pond, whose business is the manufacture of chemical products. Now much has been murmured about some family connection between these two corporations, it may well be that one exists, but it matters not in my submission. Suffice it to say that prior to the disposal of the property by Industrial there was a much more serious disposal by Caustic Chemicals of the substances shown coloured blue on the Master Plan.'

'At the present state of knowledge we cannot say that Industrial were aware of the chemical disposal, no doubt we shall in the course of time. Certainly no one else in the picture knew until one fateful day approximately a year later when Daker's Diggers decided to extend their showroom for excavatory equipment and the like.'

'Soon after they started digging, people, and animals, in the immediate area began to suffer strange effects. Men started slavering at the mouth. Their testosterone levels rose sharply and they were much more inclined, even driven, to sexual activity. Farmer Thomas's pigs on the green land began to die of exhaustion rather than poisoning or suffocation. They died if you will excuse the diversion into flippancy, with a smile on their snouts.'

'Farmer Thomas in the main proceedings claims damages upon the principle that the gasses having escaped from Mr. Redfield's land, Mr. Redfield is responsible. The claims of the other Plaintiffs Ms Winsome, Mr. Beamish, the ladies from the retirement home, and the under gardener Frobisher et al all follow suit. Mr. Redfield has joined the Buttersoft Council who watched over, and licensed the various developments, and who incorrectly answered enquiries made of them by Mr. Redfield's solicitor prior to purchase. He has also joined the former owners Industrial Investments Inc and the Chemical Company, Caustic Chemical Corporation.'

'Now we come to the purpose of this application, which may already have become apparent to your Lordship. Mr. Redfield says, 'I am innocent. I did not deposit chemicals on this land. I did not know chemicals had been buried out of sight on it. My surveyors on purchase did not see it. Neither the local Council nor the vendors, Industrial Investments, informed my solicitors about the blue substances. Finally I do not even have the right to possession of the land as Dakers Diggers have exclusive possession of the entire area. He continues with a plea to the Court. Do not rope me in to a major piece of litigation to which I should not really be a party at all. Let me go home. My learned brethren will try to force feed you with the case of Rylands-v-Fletcher, my Lord. May I respectfully suggest that you do not swallow? In that celebrated case the owner of the land also occupied it. He knew of the water and diverted it so that it flooded the Plaintiff's land. This case is entirely different. I ask that the case against Mr. Redfield be summarily dismissed or that judgement be entered for him as first defendant to the writ.'

'Thank you Mr. Hammond delivered with your usual panache. Yes, Mr. Sands?'

'My Lord I represent Dakers Diggers second Defendants in this case. I echo the sentiments of Mr. Hammond save that I contend that mere leasing of the land, and even innocent digging on it, which unbeknown to my clients, releases hidden chemical gasses should not impose any greater liability upon Dakers Diggers. I also request dismissal of the claim against my Clients.'

'And Mr. Harvey Price for Buttersoft Council?' the Judge peered over his spectacles at the row of Counsel before him.

'Ahem. Your Lordship as Counsel for the Council, I oppose both the joinder of my Client as a Defendant third party, and the release of either of the Defendants who have already spoken from these proceedings. The Council did not seek to mislead in its replies to Enquiries, but does disclaim liability for negligent answers in any event. As our state of knowledge stands at this time we cannot say we knew of the Chemical disposal any way. In the circumstances I seek a release from the effects of the Third party notice and of the Council from these proceedings.'

'Mr. Newett for Industrial Investments? Thank you.'

'My Lord, Industrial Investments do not admit knowing about these chemicals. They say 'We simply sold the land to Mr. Redfield. It was up to him to check it over and it is his responsibility to ensure nothing illegal occurs after the transfer of the property. He may have effectively transferred those obligations to Dakers Diggers, but that is none of our concern. We dispute the third party notice and ask to be released. For the reasons stated we object to the release of Mr. Redfield and certainly of Dakers Diggers. Thank you my Lord.'

DP Underwood rose to his considerable feet (size 17 by all reports). He was a tall fair-haired man of about 45 and he had a reputation for acerbic wit and an enviable ability to reduce evidence and witnesses to a shrivelled heap by the application of his cutting style of crisp cold logic. An ascetic in his private life, he had little in common with the Godfrey Hammond warm, expansive sanguine style. These QC;s were the butts of a joke of their contemporaries who quipped, "they are like chalk and ham!" Cheese at least can look like chalk but the taste is very different! He adjusted his spectacles and looked up at the judge. Taking time to straighten his papers, which were, in fact, in perfect order. He began:

'My Lord I represent Caustic Chemical Corporation. I may say on behalf of my Clients that they do not for a moment deny that they were lessees of what my learned friend has chosen to describe as the land edged red on the Master Plan. Nor do they deny that their business was that of the manufacture and sale or distribution of chemical compounds. For that matter they do not take issue with those on any of the other sides in this case regarding the effect of the gasses in question upon animals and human beings. My Clients simply deny that they buried the substances coloured blue on the plan either during their occupation of the land edged red or at all.'

A sharp intake of breath echoed around the Court. Even the Judge pushed his wig back on his head too far and it tumbled to the floor. The usher rushed to reclaim it for the honourable Mr. Justice Wigfield.

'My Lord' Underwood continued. 'My clients have been characterised as the villains of the piece without the benefit of a proper hearing. This is the first opportunity that we have had to set the record straight on a matter of basic principle. Anyone who had sought to make a proper investigation into the history of the use of this land, and the buildings upon it, could have discovered that, prior to my Clients occupation, which at best lasted a year, another chemical company, Testube Investments Limited, had previously occupied the site. All this occurred prior to a consolidation of its operations, which involved carrying on all its work out of its Sheffield outlet. Now, by strange coincidence, since then my Clients have purchased that company. However, the subsequent purchase of the company shares or stock cannot make my Clients personally liable for anything that Testube Investments may have done beforehand.'

'Now I realise that following this hearing any of the parties to this already multiparty proceeding may chose to join Testube Investments also, but that is no concern of my Clients. As to the question of Mr. Redfield's departure from these proceedings, my Clients have no axe to grind either way. On the question of costs alone, there would appear to be little point in keeping him in the frame, when someone else is certainly more likely to have to shoulder the blame. From where I am standing either Dakers Diggers or Testube Investments would appear to be likely nominees in this regard.'

Duncan Sands QC raised himself, smoothed his silken gown and began.

'My Lord I must object to my learned friend's suggestion that my Clients are to blame for the emission of gasses from substances negligently or malevolently buried either by his Clients or one of their offshoots. We all hear his attempted exculpation of Caustic Chemical Corps but are we, is the Court, to really believe this eleventh hour vindication? I think not, my Lord. On the balance of probabilities, Caustic is liable. It may have to share responsibility with Testube, but in the absence of direct evidence of who buried the blue substances and when, we shall have to rely on the balance of probabilities.'

Mr. Justice Wigfield scratched his head under his wig. 'Anyone else have anything to say on this issue?'

The Ham lifted his bulk and placed his overhang comfortably on the desk in front of him where it was shielded from public view by the lectern, upon which he leaned heavily for support.

'My Lord I agree with much of my learned friend Mr. Sands' argument. No evidence has yet been presented of course. However, I hazard that Mr. Underwood may have a problem proving on the balance of probabilities that his client, which had exclusive possession of the land edged red for a year, and whose business is the manufacture of chemicals, did not in fact bury the blue substances. Of course their acquisition of that company upon which they now wish to shovel the blame, much as I fear they originally shovelled the blue substances, means in terms of rough justice that they now should take responsibility in any event. They will however, play the corporate veil card if it suits them. Here I mean that they will insist that they are an entirely separate entity from their acquisition Testube Investments Limited - although they own them.'

'Naturally, it does not take a genius to see that if Testube Investments is a disposable item, without a strong asset base, it will cost them less to allow that company to shoulder the blame. They may not wish to have it fall upon Caustic whose pockets appear to be much deeper. You will excuse me my Lord if I demonstrate a certain cynicism, a sharp scepticism, about the sudden belated revelation that Caustic disclaims knowledge or responsibility for the blue burial.'

'Anyone else have anything further to say?' Mr. Justice Wigfield enquired. No one spoke.

'Very well. This is a case where chemicals buried by a person or persons unknown on land now belonging to the First Defendant, Henry Redfield. Redfield is a solicitor who doesn't practice law much now, but who certainly doesn't dabble in chemical burial. Chemicals have been inadvertently revealed during excavations carried out by his tenants Dakers Diggers represented by Mr. Sands. Dakers Diggers now second defendants, were extending their showroom where they sell excavating and some farming equipment. The blue substances, uncovered by the digging, gave off gasses. Adjoining landowners shown on the plan and passers by down the adjacent road have suffered ill effects from unknowingly inhaling these gasses. The effects are vastly increased sexual desire or proclivity, sometimes becoming an irresistible urge, or so it is alleged. Dakers Diggers have a lease of the land edged red on the Master Plan and that lease gives them the right to exclusive possession. Mr. Redfield cannot enter upon the land except by invitation or for limited practical access, purposes, which need not trouble us here today.'

'Now prior to Mr. Redfield's ownership, and Dakers lease, the red land as I shall now call it, was occupied by Caustic Chemicals Corp, an American company, and owned by Industrial Investments Inc, another American institution. All along it has been assumed by the parties to these proceedings that Caustic (now third defendants) being a chemical company must have buried the blue substances that have given rise to the emission of gas and this action. Mr. Underwood now removes his top hat and pulls out a rabbit. He says that Caustic deny all knowledge of the substances. He points the finger at Testube Investments, which his clients have bought by coincidence recently and says "it was them as done it!" Counsel for Industrial Investments Inc says we didn't know and we are as innocent as Mr. Redfield. We just took our rent from Caustic. The Buttersoft Council say we didn't authorise the disposal of the chemicals nor did we know about them.'

'What a surprise! No one knows. No one wants to know. Well, let me tell you gentlemen that this Court wants to know. Now I accept Mr. Redfield's position and I have decided that, having heard legal argument from all sides, that Rylands-v- Fletcher does not apply to his case. Mr. Redfield had let the land. He could not enter it if he wanted to. The letting occurred, I understand, on, or before, completion of his purchase so that he has never had the right to enter upon it. It is just an investment to him, as shares in any publicly quoted company are an investment to another. Holding those shares does not make the shareholder liable for acts of the company. It is true that Mr. Redfield has rights that he can enforce under the terms of the lease, but Dakers Diggers did not put the chemicals there and the lease may not provide the power to force them to remove the chemicals.'

'Accordingly I enter judgement for Mr. Redfield as far as the claim relates to him and award him costs. However, I will defer dealing with the question of who shall pay those costs until final judgement is given in the substantive claim. I imagine that Mr. Underwood will wish to consult his Clients about the further disposal of these proceedings from their point of view. In the meantime I grant leave to him, to and to Farmer Thomas and the other Plaintiffs, Winsome, Beamish and various inmates of the Westchester Retirement Home to join Testube Investments as fifth defendant to these proceedings.'

'Although there is no formal application before me to release Dakers Diggers from these proceedings, the question has been touched upon. I must say that, at this point of time, I am not prepared to consider such a course. Having regard to the law relating to the Plaintiffs' case, it may still be said that Dakers Diggers, albeit innocently, caused the release of the gasses which led to the injury or loss complained of.'

As regards the question of costs for the other parties these shall await the final judgement in the case. Thank you gentlemen good morning!'

The Judge rose, and the entire Court with him. The lawyers bowed to each other as is the custom and Mr. Justice Wigfield left the Court. Henry, Dimitri, Josephine and Isabel danced in the street outside, behaviour that did not escape the notice of either the press or the television cameras.

'Mr. Redfield! Mr. Redfield! The calls competing with one another for priority. A microphone was shoved into Henry's face. 'What are your feelings Mr. Redfield now that you have won your application?'

Henry turned briefly to smile at Josephine. Then with the magnificent backdrop of the Royal Courts of Justice behind him he said, 'My victory today was one for common sense. My duty however, is to pick up the torch for the real issue here. Pollution.'

'The chemical companies in there [the Court] will seek to wriggle out of responsibility by pointing at each other and away from themselves.

We cannot allow them to run and hide. In the United States there has been a belated move to compensate some of the world's millions of cancer and serious illness sufferers who can show that cigarettes caused their problems. The tobacco companies have had to start digging deep into their bottomless pits of retained profits, to pay for the damage and injury which was the real cost of those profits.'

'A far more serious hazard is presented by those who would pollute our drinking water, our rivers and seas, the food we eat, and the air that we breath. Cigarette smokers at least volunteer to fill their bodies with nicotine smoke. We, the general public are innocent of any complicity in the wider struggle against the chemical, industrial and nuclear wasters that feed off the public body for their profits.'

'Now is the time for all right thinking members of that general public to come to the aid of the public health. Let us not be satisfied by the government of this country, and others around the world, offering to tickle the problem by a little sop here a little clean up there. Now is the time for the governments of the world to firmly grasp the nettle. What about the cost you say? Well I say tax the chemical companies for a start, fine them so heavily that they reel from the blow when they step out of line. Then it must be said that the rest of us will also have to pay for the clean up. The money must come from somewhere. Instead of spending our money on more weapons, which will finally be dumped and replaced, lets spend that money on cleaning up the mess. When the job's done the same source of income can be spent on improving our hospitals and schools.

This can't wait. We need action now. I fling the gauntlet down in front of the Prime Minister and demand satisfaction on behalf of all right thinking people in this country. Penalise Polluters Promptly. Imprison the iniquitous infidel. If people die or become ill as a result of such activity, how is that not a crime as any assault or murder of the more conventional type is? March on parliament now, if your green and pleasant fields mean anything to you!'

'Strong words from Henry Redfield who, as you heard, has been released from the battle over the gasses of Buttersoft. We shall be asking the Prime Minister for his response to this challenge on News Extra. Now, from the Royal Courts of Justice in the Strand this is Rudolph Rushton handing you back to the studio.'

LUNCH AT NO. 10

Dimitri led Henry and the girls to the car. 'Lunch at Langan's Brasserie?'

'Why not?' said Henry relaxing back into the supple rich leather of the front seat next to his friend. Josephine leaned forwards and stroked his hair. Well done young man and then she whispered 'to the victor the spoils...'

Henry smiled at the thought of relaxing with his love later but the adrenalin still flowed through his veins like hot lava. Just then his mobile telephone, which had been switched off in Court, rang 'God save the Queen'. He flipped it open and said 'hello, Henry Redfield here.'

'Hmmm. Mr. Redfield this is the Prime Minister.' Henry sat up bolt upright. 'Yes sir,' he replied.

'You've caused quite a rumpus with your speech today. Made me feel quite uncomfortable I can tell you. No, there's no need to apologise. You would hardly be sincere. What I like about you so much is your sincerity and your conviction for this cause. You are undeniably right. We must act, and act now. The trouble is that among my motley crew of ministers there isn't one with your powerful instincts on this matter. I'll be blunt. We can't beat you on this, so why don't you join *us?* We have a safe seat coming up for a by-election in two months time. Highbury and Edmonton. Yes the incumbent is emigrating. Yes, didn't you hear? He won the lottery!' Yes. Well what about it Henry? Is it yes or no?'

'Prime Minister this is an incredible surprise to me and I know I should go away and think about the offer you are making. Two months to the election is not long enough for second thoughts. On the other hand, I am committed body and soul to this issue of cleaning up pollution in all its dreadful aspects wherever and whenever it can be found. So the answer is a definite "Yes!". When and how shall we begin?'

'Why don't you and your friends start by coming to me for lunch. Security will expect you. I understand from the car on your tail at this minute that you are in Rolls Silver Spirit registration W1 NIT. How appropriate!'

'Very good Prime Minister we shall see you in a couple of moments then.'

Josephine and Isabel looked aghast. 'How could you do that Henry. Isabel and I don't have time to get changed! How can we meet the Prime Minister and his wife looking like this?'

'But darlings you both look superb. I just wonder how he will be able to concentrate on the important matters of state when you two are such a distraction' laughed the Greek.

Josephine wore a smart navy blue Chanel suit with white trimming and white stockings with navy shoes and accessories, whilst Isabel was stunning in a red and black ensemble. They had both worn hats in deference to the solemnity of the occasion in Court. Dimitri was outrageously dressed in a bold American check suit, the trousers of which some golfers might choose, but as a suit it was a riot. The Judge had pulled a face when Dimitri entered the Courtroom but had chosen to ignore the offence.

The police were waiting for the Rolls and led it toward Downing Street. The Prime Minister and his wife were at the front door uncharacteristically to greet their guests. As his wife was fluent in French the girls felt instantly at home. They wandered into the kitchen to review the luncheon arrangements. The PM led the men into a lounge area that Henry recognised from certain broadcasts to the people made over the past year.

'I have invited the constituency chairman from Highbury and Edmonton over to chat about your candidacy. You will have to go before a selection committee, but with the high profile that you have just created for yourself there won't be a problem. Now Henry, the moment that you get a seat in Parliament, I plan to offer you a Junior Ministerial office in the Environment. Let's see how you cut your teeth on that before we consider anything higher. Now also at lunch today will be an old acquaintance of yours, Norris Parker. Like you he has tied his standard to the mast on this difficult issue of pollution. Although he won't be entering politics for the time being you can work with him and his connections.

By the way, the President of the United States was on the telephone a while ago. He saw the broadcast and was impressed. He is looking for someone to start the drive for change in the USA and hopes that you will visit him to discuss the issue in due course. Henry congratulations! You have arrived!'

'Prime Minister thank you for your confidence on such small evidence. Having said that, I can assure you that you will not be disappointed. Changes are coming and legislation will augur those changes. I can't wait to get to work.'

'Oh here's Peters from Highbury. Hallo David how are you? This is Henry Redfield. Have you seen the broadcast? Oh you have - good! Let's go into lunch now I'm sure that we are all ravenous. Hallo here's Parker too - good! Let's see what the girls have rustled up for us.'

The lunch passed off very well and was surprisingly informal. Simple hors d'oevres of avocado vinaigrette or melon with Parma ham for the carnivores, followed by a huge mixed salad, lightly tossed, for the veggies, and Thai chicken and mange tout, small sweet corn and new potatoes for the rest. the Prime Minister generously gave an initial toast in champagne (*Veuve Clicquot*) to Henry and his electoral and legal success. White Bordeaux added a touch of light merriment to the main dish, with an alternative red from the same chateau for those that preferred it. The girls laughed and giggled in their native tongue with the PM's wife giving measure for measure. The sun slipped a few welcome rays through the French Windows and added further warmth to a delightful occasion.

Parker 's editorial was discussed at length, but he agreed to withhold news of Henry's move into the world of politics until the PM gave him the signal. He was really pleased that Henry had espoused the cause that was so dear to his heart too. Pleased for the opportunity for a rest personally from the avid and unending physical demands of Sharon, his new wife to be, he stretched his long legs under the table and relaxed.

Dimitri was surprisingly subdued until just before the time had drawn near for them to take their leave. He turned to the Prime Minister and said 'I am proposing to enter politics in Greece you know, I have decided to adopt Henry's banner "The fight against Pollution". Of course it will take me longer, and Greece is not, unfortunately, as alive to the issues yet as you are here and in the United States. Our belated protection of the

Parthenon in Athens is a beginning, but we have much more to do. Athens had become synonymous with the word smog, which was originally a London born concept, adopted also by Los Angeles. Now in Athens the atmosphere is putrid. I shall fight the good fight in my corner too.'

The Prime Minister uttered words of encouragement in his effective individual manner and then bid them farewell. Photographs were taken on the doorstep, which now adorn the wall furniture of each of the visitors.

The by-now 'famous four' drove out of Downing Street and were observed by the cameramen who are virtually permanent fixtures at the end of the street. Not stopping to chat, Dimitri, who had hardly touched his wine, drove to the Hilton. Upon arrival in his suite he took Henry to one side looking more serious than the lawyer could remember.

'Henry I am planning to return to Greece tonight. I am putting Takis Yeromoschos, a trusted cousin of mine from Salonika in charge of the management of the scientific project in my absence. The main research is complete now, it is a matter of patents and licensing from the health authorities around the world. That will take time. I cannot allow delay to interfere with my move into politics. I did not tell the Prime Minister that, with other family connections hard at work, I have already, unofficially, been offered the position of Ambassador to the United Kingdom. I may take it rather than enter parliament, as it may be a quicker route to the top.'

'Wow Dimitri! I am impressed. Go for it. To think I shall soon be sipping champagne at the Embassy on a regular basis. The campaigns we can plan. Terrific news.'

'Hang on Henry! It's not official yet. You must not tell a soul! I will call you as soon as I am officially appointed. Then I will be visiting your PM again, and sooner than he might have expected!'

'You will have to sort out your personal life now Dimitri. Either divorce Vicky or reconcile. You can't have your private life on display after your appointment.'

'Already done. I have told Isabel, although we are great together I have responsibilities and must fulfil them. Perhaps, if she wants to wait, our time may come later.' Dimitri was, nonetheless, sad and introspective at the thought.

'She must be very upset. I'll have words with Josephine and find out for you. Much as I love Isabel too - as a friend of course, I think this is the right decision' advised the lawyer.

ON HIGH AT HIGHBURY

Upon the go-ahead being given by the PM, Nosey composed a very favourable piece on Henry and the forthcoming by-election, for which he had declared his candidacy. Congratulating Henry on his strong positive stance on the question of pollution, Nosey decried the reactionary politics of his main opponent Major George Hamilton Cruikshanks. Cruikshanks wanted not only to revive fox hunting, he actually had espoused the suggestion that bear baiting and cock fighting be made legal again. It seems that his private interest was in snail racing. His wife insisted on wearing silver fox or mink coats even when shopping in the local supermarket. The Major's strongest cause was the reintroduction of conscription. Still sporting his army uniform and a monocle he would climb onto his soapbox at the hustings and cry:

'Put them in the army, that's what I'd do. Get them off the streets and the dole and give them some square bashing to think about. The whole lot either need a haircut or enforced growing of the stubble. Any earrings in any part of the body will be ripped off. Vote for me and I'll make England great again. I'll show the Bosch. Think they can out-produce us and win the economic war do they? I'll put soldiers in the factories 24 hours a day on shift work. We'll show the blighters.

And this European Union nonsense. I'd get rid of that right away. We 'd have the support of the Falklands and other strategically placed members of the Commonwealth. Let's get out whilst the going's good!

Nothing wrong with our beef I'd force-feed it to the convicts and the conscripts alike. A dose of BSE every now and again won't hurt. Too much drivel is being spoken about pollution. What is it? Just a few germs. If you don't expose your children to it they won't build up immunity. Of course you'll lose a few. Doesn't matter. That's the natural order - survival of the fittest.'

The election was an exciting time for Henry. He was there waiting patiently for the final votes to be counted. When the Chief Returning Officer approached the microphone to make his announcement.

'As Chief Returning Officer for the London Borough of Islington and Edmonton I declare the votes cast for each candidate were as follows:

Sykes, Frederick James ------------------ British National Party 205
Brown, Lillian Jane--------------------- Liberal Democrat 4,599
Cruikshanks, George Hamilton ------- True Blue 1,001
Meadows, Daisy Rose--------------------Green Party 3,243'

Applause followed every announcement thus far, often just a trickle, but tension mounted as the final declaration was to be made. The returning officer cleared his throat.

'Redfield.' A cheer went up in anticipation of the result, but breath was held and hearts pounded nonetheless.

'Redfield, Henry Victor--------------------Labour 24,837

And I declare the said Henry Victor Redfield elected as the Member of Parliament. for the constituency of the London Borough of Islington and Edmonton...'

Cheers, shouts of support, and hoots of derision from the youngsters were to be heard both inside and outside the hall. A group began singing the "Red Flag" and 'God save our glorious Green!'

The telephone rang, and Henry scrabbled about for it in his briefcase.

'Well done Henry, you got in with an increased majority. That's most unusual in a by-election. Normally there's a bit of a kick against the ruling party. Again I am impressed.'

The Prime Minister put down the telephone and wondered how long he should wait before dropping Henry into the deep end. A month perhaps. There were bound to be a few bruised shins over the appointment of a new boy to a pretty senior post too quickly. Never mind.

The appointment of Dimitri Loukopoulos as Ambassador for Greece to the United Kingdom was announced on the evening news. It had come as a complete surprise to the PM. He told his wife, 'I only met the chap last month. He didn't mention a word about this. He is keen on the environment and curbing polluters too. Capable of making a big noise,

Henry tells me. I think he was being a touch ironic about that, as Dimitri kicked him hard at the time, but we shall see.'

As the months passed Henry became well known in the corridors of power. He made a fine junior minister. He introduced legislation imposing heavy penalties on the polluting chemical and industrial offenders. A broader inspectorate working together with local water boards carried out regular tests of the quality of all water reservoirs, lakes, rivers and the seas. Soil in agricultural areas was subjected to random tests. Litterlouts now face possible imprisonment, and refuse disposal units had to show how they were dealing with the different grades of refuse that they collected. Recycling took on a new face, animal and vegetable waste being converted into organic fertiliser with a by -product of electrical power or energy. Properly managed, even the greenhouse effect could be reduced.

Each day new ideas were being investigated. Real progress was being made. The government was subsidising the production of cars driven by solar and electric energy. The Japanese had now produced a really small cell with a computer microprocessor built into it, which enabled recharging also through the momentum of the wheels. Once the car was under way, the energy created by its own momentum carried it onwards whilst batteries recharged through the motion created. Cars were now being forbidden access to more and more areas in the City. Improvements in public transport had made it very attractive for the customer in terms of stress-free travel and savings in money and fuel.

Always have an eye to clean and safe energy was Henry's approach. The quality of the air in central London began to improve noticeably. Henry's popularity grew. Parker of the Press as he was still known was always praising Henry for this or that, and others had learned the wisdom of following where Nosey led.

Finally the main case regarding the Buttersoft gas leaks had come to Court. Both Caustic and Testube were found to be responsible despite their antics in trying to cast the blame on the other.

On the auspicious occasion of the final day in Court Judge Wigfield in his sternest possible tone exclaimed

'A plague on both your houses! There is no doubt that one of you two Companies buried these chemicals. Trying to cast the blame on the other will not wash with this Court, especially as you are connected companies. Hiding liability after hiding the chemicals demonstrates a character that this Court deprecates in the extreme. I can only hope that criminal prosecution will follow this event. I find for the Plaintiffs against both Companies equally.'

Dakers Diggers escaped having a judgement registered against them.

Damages were not huge as Farmer Thomas could not show more than an initial loss, but general damages of £50,000 were awarded to him in addition to his particular losses and his costs. His pig farm has flourished and rumour has it that he now wishes to buy adjoining land to extend his endeavours. May and he are married and have a baby boy born weighing twelve pounds! In view of his proportions and the tradition in the Farmer's family they have named him John.

Wpc Winsome got a handsome award of £250,000, and is now courting with the barrister, Davenport. She has resisted attempts to persuade her to model panties for a living. Beamish was awarded £100,000, although in his case there was considerable doubt about the extent of the influence of the drug, after two weeks in clink, his conviction was overturned on appeal. Ladies who spot him in the supermarket or large convenience stores try to avoid bending over in his immediate vicinity.

The ladies at the retirement home were awarded £10,000 each and the assaulted young men received £150,000 each. The Retirement home has had to find replacements for two staff, but have put up their guest rates.

There was no doubt that the Defendant Companies had been subjected to penal damages because of their attempts to wriggle out of responsibility. They appealed to the Court of Appeal.

In a unanimous verdict the Court of Appeal upheld the decision of Mr. Justice Wigfield on all counts and further recommended an investigation into the affairs of the two companies by the Director of Public Prosecutions. There were criminal penalties for pollution and the judges felt that there was also a possibility of evidence having been suppressed. So the investigation continues.

The aptly named and gross, Gassman has been retired by the Caustic Chemical Corporation, who can now ill-afford his expensive dinners and sojourns at the Hyde Park Hotel. Rumour has it that he has immigrated to the West Indies with a waitress/cook whose speciality is spaghetti bolognaise. It seems that she is quite clumsy for a waitress, often dropping the spaghetti into some lap or other, leaving Gassman to pick up the pieces.

Golde Lox has retired from modelling having married the headwaiter of one of the better London Hotels, as he is now. Their marriage has proved satisfying for both parties. They have recently moved to a detached house owing to complaints from their former neighbours about strange noises disturbing them in the dead of night. Yes, the Hardings are a happy couple.

Dai and Doris are the proud parents of three children who have all learned the Welsh language. Doris still does the odd bit of modelling but of clothes for the more generously-built, or matronly lady.

Norris Parker has done well for himself winning awards for his articles and short non-fictional works on pollution, now lives with Sharon in London, not far from Fleet Street where his editor is of one of the well known National Newspapers. They do not have children and friends and relatives alike have, knowing Nosey's reputation of old, enquired as to the reason. Little is known, but there is a murmur that Parker has asked Henry for a supply of the wonder drug.

Henry, now married with two children a boy and girl, has a directorship in The Anglo-Greek Drug Company (AGD) and a senior position in Gerard Boucher's Group which goes from strength to strength. The Fabergé egg, which Henry had so admired in Boucher's Mayfair residence, was the Frenchman's wedding gift. Mind you Gerard had to fly out by helicopter immediately after the ceremony for a meeting in Rome. He was present, all in all, for fifteen minutes.

Dimitri is now back in the bosom of his family, but has taken a residence in London as befits a fully-fledged ambassador. He is often obliged to make short trips to France to consult with colleagues there. In view of this requirement, he has also taken a flat in Paris. His PA in Paris, who looks after the apartment in his absence, bears an uncanny resemblance to Isabel.

The Public Health Authorities in the USA (the FDA), and in the various countries of Europe, have licensed the new drug produced by the AGD. The Anglo Greek Drug Company owns the rights to and distributes the drug, and has in clinical trials clearly demonstrated that it offers a cure for impotence and low libido. The drugs are only obtainable in limited dosage on prescription; nonetheless the demand has been unbelievable. What a hoot!

Lightning Source UK Ltd.
Milton Keynes UK
UKHW011830200123
415700UK00001B/53